READER'S REVIEWS

Loved this book; great read!!! The most powerful lessons for me from Rob's stories are how many events in our own lives have made us who we are. We have all been scared and hurt, as well as felt success and failure. For me, I feel that I have learned as much, if not more, from failure as I have from success.

Nancy Grace, Avon, CT

What a book. Life, learning while living. Riding the Boneyard, The Mudders, and Enos Pond. Simpler times when there was lots learned from our classrooms of life. His best book ever. An excellent read!

Jeff Sims, Lakeside, TX

Rob's writing makes me nostalgic for a time when I wasn't even born. It's a gift to be able to share and evoke the past and make it feel real. I never took a death ride on a toboggan or played in a band, but you take us along with you in your memories.

Lisa Sprague, Enfield, CT

I have spent many breakfast mornings in a booth at a Lutherville, MD, diner, listening to Rob's stories. The stories are always rich in detail and meaningful. When you read his stories, you'll feel like you are sitting in that booth with us.

Al Fick, Bath, ME

Rob's journey through "slightly uncomfortable places" in his "Classrooms of life" is an inspiring and wistful memoir of post-war New England childhood.

Marie Kolczynski

What a wonderful collection of stories teaching us that small moments can be powerful in shaping us as humans. Living in Holyoke, MA, it was fun for me to be brought back to Mountain Park, Riverside Park Speedway, and the landmarks of Simsbury, CT. No matter where you make your life, it's the people you meet and the kindness you show that write the true story of how one makes a difference. Rob, thanks for the lessons!

Linda Brown-Provost, Simsbury, CT

Oh yeah, "The Elephant Remembered." What I really enjoyed was the author's honesty with himself. No sugarcoating here. The stories are witty and comprehensive. The attention to detail and recall of names and dates is impressive. I'm glad he took the advice to write it down before it's forgotten. Well done, Rob!

Karen Paglia, Baltimore, MD

Rob Penfield captures the essence of life in Simsbury, CT, during the dynamic 1950s and '60s, transporting readers to a bygone era of simpler times. The vivid descriptions of characters allow readers to feel each story's surroundings with remarkable clarity. His level of detail is truly impressive. The perspective of a curious young boy navigating his world. For those with ties to Simsbury, it's a must-read journey through familiar streets and shared memories.

Patrick Sullivan, Simsbury, CT

Rob has done it again. Every story is a page-turner.

Tony Connor, New York, NY

SLIDING DOWN THE RAZORBLADES OF LIFE

A Book of Stories

Rob Penfield

atmosphere press

2024 Robert Penfield

Published by Atmosphere Press, Austin, TX

979-8-89132-437-4 (Hardcover)
979-8-89132-436-7 (Paperback)
979-8-89132-438-1 (ePub eBook)

Library of Congress Control Number: 2024917432

Cover Design by Matthew Fielder

Tree icon by Freepik. Baseball icon created from assets by lamyae chnifar on Vecteezy. Baseball cap icon by adeer hussain on Vecteezy. Checkered flags icon by Kadal Gurun on Vecteezy.

Atmospherepress.com

THE DEDICATION

The dedication for this book was an easy task. It's for all those kids I grew up with in my hometown, Simsbury, Connecticut. We shared learning with each other every day of our lives. We taught each other how to live. On our streets, in our neighborhoods, and in the woods. At Eno's Pond and Memorial Field. At Holly Farm. The field at Northfield Circle. South School, Snake Hollow, Central Grammar School, Memorial Field and Pool. All those places where you would find us on any day.

Playing and fighting. Laughing and crying. Living and learning.

I remember Stevie Pileski, Nancy and Alice Westerberg, Jim Lombard, Ruthie Campbell, Freddie Peckett, Bruce Parliman, Donnie Devine, Linda and Lois Ferraresso, Patty Hunt, Brian O'Donnell, Ray Nagy, Donnie Kibbee, and the rest of the Seminary Road gang.

There was Gene Kearns, Tommy and Mary Hanley, Robbie and Bruce Elliott, Billy and Davy Davis, and Diane and Gary Formaggioni on Northfield Road. Billy Rohrer, Bobby Bagshaw, Bobby Newbold, Johnny and Linda Coleman, Jane Holmes, Ben Bode, Carolyn Guite, Georgie Falkner, and the rest of the Northfield Road mob. Jim and Bruce Hammond, along with Jimmy Tuller, from Barry Lane. Bobby Forsyth, Mike Butler, Ray Tooker, Jimmy Gagnon, Bobby Moran, Margie Sholes, Sharon Tetro, Ricky and Ronnie Roach, Peter Viets, John Curtiss, and Dickie Pettee from nearby streets.

Also, Bruce Messenger, Ronnie Krogh, Jay Humason, and Vinny Cayne. Tommy, Timmy, and John Vincent. Joe Garrity, Butchie Clapper, Johnny McClure, and Charlie Shaw. Along Firetown Road, there was Joe Kobza, Mickey Zacchera, Jimmy Dearden, Joe Bonczak, Kurt Swensen, Roger Thompson, Dave Iskra, Kurt and Ralphie Boehm, and Dougie Newton.

There were many others from West Simsbury, Tariffville, and Weatogue I got to know through Cub Scouts and Little League. And whether anyone cares to admit it, those kids of the 1950s had a subtle and positive impact that contributed to change in Simsbury. We were the future and put our fingerprints on so many things that are the town of Simsbury today.

We took learned skills from our outdoor classrooms to school. I learned from teachers, and my skills improved. At Central Grammar School, my fifth-grade teacher, Alice Goodwin, taught me the importance of commitment. That when you made a promise to someone, you kept that promise. A virtue I came to appreciate throughout life.

In junior and senior high school, it was Russ Sholes, Bob Pellitier, and Ed Lowndes who offered support. Joe Kane was a wonderful teacher and person. He always had time and listened to what I had to say. His suggestions were always sincerely appreciated.

I learned the keyboard's "home row" from my typing teacher, Ruth Schultz. She let me type assignments using my own unique style. My English teacher, Maggie Wade, allowed me to write thoughts in my own aggressive and creative way. Bob Amstutz, who always said yes when I asked for help, kept prodding me to use my talents. Eventually, I listened to Mr. Amstutz and followed his recommendations.

Science teacher Don Burnett became an unexpected exclamation point. From him, I expected detentions for my ways. What I got was a surprise mentor who had always wanted to help. He helped me to recognize it was time for me to get into the game. It was Mr. Burnett who told me that many in the school's system had been waiting for my talents to "wake up."

In my professional life, I owe thanks to Lou Ball and Caris Carr at the Farmington Valley Herald for their support and friendship. As a management consultant, I had the good fortune to work with and learn from Jack Best, Richard Kristensen, the late Carl Hamlin, and Roy Klotz. Their patience and professional support molded me into a world-class management consultant and developer of financially successful business training programs. The late Gene Yoksh from Katy, TX, picked me out from a group of more than a hundred candidates and hired me to a training position for Citibank Maryland at a critical point in my life. An opportunity that eventually led me to start my own company, RSP Training Ltd., a business I would run for 28 years.

All those wonderful people. I learned from every one of them.

Their support from as far back in my life as I can recall was critical to my development. The lessons learned from those folks got me through lots of tough situations and lifetime decisions. That lifetime battle with survival.

Simply, to all, "Thank You!"

THE BOOK'S CONTENTS

THE PROLOGUE
FROM ROB PENFIELD

THE REASONS WHY EVERY DAY
I FIGHT TO LIVE

A horrible fact is I may have killed a human being in Vietnam.

One of those times of self-awareness, judgment, and excruciating mental pains we all experience during our lives. Times of opportunity when we take uncontrolled rides and painfully "slide down the razor blades of life."

Emotional episodes producing memories and creating lifetime debts we now own. Payments we now endure for those things we did and said during our lives. Some of those debts, we can never fully repay.

These events occurred during a time when I felt strangely comfortable with being slightly uncomfortable. A Rubicon of sorts in a rather confusing way. Times when a little bit of our soul is chipped away and lost somewhere as we pass through one of those many junkyards of life.

Now, they're my memories. Some I struggle to remember. Others I am trying to forget. Debts I must forever endure.

I've written a book of stories about times in my life and some of those memories. Lessons I learned during my life's journey. Lessons associated with the good and the bad. Those debts we now owe. Those many razor blades we rode.

Memories of Vietnam are a terrible compilation of painful thoughts I've carried with me for over 50 years. I'm a veteran, and I carried a weapon. I was trained to kill, hoping I'd never have to.

Forever wondering if the person I shot was an enemy VC or an NVA regular. Maybe it was a little girl carrying hidden explosives strapped between her legs. Perhaps it was a dog. A local civilian or a Cambodian or Laotian mercenary. I'm not sure. You see, it was dark and happened so fast. We quickly moved on. It's the pain of not knowing what I did. That's what makes those memories even worse. It's why the stories I wrote and now offer to you about lessons learned during my journey are so critical to my sanity.

Rob Penfield Archives
The Author in Vietnam
Christmas Eve, 1968

As a soldier, I was trained how to fight. How to survive. Then, it's over. Nobody trains you how to forget. How to make those memories go away. How not to remember. So, they don't go away. They just linger. Like those painful lifetime debts.

And that makes my stories, my memories about the good

2

things, harder to remember. And memories of the bad things I want to forget, more painful. I've searched for a balancing point to manage an acceptable perception of the good and bad memories. That balancing point is never in the middle. Sometimes, it's nowhere to be found.

I can rationalize my military memories. Listen to those who say my actions were justified. It was war. I was protecting myself. It was either us or them. Rationalizing is never a good balancing point. When I have used it, I feel a coward.

Yeah, well, no matter if it's rationalized or not, that doesn't make it any easier when every night I close my eyes, trying to fall asleep. Those awful memories come screaming back into my head. Because I was never taught how to forget. They come back, as they've done every night for over 55 years.

And I'm tired.

I'm one of the more fortunate veterans. I have my hands, arms, my legs. My eyesight and most senses. Able to work and think in a cognitive process. Not a victim of brutal disabilities. Catastrophic injuries from war. Single and double amputees. Head injuries. Burn victims. Paraplegics and quadriplegics. Veterans existing in living comas. Like I said, one of the fortunate ones.

Yet, deep inside, like so many others, I'm wounded.

Ever since that horrible time, I've lived and interacted with others as if Vietnam never happened. My storefront appearance is fine, though I live with pain that the best of my words cannot begin to describe.

So, I turn to my stories. Those valuable lessons learned during my classrooms of life, that gave me the strength and confidence to face life's challenges. On any given day, I'll cling to one good thought or memory. One so strong it helps me manage the day. Control the triggers for lots of bad memories.

Professionally, I worked as a sportswriter. I attended some of the greatest spectacles in sports. Writing stories for major publications. Hoping my work will ease the pain of some of those memories.

Commercially, I was an effective management consultant.

Building business training programs in every US state and Canadian province. Worked for over 200 clients in 30 countries worldwide. I saved businesses and industries millions of dollars. Stayed busy so as not to dwell on painful memories.

I survived using lessons learned from those six hours a day of classroom discipline. That standard package every teacher is conditioned to deliver. The larger portion of learning, those 18 hours away from school, are my classrooms of life. Self-learning, discipline, and creative skills for thoughts, words, and deeds. Real and impacting communications. When and how to make decisions. How to identify on-coming omens. When to fight and when not to. How to survive. How to love. How to like. Sometimes, just knowing how to exist with those lifetime debts that can never be fully repaid.

There were days I got by on lessons learned. A remembered thought that controlled my triggers, like a World Series I attended in Boston. The NCAA Final Four in Philadelphia. A Super Bowl game I covered in Houston. A long-ago girls' historic field hockey game in Connecticut.

I'd recall a training approach I designed that saved thousands of lives in India. A blueprint reading program I created. It elevated a man with third grade reading skills to a supervisor of 25 people. Or my adding a simple change to a drilling program that saved an oil company a million dollars per day. I remember the sports stories I wrote and the millions of business dollars I've been given credit for saving.

Often, I'd wonder. The sum total of all those accomplishments. Are they worth the killing of a human life?

I hope, never again, to be manipulated into a situation where I may be called upon to take a life. Unfortunately, in our lives, there are no guarantees.

Only those memories! Those pesky little lifetime debts.

I'll share with you a story of how I learned to work with people. To do my work the right way because the cost of cutting corners and cheating is too high. I learned this lesson from a high school football game played in 1959. A lesson that kept me alive in Vietnam.

I will tell you about the impact of truth and honesty. A lesson learned because one day, I did my homework the way it was supposed to be done. I'll share with you stories about the virtue of patience. Like when you go fishing or in so many other activities in our lives when we, the world, always seem to be in a hurry to go nowhere.

Another story will talk about banding together as part of a rock 'n roll band. A simple lesson of give-and-take.

I'll share with you a story about kindness. It's still out there today. The lesson learned is you may have to search a little harder to find it. Another story will talk about the reality of guardian angels. And I will tell a story about the simple but lasting effects of commitment and planning.

I will tell you of these stories and lessons learned and hope you'll understand.

Oh, I guess, over the years, I survived OK because of lessons learned. Yes, I still live with those frictions of life, like that awful killing day. The memories of those forever debts and sharp razor blades that never go away.

They just ... never go away.

Tom Lehrer, satirist and musician, sang of the gilded paths of education in his 1960s song, "Bright College Days." His comical, deep-rooted view of life's preliminary education and the expectations for receiving a diploma in life. The partial understanding of the eventual prices we all must pay for that fractured, half-assed approach to learning and self-anointment. An ignorance of the protective guardrails that surround and protect us.

So, like others before me, there I was, as Lehrer had said. Once a soldier, a student, now a graduate. Giddy, confused, and clutching my life's diploma. The owner of all my memories and those hard-earned debts from living.

There are always good and bad memories because there's always that painful need for balance. Hoping the lessons learned from my classrooms of life will help me to survive. Perhaps help the reader to survive, too.

And despite all our good fortune and freedoms to learn, what remains is the horrible fact that we, and our world, continue to slowly kill each other.

More memories ... more debts.

And all the while, we are, as Lehrer so mockingly sings, blind and blissfully, "sliding down the razor blades of life."

STORIES FROM LIVING
AND
LESSONS LEARNED

"FOR THE PEOPLE"

1

THE MUDDERS,
SOMEWHERE IN TIME

A STORY FOR ALL THE DREAMERS
AND BELIEVERS

I admit that I am one of those dreamers who believe that everyone has, or at one time had, a guardian angel. Someone or something that watches over the ways and means of our lives. They protect and guide us while existing in a parallel zone that runs concurrently with our realities as we plod along during our lifetime of mediocrity.

That all-too-short journey of earthly pilgrimage that is our life.

We're not sure where guardian angels come from. They may enter our lives as a childhood thought or a bedtime story read to us by a loving grandmother. Maybe as a harmless playmate we've created in our head and who lives under our bed. Or in a corner of our closet. A voice from our chest. An echo in our minds. Coming to us as a small bird like a finch or a wren. Or larger creatures, like a mythical gargoyle or a Mothman.

Some may be with us before we're born. Their aura is a part of our moms. At the hour of our birth, they gently put your mom's hand into the hand of God. Together, they walk with you through the valley of the dark shadows and into this world, giving you life. A debt that can never be repaid.

For others, they arrive at a myriad of times. When we take our first shaky steps. During that first life-threatening illness or death of a loved one. When we fear for the first time. In times of pain or physical abuse. When we learn how to say YES, or when we learn how to say NO!

Our protectors may also come when we least expect it.

As an unusual chill in the house on a summer's day when your dad's at work and your mom's shopping. In school, when you surprisingly know multi-word answers to questions on a test you didn't study for. A fight with a bully. A sense of hate or racism. Or when one of your toys moves without you touching it.

Always, it seems, they arrive at times when we're still too young to understand.

Guardian angels can be ghostly apparitions like the tiny balls of light known as Foo Fighters that were experienced by WWII bomber pilots. They can be a soft, wispy breeze that gently kisses our forehead. A ray of sun on our faces as we walk on a sun-lit path. They can be unseen shadows creeping along a wall. Inanimate objects, like a sign, a tree, a chair, a picture hanging on the wall, or an old fence. Something you notice that seems out-of-place. Or something that seems a little too familiar for no reason at all.

They'll appear and disappear within a heartbeat.

Guardian angels, though kind with intent, are self-indulgent, uninvited guests. Arrogant deciders of what is universally good and bad. Their presence can be a sign or an omen. They can influence results. They can make you happy, and they can make you sad.

And, of course, we know guardian angels are neither real nor alive.

Then again, sometimes, they're as real and alive as you and me. A living, energy-driven, self-apparition of physics.

Just like the Mudders!

His name was Maddy, and he was a Mudder.

For all I know, he may have been, or still is, my guardian angel. It was 1951, and I was five years old. That fall, I would enter kindergarten at Central Grammar School on Massaco Street in my hometown, Simsbury, Connecticut. That's when Maddy the Mudder came into my life.

The Mudders first appeared in Northwestern Connecticut's Farmington Valley about 1650. Nobody really knew where they came from. They just appeared one day. Many landowners in the north end of Simsbury were descendants of the Isaac Owens family, who purchased the land during the valley's Indian wars. Mudders worked farms tending to the crops. They were a strange group who set up camps along the banks of the Farmington River. They lived off what the land and muddy waterways of the river would provide.

They were rarely seen together. Preferred to work alone and exist individually. All Mudders appeared to be males and seemed to come and go in a flash. One minute, toiling in the middle of a sun-drenched cornfield. Moments later, seen working on the other side of the farm. They weren't local Indians. Didn't seem to have any European affinity with no known relatives. Didn't barter or appear to use money. They were there, though they just didn't seem to belong to the times.

Their clothes were different from what the settlers of the times wore. They appeared disheveled and somewhat confused and always were covered with dirt, mud, and other grime. Their language was rather strange. When they spoke, their words and delivery were odd. Like speaking sideways or backwards. They spoke a form of English delivered out of sequence, along with odd sounds and gestures.

Farmers began referring to them as "those Mudders," and the name stuck.

Today, there's no mention of the Mudders in Simsbury's history. Nothing in the local library that will tell you anything about them. No documents of their existence or crude sketches of their appearance. Oh, there remain a few piece-meal memories with a few folks. Bits and pieces, really, and now quietly fading. Soon, they'll be gone. Lost forever in time.

Whatever the cost of perpetuating the memory of the era and these strange people who are a part of history, that price is cheap compared to the loss of those memories as a result of ignorance and avoidance of today's population.

Yet, three hundred years later, in 1951, those Mudders were still in town.

It was a Saturday in late June 1951. My dad promised to take me fishing. It would be a busy day for him. He also had Little League practice with my brother that afternoon behind South School in Weatogue. He wasn't sure where we were going to fish. Friday, he gassed up the family Pontiac at Vincent's Tydol station in the center of town. He spoke with another man at the pumps about fishing and asked for some good spots to take a five-year-old.

The man was from Tariffville and gave my dad a few suggestions. One being the cold spring-fed brooks that flowed from the Meadowlands into the Farmington River. Just north of what locals referred to as "Nigger's Elbow." The elbow was about a mile north on the town's main road, Hopmeadow Street, also referred to by the old-timers as the College Highway.

"That's a name people say?" asked my dad, referring to the racially abusive tag for the bend in the river. The man hung his head and nodded. With a stern look on his face, he added a suggestion.

"If you're going to be eating, bring extra food. You may need it."

"Why?" my dad responded.

The man gave my dad a hard stare and said, "The Mudders. You may run into one, and he's gonna want to eat, too." The stranger then took his change from the gas pump jockey. Got into his car, a shiny black 1949 Custom Ford sedan. He drove north out of the station onto the College Highway towards Tariffville Road and the river.

"Nigger's Elbow," said dad slowly in an astonished way, shaking his head. My dad, Canadian by birth, had worked with Blacks in the farm fields of Southern Canada and New Hampshire. Worked with Blacks at the Hartford Gas Company and Hamilton Standard. Played ball with and against Blacks, beginning with his years at Riverside Military Academy in Georgia, then in Florida for the Hartford Gas Company, and for Hamilton Standard and Pratt & Whitney. He had no issues with people whose skin was different than his. The name used by locals left a foul taste on my dad's tongue.

To his thoughts, my dad added, "Mudders! What the Hell is a Mudder?"

Mom got me out of bed around 6 AM. I put on my fishing clothes and headed for the kitchen. Dad was drinking coffee and having a sugar cruller. I had a bowl of cereal and a glass of orange juice. I told Dad that on Friday, I'd gone out into the potato fields behind our house and dug worms for fishing. I proudly announced I'd found 15 worms. I described them as "real nice squigglers." A wormy term I'd heard on the radio.

We listened to WTIC's morning radio show. Bob Steele came on with his segment, "Speaking of Sports." I was already a baseball fan. Steele told me my Red Sox had won the opener of a three-game series at Fenway Park against the White Sox, 6–5. Mel Parnell was the winning pitcher. Ted Williams had two hits.

Dad said the Red Sox were now five games behind the White Sox in the standings. Williams was hitting .322 but struggling to catch Ferris Fain, who was leading the league with a sizzling .362 average for the lowly Philadelphia A's, who were mired in seventh place.

Mom asked what we wanted for lunchtime sandwiches. I wanted a PB and J. Skippy Peanut Butter with Welch's Grape Jelly. Dad chose ham and cheese with yellow mustard. Mom added a bag filled with State Line Potato Chips and packed a few chocolate chip cookies she'd baked the night before.

My dad, in a hesitant manner, asked if she would add another sandwich. He had remembered the stranger from the gas station saying to bring extra food. "Are we feeding the animals, too?" asked Mom.

Avoiding eye contact, Dad answered, "You never know what you might run into out in the woods." Mom put another PB and J sandwich into the small knapsack and a few extra cookies. I filled my old army canteen with cold lemonade from the fridge.

We put our food, fishing poles, and gear in the trunk of the Pontiac. We also loaded our boots, the shoulder bags that served as small tackle boxes with extra stuff like fishing line, hooks, leaders, sinkers, and bobbers. We added a few lures, a small can of oil, and Band-Aids. We headed out at 7 AM and traveled north on the College Highway. We turned right onto Tariffville Road. Crossed the railroad tracks and pulled into the parking lot in front of the Old Well Restaurant. My dad knew the owner, Arnold Daden. My dad had permission to park there when we would fish the area.

We grabbed our gear and set out on what would be a ten-minute walk through the meadowlands towards the river. We passed the spring-fed pond known as "The Grove." It was surrounded by marshland and quick mud. You could only fish this pond from a rowboat. Eventually, we came to the brook. It was small and shallow yet continued to widen as we moved along the path towards the river. We reached a point where the brook was five feet wide and had nice holes for fishing. Amid fallen branches where the water passed under a tree trunk that jutted out from the shore. My dad called these holes "trout motels"!

We crossed over the brook to the east side, which offered a better angle at working a hole. As we fished downstream, I kept lagging behind, looking over my shoulder. "Quit lagging," said my dad. "Whaddya doing back there?"

"Looking at the man," I answered. "A large man dressed in black."

I felt my dad's hand on my shoulder and saw he was looking back on the path we had just walked. We hadn't entered the woods yet, so it was open land. Not many trees. "What man?" he asked. "No one there."

"He was there. Honest," I said, looking back on the path. "Big man, dressed in black."

We worked our way downstream. I learned how to bait a hook for the type of hole you were about to fish. Dad showed me how to work a hole with my small casting rod. Slowly releasing my line, letting my bait flow naturally with the current. How to hold the line in my left hand so I could use two or three fingers to slightly tug on it. See if there was anything on the other end tugging back. He taught me how to read the dark water currents.

He explained how wet grounds were helpful for us. It softened our steps as we walked so as not to alert fish who could sense the impact of people walking along the banks. That a partly cloudy sky was good for fishing, as we didn't cast shadows on the water that fish, especially trout, could sense.

All the while, I kept looking back over my shoulder. Trying to catch a glimpse of that large figure dressed in black that I knew was following us.

We decided to stop and eat. Found a wonderful spot. A small clearing along the east side of the brook near the river. We dug into our food supplies. Talked about the brook we had just fished. My dad checked his watch. He had to be back home by 1 PM. Change clothes and get to the ballfield for little league practice. We would finish our lunch, then fish upstream as we worked our way back to the car parked at the Old Well Restaurant.

Dad had his back to the path, rummaging through his tackle bag. I had my head down, pouring more lemonade into my small metal cup. I heard a sound and looked up. Startled, I sucked in a quick breath of air, and my mouth hung open. It was as if he materialized right out of thin air.

Standing just ten feet away from me was the large, strange man, dressed in black.

"Lo, Maddy is," he said in what sounded like a voice from a machine. His left hand was waist high. He appeared to be waving at us by wiggling his fingers. I was pretty sure "Lo" meant "Hello." And I guessed his name was Maddy. His manner of speaking was different and hard for me to understand. I lifted my tiny left hand and wiggled my fingers. Kinda waving back at him. "Lo," I said. "My name is Rob."

"Roo-oooob," he said, drawing out the o's in my name. "Good, Good."

Maddy's appearance was strange. Different from others. Jeez, different from just about anyone I'd ever seen. He was big. Like a phonebooth. Six foot six and 250 pounds. His clothes were odd. He wore funny-looking overalls. Kinda like the Levi bibbed dungarees I wore, but different. Mine had two straps. Each came over each shoulder and attached to the front bib. His bib had only one strap. My jeans were blue. His were dark gray. And the material looked like he was wearing a dark burlap sack. Under his overalls, he wore a long-sleeved shirt. The sleeves came down just past his elbows. It looked like a uniform.

His clothes were torn, full of holes. On his feet, he wore, well, not shoes. They were more like ... things! Very big things. Unlike my sneakers or my dad's boots. There were no laces or structure to his footwear.

His clothes were filthy. Covered with dirt and dried mud. I knew because I'd been scolded many times for coming home with the mud on my clothes. He smelled, too, like the smells that were the woods I would come to know. And, when he sat down on the log, his clothes sounded like metal does when you bend it.

His simple body movements reminded me of something that had been built. Mechanically driven, yet functional. Like what you'd build with a kid's Erector set. Like the ones from the A.C. Gilbert Company in Westville, CT, the company that also built the American Flyer Trains for over 20 years. Maddy looked like he was built from parts in a kit that included how-to instructions.

His face was large, but his mouth, nose, and ears were small. His skin was a noticeable color of brown, rough with an orange tint, like tanned leather. But it was his eyes that made me stare at him. They were huge, without much movement, in a fixed stare. Like in some of the kids I would come to know in my youth with Downs Syndrome. Or, in later years, that eye gaze of people with autism or Parkinson's Disease. His hair was messy. Seemed to go in many directions, including in the back, where it stuck straight up. Like Alfalfa's hair in the 1930s *Our Gang* series.

My dad reached for the large knife nestled snugly in its sheath hanging on his belt. Maddy looked at him. Lifted his left hand like when you want someone to stop. My dad took his hand away from the knife.

"Hungary I'm," said Maddy. "Food me, preeze."

He ate the PB and J. "Good, good," he said, nodding his head, his entire face contorted as if trying to smile. I held my sandwich in front of my face, took a bite, and said, "Good, good!" I smiled at him. He nodded but didn't say much. We could tell he liked the sandwich. He munched down a handful of potato chips in one gulp and one of the big Tollhouse cookies Mom had baked.

When he opened his mouth to eat, I could see he didn't have many teeth. He licked his fingers, which were long and large. I licked my fingers, too, and my dad laughed. Maddy drank lemonade noisily with a slurping sound. His tongue ran quickly over his huge lips. Again, he said, "Good, good."

Slowly and softly, he began talking. I understood a few of the words spoken. Most, though, were more like sounds I'd never heard. For most folks, it would have been like listening to a foreign language. My dad asked Maddy what he was talking about. Maddy looked at him and said, "River." *Then he added,* "Monster."

He continued his story using words, hand gestures, and a small branch drawing stick images in the dirt. Dad kept an ongoing conversation with Maddy, asking questions and trying to understand what he was trying to tell us. Eventually, Dad came to understand Maddy was telling us about the little-known, three-hundred-year-old story about "The Farmington River Monster."

Maddy said he knew the monster. Had talked with her many times.

It would be the first time in my life I would hear that story. A story that became a book I wrote almost 70 years later, titled *The Monsters That Never Die*. It's Maddy who gave me the idea for the book and its title.

Maddy finished his story and said, "Monsters never die!"

He thanked us, saying the food was good and it was time for him to go. He had work to do. Needed to be finished before dark. Dad asked if he was working on a farm. Maddy gave a funny look, nodded, and said, "Faam." He rose from the log, and his clothes again made that sound of metal. His left hand was waist high. He wiggled his fingers, saying, "Bye-bye, Roo-ooob."

He walked backwards for a few steps. His giant shoe-like things that were his feet leaving lines in the dirt. He pointed at me with one of his huge fingers and, in a voice slightly different from the one he'd been speaking with us, said, "I know you." My dad had an odd look on his face but said nothing. Maddy backstepped a few more paces, again pointing and saying in that different-sounding voice, "I watch you."

I was five years old and had no idea what he was talking about.

He turned and walked away on the path towards the Meadowlands. I looked at my dad, who said, "Now, that was rather interesting." I said that I liked Maddy. He was odd but friendly. Dad said we should keep this to ourselves and tell nobody. It will be our secret. I nodded OK. We looked at the path leading to the Meadowlands.

Maddy was gone. In seconds, he just disappeared.

It was three years before I again saw Maddy. It was summer 1954, and the world was changing. I was now a ripe old age of eight and growing up.

My hero, Ted Williams, had returned to the Red Sox from his tour spent flying 40 combat missions in the Korean War. Willie Mays was tearing up the National League for the New York Giants. On Saturday morning TV, I watched Sky King and Johnny Jupiter. I drew lines on an acetate roll we could place on the TV screen during the kids' TV show *Winky Dink and You*. Mom and Dad watched TV shows *The Life of Riley*, with William Bendix; *I Love Lucy*, and *Topper*, starring Leo G. Carroll. You could walk across any backyard, and from the radio on the ledge in the kitchen window, you'd hear Perry Como singing "Papa Loves Mambo" and "This Ole House" by Rosemary Clooney. The Chordettes harmonized with "Mr. Sandman," and new styles of hard-driving music were coming from Bill Haley and His Comets.

Senator Joseph McCarthy had just been censured by Congress. His personal witch-hunt for Red Communists within our American structure came to an end. Roger Bannister broke the four-minute mile in track and field. *On The Waterfront* and *White Christmas* were the big movie draws. Eggs cost 59 cents a dozen. Gas averaged 25 cents per gallon. A candy bar was ten cents. Stamps, five cents. Put a quarter in a cigarette machine, and a pack of cigarettes dropped down along with two pennies in change and a pack of matches. Try to explain that to somebody today.

The Vietnamese Communists now occupied the upper regions of what today is North Vietnam, after defeating the French at the Battle of Dien Bien Phu. The Supreme Court ruled in the Brown v Board of Education case. Their finding was that "Separate but equal is inherently unequal when providing public education and that segregation violated the 14th Amendment." Guess folks in our town lost that decision somewhere downriver from "the Elbow."

Ellis Island's immigrant processing center closed. In August, Hurricane Carol barreled through New England, killing 70 people. Pudge Heffelfinger, Yale's first-ever All-American football player, died. Jonas Salk's first inoculations against polio took place in Pittsburgh, PA. For the first time, NBC aired the Rose Bowl parade and game in "living color." The Dow Jones Industrial Average hit an all-time high at 382.7.

During that summer of my eighth year, I was promoted from Blue Team One in the minor leagues to the Little League Giants in the major leagues. The team was managed by my dad, and I was now playing alongside my brother Pete and his friends.

And on a beautiful day in late June, I would once again see Maddy at Eno's Pond.

He was carrying a huge tree trunk along the northern bank of the pond. A hunk of wood that would normally take two or three guys to carry. He wasn't looking in my direction. Yet, he stopped. Dropped the tree trunk. Turned his head and hollered out, "Roo-oooob."

I was sitting alone 300 feet away on the pond's east side. How he saw me, even recognized me, was uncanny and a little weird!

He came over to me. Stayed for only a few minutes. Ate two chocolate chip cookies. Sipped Zarex from my canteen. A mixture that came in multiple flavors. Z was an old-time New England product. One-part Zarex sweet syrup, seven parts water. It was sweet and tangy. Maddy licked his lips. Before leaving, he gently touched my shoulder and said, "Good, you!" He didn't ask me if I was good. You know, in that perfunctory way when people make conversation, asking how things are going and if you're doing OK.

Instead, he told me I was good.

He gave his waist-high wave, wiggling his fingers. I waved back. He returned to the log. Picked it up as if it were a small branch. It had to have weighed hundreds of pounds. Hoisted it onto his shoulder and, with machine-like precision, disappeared over the bush-lined incline we kids knew as Williams Hill.

I had this strange feeling that Maddy was always where he wasn't supposed to be. Or where I wasn't supposed to be. It was confusing, and for the first time I could remember, I asked myself, "Maddy, where do you come from?"

Harold Tetro was known throughout town as the "Moleman." He did odd jobs like digging ditches, thus his nickname. Folks also knew him as "the Egg Man." He had a small chicken coop at the bottom of Seminary Road and a flock of chickens. Some days, he'd walk the neighborhood selling eggs for 50 cents a dozen.

In 1955, the drywell in our backyard caved in. It had been installed in 1948 as a wooden structure. New structures were now required to be steel. Harold dug out our old drywell in preparation for the new one. We always fed him and provided snacks. One day, I sat with Harold in the cool of a shade tree during his break. He dropped a bomb on me during our talk.

"You know about the Mudders, don't you, kid?" said Tetro, looking into my eyes. "I know cause I seen ya in the woods talking to one of 'em." I nodded, admitting that I did know one, asking why he had an interest in talking about the Mudders. Even for a nine-year-old kid, his answer was riveting and a little scary.

"Kid, they ain't from here, ya know," said the Moleman.

"Where they from?" I asked.

His answer: "I dunno. Mars or Jupiter. Sumpt'in like that."

In the fall of 1955, my dad was adding a porch and garage onto our house. A co-worker at Tracy, Robinson, and Williams Company in downtown Hartford offered to help with the roof's finishing touches. The final plywood sheets, tar paper, and shingles. The man's name was Art Hube, and he lived in Newington.

Over two weekends, Hube, his wife, and sons, Artie Jr. and Danny, came to Simsbury. And, along with other folks from the neighborhood, the roof was finished. As payback for the help, my dad agreed to help Art during the following summer. Hube was building a lake house near West Hill Pond in Barkhamsted, CT.

On two weekends in 1956, we stayed with the Hube family at the lake. My dad and mom helped with the building. We kids would work in the AM, then head for the lake in the afternoon. Artie Jr., Danny, and my brother would swim out to what was known as the Gray Raft, about 25 feet from shore. I had not yet learned how to swim, so I stayed close to the shore.

But the lure of the raft and all the fun those kids were having was too much. I paddled out to the raft in an inner tube. The raft was always fun for kids, with lots of energy and horseplay. I hung close to Danny, who was a year older than me. The activities got aggressive, and I was caught up in a pushing match between groups. Suddenly, I was flying off the back of the raft into the water that was seven feet deep. And I couldn't swim. Oh, I could dog-paddle and stay afloat if I absolutely had to. But the suddenness of events had put me into a scary situation.

I bobbed in the water, hollering to Danny. I could muster but a whisper as my mouth filled with water. I went under. Surfaced and again went under. This time, I could sense that I was sinking. I held my breath. My eyes were open. I could see the bottom of the raft as I sank deeper. I felt my foot hit the sandy bottom. I started to push myself up when, suddenly, I was propelled upwards. Exiting the water waist-high at the corner of the raft. I grabbed hold. Held on for dear life. Holy shit! What had just happened?

I climbed onto the raft. Carefully made my way to its corner where the inner tube was still tied to the ladder. I got into the tube and paddled back to shore. That's when the real fear of what could have happened set in.

For the remainder of the weekend, I was rather somber and a recluse. Mom sensed something was wrong. She smiled at me, sensing I didn't want to talk. So, she didn't ask.

I never told anyone about the incident.

During the summer of 1957, I learned how to swim. My instructor was a terrific young man from Simsbury named Donnie Marshman. He worked for Director Jack Geason as a lifeguard and swimming instructor at the new War Memorial Pool at Memorial Field. And, as I have often said, nothing good ever lasts. Marshman, a Springfield College athlete, would die from a severe head injury incurred after falling from gymnastic equipment in the old college field house.

Over the past 65 years, every time I've gone into the water, I think of Donnie Marshman.

Maddy appeared one day in 1957. I was fishing Eno's Brook with Roger Thompson. What today's townsfolk refer to as Owens Brook. We reached a point known as Skunk Cabbage Bend. It was easy walking along this stretch. Rays of sun filtered through the trees, yet a cool breeze always blew through the area.

Roger moved ahead of me, down the brook to deeper water. I had to relieve myself. What we kids would refer to as having to "take a shit." This was a good spot because we used the large skunk cabbage leaves for toilet paper. I relieved myself and used the cool waters from the brook to clean all the exposed body parts.

Just as I was about to resume my trek downstream, Maddy was there in front of me. He just appeared out of thin air.

"Lo, Roo-oooob," he said with his usual waist-high hand wiggling of his fingers.

I answered back, "Hi, Maddy," and then I asked, "Why are you here?"

"Watch you," he said.

He ate half my sandwich and drank most of my grape soda. We talked briefly about the woods and brook. Then he said it was time to leave. I should rejoin my friend, Roger. I walked down the brook about 50 feet. When I turned and looked back, Maddy was gone. Roger said he heard voices and asked who I was talking to. I said that I was talking to myself. Roger never saw Maddy.

I would see Maddy three more times during 1957 and 1958. During one meeting, I took a stick and wrote my name in the dirt. It appeared as Rob. I said to him, "Me, Rob," as I tapped my chest.

Maddy took the stick and began etching in the dirt next

to my name. What appeared looked something like $\sum$ ϵ $\mathbb{F}$ ω $\mathbb{F}$ † □. He looked at me with his X-ray-type eyes and said, "Maddy, me. I make rain, tooooo-ah."

I thought, "Wow, he's the Ted Williams of weird."

Ed Fellows was Simsbury's long-time chief of police. He was grandfatherly. An old, leathered face of lines and wrinkles. A nice man who always seemed sincerely concerned about people, especially kids. It was May 1959; I was thirteen. I'd just exited Weldon Hardware and was walking towards Hopmeadow Street.

I heard someone call out my name. I looked back and saw Chief Fellows calling out to me from one of the town's police cruisers sitting at the traffic light on Station Street. He was driving a gray and weather-beaten 1958 Ford four-door sedan. We kids referred to a cruiser's backseat as the police pigpen. He waved for me to come to the car. When I got close, he said to get in the cruiser's front passenger seat. I followed his instructions.

He drove a short distance and turned up the hill onto Library Lane. We pulled in behind the Simsbury House Inn and parked behind the old horse barn most folks referred to as the Carriage House. I sat quietly, nervous but curious. The chief sat quietly for a moment, looking out over the steering wheel. He looked at me and spoke. His voice was low in tone and calm.

"Rob, I want to talk with you," said Chief Fellows. "You don't have to answer any questions if you choose not to do so," added the police chief. "I won't be angry if you choose not to talk. I'll understand. OK?"

I looked at him and nodded.

He asked me about the Mudders.

He wanted to know if I'd ever seen or ever met one. I didn't lie and said yes, I'd seen one a few times, first with my dad when I was five years old. And always in the woods near

Enos Brook. I told the chief that I called him Maddy because he told me that was his name.

Chief Fellows asked if I ever saw Maddy or any Mudder commit a crime. I was confused by the question. Not sure how to answer. About the only thing I could think of was Maddy always ate my food, even my extra chips and cookies. Fellows looked at me and broke into a wide smile. He laughed out loud. Pushed his cop hat up on his head with his thumb. Muttered a comment that eating someone's food is probably not a crime. He adjusted his hat. Then, Simsbury Police Chief Eddie Fellows asked me the question that was really on his mind.

"Rob, do you know, er, well, what I mean is, do you have any idea where they come from?" asked Fellows in a surprisingly soft voice.

I swallowed hard. I was afraid to look at the chief, so I looked straight ahead through the windshield. I answered, "Well, Harold Tetro thinks they come from Mars. My friend Stevie Pileski believes they are some kinda machine. You know, like a robot. Frank Passini says they come from the clouds. And Maddy told me he comes from between the trees. He told me it's a place where I cannot go."

There was a long silence inside the cruiser. Chief Fellows inhaled deeply. I swallowed hard. Somehow, I found the courage to ask, "Chief Fellows, where do you think they come from?"

His mouth opened, but he spoke no words. He blinked his eyes a few times. Wiped them with the back of his hand. Gave me that grandfatherly look. Hard eyes, soft smile. He looked a thousand years old. He put his hand on my shoulder and spoke. His answer was blunt and poignant, and I will remember it till the day I die.

In a soft voice, he said, "Well, Rob, they ain't from this planet."

In Simsbury during the 1950s, if you needed your lawnmower fixed, you took it to Frank Passini. He had a small repair shack in the cornfields off Firetown Road, just north of Seminary Road. Today, that's near the intersection of Branch Brook Drive and Cornfield Road.

Frank was a simple man. He was friendly, a hard worker, and a whiz at repairing small engines. The repair shop was a second job and kept him busy, and he enjoyed the work. He did repairs for a paltry amount, often accepting whatever folks could pay. Sometimes, payment was food, like a chicken or freshly caught trout from one of the local brooks. A pie, cake, or fresh produce from a home garden. Those were different times in Simsbury.

Over the years, Maddy had been at the shack, especially when Frank had a backlog of work. Maddy was a whiz with mechanics, power sources, and gasoline engines. Frank paid Maddy cash under the table for work performed. Maddy was confused and didn't understand the money Frank gave to him. The paper bills or the coins. Frank had to teach Maddy about money. What it was, and how it was used.

Once, Maddy pulled paper bills from his pocket. When Passini saw them, he could only stare, open-mouthed. They were silver certificates from about 1920 or 1921. Another time, he had pennies. Indian Head pennies from the 1890s. Maddy said he'd been given money by others over the years but never used it.

Lee Hutchinson was the chief of the Simsbury Volunteer Fire Department. There's a story that Hutchinson watched Maddy work on a roto tiller in Passini's shop. Maddy, using water as a base, mixed ingredients from other bottles into a tin can. Smelled it and touched it with his lips. Poured the concoction into the tiller's gas tank. The engine ran like a top. He had created gasoline out of water and blended it with other minerals. Like TV's Jed Clampett of *The Beverly Hillbillies*, perhaps an oil company would have paid Maddy millions of dollars for his skills.

Frank Passini always knew Maddy was not from this earth.

I remember one meeting with Maddy. It wasn't the best time we ever met. Or the most fun time. What I remember … it was the last time we'd ever meet.

It was a Wednesday in August 1959. A hot and hazy day with a chance of afternoon thunderstorms. I was alone, fishing Eno's Brook. Near Rock Falls that was close to an area us kids called "the Graveyard of Old Cars." I was sitting on a log, pulling fishing line through my poles' eye loops. I had gotten my line hung up on a submerged branch. I hadn't been able to loosen the hook from the snag, so I had broken the line. I was now replacing a new leader and hook on my line.

Since I had gotten out of bed that morning, I'd had this odd feeling. An omen of sorts, a sense of sadness. Don't ask me why. I don't know how to put it into words. An uneasiness that kids have. I had my Motorola Transistor Radio with me. Listened to the songs of the day. Bobby Darin sang "Dream Lover." Wilbert Harrison did his classic "Kansas City." A pulsating organ-and-saxophone instrumental "Red River Rock" by Johnny and the Hurricanes.

Out of nowhere, Maddy appeared.

Without his asking, I dug into my small knapsack. Handed him half of my bologna and cheese sandwich with lettuce and yellow mustard. I also gave him a few potato chips. He gobbled them down and licked his lips. Washed it down with lemonade from my canteen.

He seemed fidgety. Kept looking around the woods. At the trees, the skunk cabbage, the graveyard of old cars. He didn't speak. That was unlike him. So, I spoke to him.

I asked, "Maddy, what's wrong?"

He looked at me with that pale face, odd lips, puggy nose, and large eyes. Mussy hair pointing in different directions. Funny overalls. Large feet and his shoe-like things. His clothes matted with grime, omitting the strong aroma of the land. He said, "Go soon. Home I. Trees." He pointed toward some trees and said, "You no go to."

Pixabay Archives Image
Maddy Lived Between the Trees...
A Place He Said I Could Not Go To

I was 13 years old. What did I know? The reality of what he was saying wasn't registering with me. OK, he was going somewhere. He wasn't a close friend. A best friend. A buddy or anything like that. He was Maddy. Someone or something that I knew from the woods. And he was getting ready to go somewhere. Yeah, OK.

"Watch did I," *he said.* "You. Now you good ... good."

I stared at Maddy. Ate my sandwich. Chewed slowly. "How'd you watch over me? What did you do to watch over me?" I asked, my voice rising with a tad more energy. Hell, we'd seen each other just eight or ten times over nine years. I just wasn't old or mature enough to grasp the situation he was referring to, in this case, my life.

"I push you up. The water. Fall off float wood." His words took a few seconds to resonate within me. Then, the memory of that day at West Hill Pond came into focus. When I fell off the raft into the water on the deep side and almost drowned. Sinking to the bottom. Sun disappearing above me. Then, rising quickly to the surface. Whoa, wait a minute. Holy shit. *HOLY SHIT!*

He said, "Wood thing. That day. Snow. No crash. No hurt." Again, I had to press my memories, remembering the day we

29

were, for an unexplainable reason, able to steer our toboggan and get it turned before we ran into the large pine tree at almost 40 miles per hour on a path we called the Boneyard.

I asked, "How do you know that? How, Maddy?" I wanted to know. He looked at the trees. He put his hands over his eyes. Strange sounds emanated from deep inside him. He appeared to be sad. I saw water on his huge fingers. Tears.

Maddy shook his head and hands. I took that to mean my question of how wasn't important. I didn't need to know. We exchanged a few words. He reached out and gently touched my arm with his huge fingers. My Motorola transistor radio played "Put Your Head on My Shoulder" by Paul Anka.

Maddy nodded and said, "Good, good." Then, it was time to go.

We rose from the log. His clothes making a noise like metal. He put his hand out, wanting me to take the lead. As I passed by, he gently touched my shoulder and again said, "Good, good!" We walked the path next to the brook for about 50 feet. I was about 10 feet in front of him. I could hear him talking and humming a sound like the music from the radio. Again, I heard him say, "Roo-ooob, good, good." I turned to ask him a question.

He was gone.

I stopped. Spun around a few times, searching the woods. Called out his name five or six times. My arms flailed and I slapped them against my thigh. Hollered out his name. I stood there staring at the spot where I had last seen him. My heart was beating in my chest. And it hurt. Like all those other times, he had just disappeared into thin air. And I knew he was gone.

Somewhere between the trees.

Thursday, I rode my bike to Frank Passi's lawnmower shop. Frank was working on a Briggs and Stratton engine. As I approached, he looked up at me. The smoke from his cigarette floated upwards. He squinted his eyes. He took the butt from his mouth and acknowledged my presence with a friendly nod.

He continued working on the engine. I waited for about 30 seconds, then said, "Frank, Maddy's gone. Said he was going back to the trees."

Frank loosened a bolt on the engine, then stopped. The wrench dropped from his hands. His head drooped, and his chin fell to his chest. He held the cigarette between his fingers and stared at the ground. Took off his baseball cap and tossed it onto the workbench. Stayed in that kneeling position for a while. I could see his back rising up and down. Like it does when somebody's crying. He was hiding his face with his right arm. He slowly rose up, a blank stare on his face. Walked toward the front door of the shack and out under the overhang. I followed, staying a few feet behind.

He stood outside the shack, staring at the blue skies. Those wondrous white puffy clouds that looked like cotton balls. So white and fluffy, floating slowly by, just above us. Seemingly so close to the ground that you could almost reach out and touch them. His head was tilted upwards, looking at the sky. I waited a minute before I dared speak. "Frank," I asked softly, "where is he? Where'd he go?"

Frank breathed hard and sighed, "Up there somewhere," he said, nodding his head towards the clouds. "He's there, or there, or over there," he said as he half-heartedly pointed with his cigarette hand. "He's somewhere out there in time." Frank made a sad, mewling sound. Turned and walked away from the door towards the tall rows of corn surrounding his shack. He stopped and turned towards me. I could see tears rolling down his cheeks. He wiped them with his sleeve.

"Ya know sump'in', kid? He could make it rain," said Frank.

"Rain?" I wondered. Were Frank's tears the rain?

I rode my bike home. A little afraid that I might crash because I was trying to catch a glimpse of the clouds in the sky. Blinking my eyes. Wiping them with my sleeve. Afraid that I, too, might rain.

The idea of having a guardian angel is really a half-assed thought.

Oh, it's OK for the movies. Like Frank Capri's 1946 movie, *It's A Wonderful Life*. The symbol of a ringing bell announcing that an angel, in this case, Clarence, gets its wings after helping Jimmy Stewart's character, George Bailey, throughout the movie. Guiding him in the ways and means of the responsibilities we all inherit during our journey through life.

There are those people of religion who believe they have connections to spirits that live among us. Spirits that exist in other dimensions. The Gods!

Well, my issues are that too many of those people of religion are full of horseshit. Mainly because there continues to be an underachievement in the delivery by those gods from all those religious-talking heads. Delivery of support from those spirits to the people in today's troubled world in such dire need of those gods.

Yet, we, as a people, continue to believe in those gods because we want to believe. We need to believe. In gods and in the inherited good we all know is real. Unfortunately, there's just not enough of that inherited good to go around these days.

We all want to believe there exists a divine good in people. Because if we stop believing, then we're giving up hope. Throwing in our cards. Cashing out. Admitting the end is near. And allowing that cruel bastard I know as death to win.

No guardians. No gods or angels. No Maddys.

It's not life and death. But it is all about life and death.

All about learning and understanding the disciplines in our lives. The ebbs and flows that dictate direction and decision-making. About all the good there is in living. And, sadly, all the bad because there's always a need for balance.

Pixabay Archives Image
The Woods Were Alive With the Mudders

There has always existed a need for people to believe in stunning things that go beyond our known comprehension and everyday thoughts. "There are more things in heaven and earth, Horatio," said my dad, trying to explain the wonderments that surpass our imagination. I would come to learn his words are Shakespeare's, spoken by Hamlet to Horatio in the 13th century atop the battlements of Elsinore that defended the eastern coast of Denmark. Hamlet spoke of powerful energies that exist beyond what we have "dreamt of in [our] philosophy."

In essence, my dad was saying to me that you are born with the freedom of choice. You either believe in the great beyond, like between the trees, or you don't.

So, it's also about the confidence and depth in our beliefs in people or things that go way beyond what our eyes, ears, and thoughts can comprehend. It's a journey of natural order, survival, and tragedy. The strength to fight back and not let the bastard death be the winner. Because, simply put, it's a waste of time to put one foot forward and then let the other foot drag behind. Killing the dreams and all that wonderment so many of us have "dreamt of."

Whether I think having a guardian angel is or is not a half-assed thought, here's the skinny of my beliefs. Someone or something came into my life at a time when I was too young to see and understand much about the ways of life and the meaning of death.

He taught me without my even knowing I was learning. He protected me without my being aware it was happening. It wasn't a dream. It was real.

Real, just like the trout I had learned how to catch in the brook. One day, I went fishing and caught something from a different dimension. Maddy! Or perhaps he caught me.

Maddy was kind and ageless. Maddy was a Mudder.

Now, over 70 years later, I've come to believe he was a source of energy that manifested itself into a time traveler. He knew all about me and my life. About all my successes and failures. He had empathy for me and for what would become my pain and memories of Vietnam. And he had this human empathy for years, hundreds of years, before any of my life happened.

Then, he appeared and watched over me, saying, "Good, good!"

It's taken most of my adult life for me to understand what Maddy's presence and his intentions with my life were meant to be. Perhaps it was to give me a gift. Not a physical thing or something I could touch or hold.

It's more metaphysical. The intent of positive thoughts and deeds. A challenge for one's mind to look beyond the accepted boundaries of normal thought. To live with a clear conscience and, as Hamlet said, with all those things we've "dreamt of."

Perhaps the sheer wonder and ability to conjure gifted thoughts or ideas into beneficial paths to travel. The comforting knowledge that one's creative thoughts are real. Wishes and dreams for yourself and others can really come true.

Beliefs that you really can achieve anything you set out to do if willing to believe in yourself and others. Have a plan, play within the rules, and put in the required time and hard work.

That you don't need to hit life's target dead center to be successful. Knowing that it's OK to fail. In fact, you're expected to experience failures because that's a part of Maddy's gift.

The gift of living and learning.

I've learned all about those everyday dangers hiding out there, challenging me along the way. I learned about my willingness to adjust when needed. The punishments we all endure. Those occasional rewards we all earn. And, whether any of us cares to admit it, it's OK to believe that maybe, just maybe, we had, or perhaps still have, in our lives, a guardian angel. Watching over the ways and means of our rather short journey through life.

Like my Maddy. Out there, between the trees.

Somewhere in time.

2

EASY ED AND A STATE BASEBALL CHAMPIONSHIP

JUST KEEP WORKING AND FIND A WAY TO GET IT DONE!

Ed Lowndes was a longtime physical education teacher and coach of high school sports teams in Simsbury, Connecticut. Due to his appealing personality and his ability to get along with almost everyone, at a young age, he earned the nickname "Easy Ed." During the spring of 1963, his Henry James Memorial High School varsity baseball team won the State of Connecticut's Class B Championship.

That baseball title would be the only state championship won by the Trojans of Henry James Memorial High School. That short-lived and borrowed name was the alias for Simsbury High School between 1961 and 1967.

Lowndes' Trojans were an average baseball team. Their regular season record was 13–4. Despite finishing first in the Northwest Conference standings, they had to win their final four conference games to earn a spot in that year's eight-team Class B tournament.

In the tournament's first round, Simsbury slipped past conference foe Lewis Mills High School for a 4–3 win. In the semi-final game, they staged a thrilling comeback in the final innings to beat the tournament's top-ranked Class B team, St. Thomas Aquinas of New Britain, by a score of 4–2. The Trojans then beat heavily favored Rockville High School 2–0 in the championship game.

Rockville's Rams were one of the top-ranked teams in the state. Their starting lineup had six seniors and three sophomores. Rockville had all-state players, and three would go on to have stints in professional ball, one with eleven years in the minor leagues.

James Memorial's team of no-names was just the opposite in the scorebook, with a starting lineup of six sophomores and three seniors. They played beyond expectations. The seniors would lead by example. Those sophomores played like seniors. Nobody went on to play in the minor leagues.

They won the championship because Coach Lowndes, the leader of the pack, sat back, quietly poised, wheeling and dealing with the confidence and aplomb of a Las Vegas card shark playing with house money.

His moves were like mystical predictions. They happened quietly and quickly. Faster than kudzu growing wildly across a North Carolina highway. Almost as if Lowndes knew the outcome of his moves before they happened.

He created lineups with players seemingly out of position. Batting orders other coaches would never have dreamed of using. Substitutions and strategies that seemed ill-timed. Yet, always, his moves produced positive results. Lowndes, that crusty old veteran of 24, would see these moves in his head, as if he were mentally moving the pieces on a chessboard. Like a classic general leading his troops into a critical battle. Like a blind man reading braille. Like a baseball aficionado.

Yeah, ole "Easy Ed" just played the cards he was dealt and won it all.

Simsbury had always been competitive in baseball, typically winning more than they would lose. Usually, not enough to qualify for the post-season tournaments. Phys Ed teacher Bob Pellitier finished 9–7 in 1960 with a good team. Had an 8–6 record in 1961 with a decent core of players. He then stepped down and became the principal of the high school.

Lowndes took over coaching varsity baseball in the spring of 1962. Simsbury had a few good players, though not enough talent to compete with conference foes Farmington, Lewis Mills, and Housatonic. They gutted out a hard-earned 8–7 record. They captured the last official Little Three title, sweeping games with local foes Canton and Farmington.

Lowndes was first involved in the spring of 1961 as coach of the junior varsity team while also graduating from Springfield College. I was a member of that JV team. We were a ragtag bunch, maybe one or two good ballplayers. We didn't hit much and had little pitching. We were weak defensively. Ran the bases badly. We finished with a 4–11 record.

I was the starting second baseman. One day, Lowndes saw me shagging fly balls during batting practice. It looked like I was having fun, and he liked what he saw. Since our outfield had more holes in it than a piece of Swiss cheese, Lowndes moved me to left field. In 12 games, I didn't make any errors. Saved a couple of games with a few late-inning catches. Despite injuries, I even had a decent year with the bat, hitting .285, and led the team in runs scored and stolen bases.

During a game against Farmington, Bruce Messenger got into a shouting match with the Farmington bench. Things got out of hand and escalated into a mini-brawl. Before we could run in from the outfield to join the melee, Lowndes had run out to the mound and yelled at us to stay in place.

When play resumed, Lowndes yelled, "TIME, TIME," to stop play. When he looked at his outfielders, he saw me with my back turned to the infield. I was writing notes in a notebook for a test I would be taking in Civics class the next day.

In centerfield, Tony Connor had his face buried in his glove. He was reading a homework assignment. Over in right field, Carl Miller had his glove covering his face. Blue-white smoke coming out from under it. He was having a quick smoke.

I was told Lowndes went down onto one knee. Put his hands together as if praying. Looked at the sky and said, "I could use some help down here." When we came in from the field, he didn't yell at us. One by one, he reminded us of our roles and responsibilities to our teammates and to ourselves.

That was Easy Ed.

Lowndes' 1963 varsity team had potential, though he wasn't sure what his roster would be just a few days before the opening game and was nervous about the expectations of those incoming sophomores. Hell, he wasn't ever sure if his seniors would play to expectations.

What made his outlook more demanding was that, just 15 miles south, Avon High School had won the Class C title the previous year in just its third year of varsity competition. Avon had thoroughly embarrassed and outplayed Simsbury during a pre-season scrimmage. When asked by the *Farmington Valley Herald* for a pre-season overview, Lowndes replied, "No clue. We'll see what we've got when I put 'em on the field."

I didn't play sports during my sophomore year. Lots of reasons and injuries like bad knees, a swollen right elbow, and a sore arm. Lowndes wanted me to play JV ball, just to keep my hand in the game. I was too banged up to do so.

By my junior year, my knees felt better. The swelling had gone down in my right elbow and shoulder. I had hoped to be part of the 1963 team. Just when I thought it was safe to think that maybe I might give it another try, I was diagnosed with hepatitis. A somewhat common yet complex and confusing disease to diagnostically treat and eventually flush from one's body. Hepatitis would come back again during the ensuing years to reeve havoc on the Henry James Baseball Team.

It would bring pain, heartache, and death.

During 1963's early practices, junior Joe Bonczek appeared to be the ace of the pitching staff. He was strapping, over six feet tall, and 200 pounds. He could throw hard. A wicked, hard, rising fastball. A low fastball that kept dropping. What catchers refer to as a heavy ball.

Joe wore thick glasses and had a hard time seeing the catcher's signals. Often, opposing batters looked a bit fuzzy. Standing in the batter's box against Joe could be a little scary.

Sophomore Doug Dianis played on the varsity team during his freshman year. Now, he was bigger, stronger, and pitched more aggressively. He had a herky-jerky windup that made it hard for hitters to time and pick up his release point. He threw a variety of fastballs, curves, and sliders that, on any given day, made his pitches unhittable.

Vinny Cayne, another sophomore, was an option for Lowndes. Cayne, a lefty, threw hard, especially inside and tight, to hitters, just under their hands. But Vinny had a repertoire of what could be called junk. Slow curves. A screwball and a lollipop changeup that was so slow opposing managers would yell out the pitch to their hitters before it crossed the plate.

Senior Gary Kuckel was a four-year varsity performer. He was six feet tall, 190 pounds, and athletic, and he could play multiple positions. Gary used a homemade bat, like in the movie *The Natural*. It was made in the school's woodshop by a classmate, Craig Rowley. When finished, Rowley gave the bat to

Kuckel and said, "Here, try this one. You'll hit 'em where they ain't." A quote referring to the hitting prowess of Wee Willie Keeler, a slap hitter for the Baltimore Orioles of the 1890s.

When Gary got hot, he could carry a team. And his hits were not dinks. They were screaming liners and tape-measure home runs. He hit 'em where they ain't all right, just as Craig Rowley had predicted.

Fred Young played shortstop. One of the key positions in what is referred to as "a team strong up the middle." Young had a good glove, quick feet, and quick hands. Offensively, he wasn't a strong bat, but he did what was asked of him. The type of ballplayer every coach wants on his team.

One senior was a surprise arrival for Lowndes. His name was David Seaman. He transferred in from Oberlin, Ohio. His dad had been promoted to a senior management position at Eastman Kodak. Dave had been the captain of his high school's football team. He came with a broken forearm, injured on the very last play of his last varsity game against Massolin High School.

To deal with his injury, he was assigned to see Dr. Cannon. When he visited the medical center in the old Darling House on Hopmeadow Street, the nurse called out, "OK, Seaman." Dave rose, as did a young girl also named Seaman. She was Linda Seaman, a junior in my class. She, too, had been a transfer into our school from Illinois. Ironically, they would later learn through a social event they were related.

It wasn't until early March when Seaman decided to give baseball a try. He had lettered in baseball for two years at Oberlin. Said it was his best sport. His high school had almost won the state championship in 1962.

Ed Lowndes watched Dave Seaman play catch for about five minutes. Saw him take just four swings during indoor batting practice and watched his mannerisms around others. It didn't take Lowndes very long to say about Seaman, "He's a baseball player!" He would become Lowndes' leftfielder.

41

That gang of sophomores arrived with confidence, arrogance, and ability. Doug Dianis and Billy Rohrer had played on the varsity team as freshmen. Vinny Cayne was being looked upon as one of three possible starting pitchers in Lowndes' rotation.

Ronnie Krogh was the stand-out of the group. He threw right, batted left, and had a keen batting eye and a sweet, level swing. He could hit, could field, and was an exceptional player on both offense and defense. Krogh could play anywhere on the field, and Lowndes saw him as his right fielder.

Tim Connor was smallish in size and a solid player. He was known for his defensive prowess and knew how to play the game. Lowndes penciled Connor in at second base.

HJMHS Yearbook Photo
Sophomore Ron Krogh, Hit .325 For the Season

Bob Blanthin was a block of stone. He threw and batted from the left side and was built like a fire hydrant. He was a good first baseman with a slick glove and a quick bat and, like Krogh, could hit the ball to all fields.

If there was one sophomore who became the stalwart of the bunch, it was Jimmy Gagnon. He was the catcher. He had always been the catcher.

I had played ball with and against Jimmy since we were seven years old, growing up in the same neighborhood. Behind the plate, he would carry on a running dialogue with anyone willing to talk. He played with intelligence, and that made it tougher to beat him. He loved to play baseball, and being around him was lots of fun.

42

He wasn't a great hitter, but he could hit. As a runner, he was quick afoot, and defensively, his only rivals at the catching position during his Little League and Babe Ruth years were schoolmates of mine, the late Mike Betz, Roger Thompson, and Billy Aliski.

When it came to holding the team together during a rough patch and being that leader when it was needed, Jimmy Gagnon, of course, stepped into that role. You respected him and followed his suggestions and instructions.

HJMHS Yearbook Photo
Sophomore Jim Gagnon
Heart & Soul of the Team

Jimmy Gagnon was a born leader. And every team needs designated leaders. One on the field and on the bench.

During a key moment in some games, Ed Lowndes would look off into the faraway sky, and you would hear him say, "C'mon, Jimmy. One, two, three, and take the team home.

That was Easy Ed just being Easy Ed!

Playing for Lowndes' JV in 1961, I learned his need for having depth on the bench and how to use it in situations. His '62 team had lacked depth, and he was going to ensure his 1963 did not. Not just players who had ability, but also people with character who knew their role and responsibilities as a bench jockey.

The 1963 varsity team had potential with lots of unanswered questions. Most in the know didn't have huge expectations for this inexperienced bunch, especially with all the new sophomores.

Everyone except Ed Lowndes.

The pressure on Easy Ed was self-imposed. I recall a day

43

just before the season's first game. I found Lowndes in the gym, sitting alone in the top row of the bleachers. He was deep in thought. I climbed the rows and sat next to him. He looked at me, smiled, and said something like, "That's what makes you a good ballplayer. You can read the situation."

He wasn't shy with his concerns. He had embraced a self-imposed and challenging path that was demanding. Almost unrealistic. He wanted a winning team. A record of 10–6 would be OK. But he wanted better.

James Memorial would play in the Northwest Conference. Good high school baseball schools, and none was better than Housatonic Regional in Falls Village, CT. Coach Ed Kirby's 1963 team was loaded. Between 1957 and 1964, the Mountaineers had three pitchers signed by the Pittsburgh Pirates. All three would play in the major leagues. Steve Blass would spend 10 years in the majors, winning over 100 games, including two complete game wins over the Baltimore Orioles in the 1971 World Series.

Lewis Mills had a good team led by Brian Hamernick, who would go on to sign a pro contract with the San Francisco Giants. Farmington High, always a tough competitor, had a team of experienced players.

When Easy Ed was done with his thoughts, I smiled and said, "Well, let's hope for good weather."

"Let's just play the games and see what happens," was his reply. "You just never know. Sometimes, one or two of those players surprise the hell out of you." Ed smiled. Pointed a finger at me and said, "Like you. That's why you became my left fielder and lead-off hitter."

Don't know if I agreed with his assessment of me. I appreciated his kind words.

Weather conditions for high school baseball in the northwestern corner of Connecticut were status quo. Cold, rainy weather plagued the pre-season practice schedule. Early season games were played in unfriendly weather conditions.

Simsbury gutted out home wins over Lewis Mills, Norwest Regional, and a good Gilbert team. Farmington threw its hat into the conference race with a surprising road win at Housatonic Regional, 1–0 in ten innings behind lefty Vinnie DiPietro. A game played in light rain and snow.

If James Memorial saw themselves as conference contenders, the schedule quickly turned them into pretenders. Their awakening was sudden, like a punch in the gut. They traveled to Falls Village to play Housatonic. They lost 11–0. In summarizing his team's pitching performance, Lowndes shook his head, saying, "Our pitchers couldn't hit the ocean standing at the end of the pier."

Injuries compounded the loss. Catcher Jim Gagnon jammed a finger. Billy Rohrer was gimpy after a slight ankle sprain in centerfield. Tim Connor twisted his knee while running out an infield ground ball. Pitcher Vinny Cayne, in relief of Bonczek, would feel a twinge in his left arm after cutting loose with a fastball. He would cradle his arm in towels on the long bus ride home. Cayne would admit that from that day on, his arm would never again be the same.

Another embarrassing loss was absorbed at Lewis Mills, 10–2. What Lowndes would call Simsbury's most embarrassing game of the season. The "Horseshit Game." Six Simsbury baserunners would be picked off bases. Five at first base and one at second. "Actually, it was seven," said Lowndes. "One guy was picked off at first. The ump called him safe. So, he makes it to second base and, again, gets picked off."

Two days later, the Trojans lost again. Jack Frechette of Gilbert High School scattered two hits and pitched the Yellowjackets to a 3–0 win. Simsbury's record was an embarrassing 3–3. A tough schedule of games loomed ahead.

In the interim, Simsbury managed a win at home, beating Terryville behind Doug Dianis' three-hitter. Ron Krogh had three hits and three RBIs. In an 8–1 win at Canton, Bobby Blanthin had a pair of run-scoring hits to back the strong pitching of Bonczek. At Farmington, Dianis pitched a complete game. Gary Kuckel provided the dramatics with a majestic, tape-measure homerun. He used the bat he and others had made during an industrial arts class. Every coach in the conference had confronted umpires, saying the bat was illegal, both in length and weight. No umpire, including tournament umps, ever disqualified the bat. It became "Kuckel's Beast."

HJMHS Yearbook Photo
Slugging Senior Gary Kuckel

When Kuckel's homerun hit the building, a couple were walking near the structure. The guy had his girlfriend stand at the spot of impact. Went to his truck to get a tape measure. With the help of others, he measured the distance from the outfield fence at the 345-foot mark to where the ball landed. With measurements completed, the guy told both dugouts the homerun had traveled a monstrous 473 feet.

The next week threw a wrench into the league's standings. Lewis Mills beat Farmington. Housatonic lost its second game to Farmington. Gilbert beat Terryville. Mills won a wild game vs Northwest Regional. The conference was an open free-for-all. There was now a four-way tie for first. It was like trying to figure out a Rubik's Cube.

Yeah, Easy Ed and his Trojans had everyone just where he wanted them.

The math was simple. James Memorial now stood at 7–3 with four games to play. They controlled their own destiny. Sweep the remaining schedule and hope for a little divine intervention to claim the title.

Simsbury had to win the Northwest Conference championship for tournament considerations. Even if they finished in a tie for first, they would not qualify because their overall state power rankings would be below the others in their conference: Lewis Mills, Housatonic, and Farmington.

On Friday, Lowndes held a practice at Memorial Field. Less than an hour into the workout, his wife appeared. She walked onto the field and announced, "Ed, time to come home for dinner. Now!" She got into her car and drove away.

With little fanfare and few words, Easy Ed ended practice. He instructed team managers to take the equipment back to the school. Everyone complied with his instructions. Ed got into his car and drove home for dinner. Players dispersed and Memorial Field emptied.

Not a word was spoken by anyone.

On Monday, May 21st, Lowndes held a light practice. Mostly games of soft catch and situational infield practice. Ricky "Wrinkles" Burr was on the pitching mound, and a few players took light batting practice. When Lowndes arrived at practice, he carried a cardboard box from his trunk. He emptied the contents on the corner of the bench.

He had brought sandwiches and sodas. A payback of sorts

for his leaving practice early on Friday. He had gone to the high school cafeteria after lunch, told the folks of his situation, and asked if they would be kind enough to make the sandwiches. They made 20 sandwiches using various ingredients. Added a huge bag of potato chips. A few day-old doughnuts and cookies. Lowndes also brought two cases of sodas from Vincent's Service Station on Hopmeadow Street. It was a poor man's smorgasbord.

By the end of practice, every sandwich had been eaten. The chips, doughnuts, and cookies were gone. Not even crumbs remained. Every bottle of soda had been emptied.

Lowndes announced the starting lineup for the next day's game against Canton. Calmly and with a rare show of emotion, he added, "Let's win 'em all. Get this conference shit out of the way." Nods and verbal agreements ensued from all present. Practice ended. Players picked up the trash. Managers returned the equipment to the carry bags. Ed Lowndes headed home for dinner. Memorial Field emptied.

Not a word was spoken by anyone.

Simsbury needed four wins.

The first one was on Tuesday. Joe Bonczek mowed down the Canton lineup. Ronnie Krogh and Dave Seaman had run-scoring singles. Billy Rohrer made a fine running catch of a sinking line drive in centerfield. Vinny Cayne tossed his array of junk and pitched two scoreless innings in relief. James Memorial won the game 6–2.

Win two came on Friday. Simsbury played its final road game at Terryville. This one was over early. Krogh and Kuckel had run-producing singles. Jimmy Gagnon poked a bases-clearing double. Doug Dianis limited the Kangaroos to two hits in a 7–0 win.

The following week, for win three, Simsbury got its revenge

for that early season 11–0 pasting by Housatonic. James Memorial won the game, 3–0 in front of a huge and vocal crowd at Memorial Field. Doug Dianis pitched a four-hitter and struck out 10. Jimmy Gagnon and Ronnie Krogh, now hitting .325, had key hits as Simsbury took over sole possession of first place.

Ed Kirby, the Housatonic coach, was heard saying to a writer from the *Lakeville Journal*, "James Memorial, that's the best team I've seen this year. I think they're going to beat Farmington and win the conference."

Ed Lowndes, hearing Kirby's plaudits, was heard to say to *Farmington Valley Herald* and *Hartford Courant* writers, "Ya know, I think he's right."

Win four came in an almost anti-climactic manner. Behind the pitching of Joe Bonczek, they beat Farmington on Friday afternoon and captured the conference title. They finished with a conference record of 11–3, beating out Housatonic and Lewis Mills, who both finished at 10–4. Simsbury was now Class B tournament bound.

Easy Ed Lowndes reminded his players nothing is easy and that winning is hard. Told them he was proud of what they had accomplished. Happy they had stuck with the script. Lowndes said he'd keep them posted on tournament information and upcoming practices.

Ed Lowndes then went home because it was time for dinner.

Tournament pairings for Class B were announced in the Saturday morning edition of the *Hartford Courant*. James Memorial was ranked third and would open play against an old friend and conference foe, Lewis Mills.

Lowndes put the Trojans through a light workout on Sunday just to ready his team for Monday's game. They would enter the game with an overall record of 13–4. Ronnie Krogh was the leading hitter with a .327 average. Gary Kuckel was at .280, with three doubles and three homers, while knocking in 10 runs. Bob Blanthin was hitting .300, Fred Young hitting .270, and Jimmy Gagnon at .250. They were not a big offensive team, but they hit when they had to.

They were the best defensive team in the league, having committed the fewest errors. "They better play good defense," said catcher Jimmy Gagnon, "or they have to answer to me."

Hartford newspapers lavished their praise on St. Thomas Aquinas and Rockville. Despite being Class B schools, both were ranked in the top five overall high school baseball teams in Connecticut. All newspapers in central Connecticut predicted St. Thomas and Rockville would play in the Class B final.

The writers knew little about Henry James Memorial of Simsbury. Their readership was in the huge Rockville and New Britain areas. Said Ricky Burr, the Trojans pitcher who wore a wrinkled uniform, commenting on the lack of respect, "Well, that's gonna come back and bite 'em in the ass."

Monday afternoon, Lowndes gave the ball to Doug Dianis, and the hard-throwing sophomore pitched Simsbury to a 4–3 tournament win over Lewis Mills. Ronnie Krogh again led his team with two hits. In the sixth inning, he singled, stole second, moved to third on a fielder's choice, and scored the winning run on a passed ball. On defense, both Krogh and Billy Rohrer made acrobatic catches to kill a Mills rally.

The win moved the Trojans into Wednesday's semi-final game against top-ranked St. Thomas Aquinas. A sportswriter from the New Britain Herald called the high school in Simsbury to interview Lowndes. He started the questioning with a long and wordy inquiry that sounded more like a science project than a sports question.

Lowndes, listening on a speakerphone, gently shook his head, as did others in the athletic office. He took a deep breath and answered. "Look, this is a baseball game. Two teams. Same field, same rules. We'll play a game. One team will win. One team will lose."

The simplicity of the response brought silence to the other end of the phone. I remembered a day when Lowndes shared a thought with me. He said baseball can be a complicated game but with a simple approach. If you overthink it, you'll miss what it's really all about. It's about having fun.

Mulling over pre-game notes, Lowndes murmured, "They pitch it. We'll hit it. They hit it. We'll catch it." As he had said. Simplicity while having fun.

Memorial Stadium in Waterbury, a WPA project from the 1930s, was the site of Wednesday's semi-final game. As rankings had indicated, St. Thomas Aquinas looked every bit the top-ranked team in Class B.

Saints' lefty Hank Stefanowicz, with a 7–0 season record, shut down the bats from Simsbury. Through five innings, he pitched hit-less ball, allowing only one baserunner, and was cruising with a 2–0 lead as he took to the hill for the sixth inning.

That's when the wheels on the Saints' bus came off.

Doug Dianis had pitched five innings for James Memorial, but Lowndes felt he was low on gas and removed him for a pinch hitter in the top of the sixth inning. Joe Bonczek batted for Dianis and worked a walk. Steve McIntyre went in as a pinch runner. A cloud of doom then descended on the crowd from New Britain.

Suddenly, for all those Saints, Eden became hell.

It happened like a WWII blitz. Two walks, a fielder's choice, three errors, and a sacrifice. Three passed balls and two key hits, one from Ron Krogh and a two-strike single by Dave Seaman. James Memorial was now sitting atop a 4–2 lead.

"You could feel the surge," remembered Ronnie Krogh. For

Dave Seaman, it was one of those moments when frustrations finally turned positive. "I remember saying to myself, c'mon, Dave. Time to get a hit. I singled to left on the very next pitch. I saw my teammates cheering me on. Man, that felt good."

Shortstop Fred Young remembered, "You could see the energy just go out of their entire team. Even their fans."

Relief pitcher Vinny Cayne allowed an infield single and pitched two scoreless innings to wrap up the win, sending the Trojans into the state championship game.

Ricky Burr reminded folks about what the Hartford papers had written in their praise of St. Thomas Aquinas. Especially in what the Courant had failed to say about the James Memorial team. Covering the game was a Courant sportswriter named Pat Bolduc. I had enjoyed many of his stories over the years. He was a good writer.

But that day, Bolduc fell into the same deep hole as St. Thomas Aquinas. Both became victims of events that fell out of their control.

Bolduc had the byline in the Courant's three editions. His ghostwriter called in the game info for the St. Thomas Aquinas–James Memorial game. Somehow, that info found its way tagged onto Bolduc's story from another game he was covering. Regarding game actions and the names of the Aquinas players, the Courant got it right. When it came to describing the sixth-inning rally by James Memorial, it was a mess.

Every James Memorial player's first name noted in the newspaper was wrong. The sixth-inning sequence of activities was reported incorrectly. The perception was that Bolduc made the mistakes. Perception is in how situations are managed. In this case, not well by the *Hartford Courant*. The paper's switchboard lit up like a Roman candle. There were lots of complaints from readers. Bolduc somehow became the scapegoat. It took two days before the paper finally printed a box saying they were sorry for the mistakes. And by then, everyone knew all about Henry James Memorial High School's baseball team.

That included the folks who followed Rockville High School baseball.

"Glad they didn't write about me," said Ed Lowndes after reading the Courant's story. "I like my first name, Ed. Plan to keep it."

Ed Lowndes was a complicated, deep-thinking person. Gentle, yet stern and intelligent beyond perception. He was, by definition, a physical education instructor. Multi-sports guy, sweat monger, and a jock. But, oh my, he was so much more.

He could play chess with one hand while managing a baseball game with the other. Attend classes to complete his education in the morning. Coach and lead a winning baseball team in the afternoon. He evaluated talent where others saw only struggle and inability. He could crush a softball with his hands. Or gently cradle a small bird on his finger after it landed on his shoulder during a game.

With his large frame, he would crouch down next to a tiny grammar school student during gym class. With gentleness and empathy, he would lead and teach. Show them how to hold a bat, do a somersault, or play crab soccer while offering supportive words of encouragement.

Like a guru, he predicted activities and results before they happened. The day before the championship game against Rockville, he told senior Gary Kuckel not only that they were going to win but also how they would accomplish the victory. That Kuckel and his teammates would win because, like they had done all season, they would find a way, telling Gary how they would score their runs. Just exactly how it actually happened.

Ed could compartmentalize and manage multiple components simultaneously. He respected everyone. Feared no one. He was only a few years older than some of the seniors on his team. Yet, he was, at times, grandfatherly and mature beyond his 24 years.

When asked to describe himself, he simply said, "I'm a baseball guy."

Yeah, a baseball guy. But Ed Lowndes was so much more. He truly had earned the respect of so many. And he accepted, with a smile, that he was affectionally known as "Easy Ed."

The Class B championship game, Rockville against James Memorial, was scheduled for Saturday, June 8, at Memorial Stadium in Waterbury. It was washed out by all-day rains and rescheduled for Monday, June 10. The game site was moved from Waterbury to Bristol's old and venerable minor league ballpark, Muzzy Field.

In the title game, Rockville coach Ron Kozuch gave the ball to his sophomore ace, Jim Martello, who had a record of 11–1, including eight shutouts. The lanky, hard-throwing Martello had authored five shutouts in a row and was riding a streak of 36 scoreless innings.

Lowndes hadn't yet named his starter. The team exited the bus next to the ballpark. Doug Dianis grabbed Lowndes' arm and said, "I want the ball." Lowndes knew Dianis had a sore elbow. The coach pulled a ball out of a paper bag and gave it to his young sophomore. "It's yours for as long as you want to stay in the game."

Easy Ed Lowndes knew Doug Dianis would not be coming out of this game.

James Memorial didn't waste any time and ended Martello's scoreless innings streak in the top of the first inning. Ron Krogh singled to right. Stole second. Took third on an infield out and scored on a double off the homemade bat of Gary Kuckel.

In the fifth, Krogh again started the inning with an infield single off Martello's glove. Bobby Blanthin put down a nice sacrifice bunt fielded by Ram's third baseman, Alan Putz, who made a quick throw to first for the out. Due to Putz's aggressiveness, third base was left uncovered. Krogh rounded second and kept going, making it safely into an uncovered third. As the dust settled, Rockville seemed to be a bit stunned.

Remembered Martello, "You could sense something was going to happen."

Jim Gagnon, the blood-'n'-guts catcher, laid down a perfect squeeze bunt. Martello came off the mound like a cat to make the play. Taking a quick look at Krogh, who was barreling down the line from third, Martello lost his footing. Krogh scored the second run. Gagnon was safe at first.

Martello recalled the play, "I was surprised by Gagnon's bunt. Felt myself slipping as I went for the ball. Saw I had no play on Krogh. Gagnon was up the line and almost to first. So, I ate it." A baseball term meaning he just put the ball in his pocket because there was no play to be made.

James Memorial, that team folks knew nothing about two weeks ago, was now leading 2–0.

Dianis seemed to find an inner strength atop the pitching mound. He scattered three singles, walked three, and struck out seven. In one inning, Rockville had two runners on. Lowndes was heard to say, "C'mon, Doug, throw strikes." With Gagnon hollering at him from behind the plate, urging him on, Doug Dianis reached back and fanned the next two hitters on six pitches.

Henry James Memorial High School won the Class B title game 2–0. As a fitting tribute to their championship, Jim Martello, Rockville's very talented pitcher, said of the victorious Trojans, "They're the best team we've seen all year."

The bus ride back home to Simsbury following the championship game was joyous and loud. From the back of the bus came one of those anonymous shouts that are a part of any celebration. Words of happiness. Words of bravado because we're feeling strong and invincible. We'll live forever.

"We're the champs" was hollered out amid the raucous chatter.

Ed Lowndes managed a wry smile but said nothing. He

just wanted to have some time to enjoy this one. And next year, or two years down the road, hell, that was an eternity for some. Nobody knew or had any idea what would be waiting for all those sophomores two years down the road. For both James Memorial and for Rockville. Tomorrow always has surprises for all who find their way there.

Lowndes just wanted to get home in time for dinner.

In spring 1964, the Beatles owned the musical airways. A slow and steady recession was creeping its way into the bowels of the economy. A new word, Vietnam, found its way into conversations. Human rights were now on the front page of major newspapers. And James Memorial, the defending Class B state champs, managed to whittle out a record of 12–4 despite erratic play and an armload of injuries.

The Trojans used late-season wins over Farmington and Housatonic to earn a spot in the 1964 tournament. The defending champs lost in the tournament's first round to Amity Regional. In retrospect, just making it to the tournament with all their injuries was a titanic accomplishment.

Doug Dianis managed five wins pitching with a sore arm. Joe Bonczek returned to his sophomore form, winning six games. His .290 batting average included two game-winning RBIs. With a sore back and swollen knees from football, Ron Krogh hit .340, and Bob Blanthin hit .310 despite severe back pains.

Jimmy Gagnon's football injuries, his arm and a painful hip pointer, carried over into the spring along with outfielder Billy Rohrer, the football quarterback who was playing on a bad ankle. Vinny Cayne's sore arm forced him to abandon his fastball for slow, breaking stuff. As Lowndes always said, "Nothing is easy, yet these guys find a way to get it done."

That senior leadership from the previous year was noticeably absent. And those dark clouds and omens of change were beginning to form overhead.

The dark days began in the winter of 1964, building slowly. Then, suddenly rose to a deafening and painful crescendo. It happened quickly, like a piercing jab to the heart.

Doug Dianis came into the athletic office. Sullen look on his face. He told Lowndes his dad had accepted a new management position. He would be leaving Simsbury and moving to Bardstown, Kentucky, in the early summer of 1964, where he would attend his senior year of high school.

Jimmy Gagnon needed a procedure to repair his football-injured arm. Still, the football co-captain is selected to play for the East Team in the state's annual premier all-star football game, the Nutmeg Bowl.

"That says it all about Jimmy Gagnon," said Ed Lowndes.

In February of 1965, Ronnie Krogh closed out his senior year of basketball in his final game, scoring a then-school-record 40 points against Housatonic. A week later, he changed uniforms and began indoor and outdoor baseball practice. He struggled, complained about feeling tired and weak. He was nauseated during classes and after eating.

His mom saw a telltale indicator. His fingertips were slightly yellow. His eyes appeared to be sunken. She took him to Dr Cannon. The doctor took one look at Krogh and said, "Hepatitis." Blood tests confirmed the visual diagnosis. Ron's illness was in the advanced stages. Cannon pulled Ron from school and put him on long-term bed rest.

The next day, Bobby Blanthin received the same diagnosis. He, too, was sent home for extended bed rest with close monitoring. Others in the high school were also suffering in what could only be described as a mini-epidemic.

Anxious weeks passed. On Wednesday, March 24, Cannon made his planned weekly visit to the Krogh home. He saw a slight improvement in Ron's condition. There had been minimal weight gain. A lessening of the yellowish hue from fingers, toes, and lips. As the doctor was leaving Krogh's bedside, Ronnie asked how his friend and classmate Bobby Blanthin was doing.

The doctor, his back to Krogh, stopped in the doorway. He turned slowly. Removed his glasses and softly, solemnly said to his young patient, "Ron ... he didn't make it."

Over sixty years have passed. Ronnie Krogh still remembers. "I was stunned. Like being punched in the gut. Here I was, lying in bed and fighting the same illness. Bobby, 17 years old, had died. I was scared."

Bobby Blanthin had been an honors student. Scholarship recipient. A three-sport varsity performer. Co-captain of the football team and an All-Conference .300 hitter in baseball. He had been an active member of the First Church of Christ Congregational. Held the seat of Chaplin in the Order of DeMolay. Still delivered daily newspapers. He had been 17 years old and a really nice kid.

And he was dead!

Ed Lowndes heard about Blanthin's death. He closed the door to the office. He cried loudly, unabashedly, at the tragic loss of this wonderful young man.

A worker on a painting project passed the office and heard crying. He would later tell folks Loundes was pounding his fist on the desk and moaning in pain, saying, "It's just not fair. Why him? You could have taken me. It's just not fair."

We talk about time being the great healer. Time, for all the lessons we'll learn and relationships we'll encounter. Guiding us in our transformation from the AS-IS of adolescence into the prepared awareness of the TO-BE situations we would grow into as adults and encounter during our life's journey.

Time is also an equalizer, offering us an understanding of the good and the bad. The gaps between benefits and concerns. A clearer picture of life's daily demands for decision-making.

Helping with the components to effectively deal with what is sometimes viewed as *"a question of balance."*

Searching for and finding life's critical balancing points is a never-ending endeavor. Not finding it doesn't mean we've failed. It just means we must keep searching. During those searches, we mature with the understanding of knowing when it's more right for something to happen as opposed to those times when we know it's so wrong for something to happen.

There are two sides to the ledger. Sometimes, those questions for understanding are on that side of the ledger where they are easily answered. What to eat for dinner. Where to go on vacation. What to do with those on-the-job decisions. What color to paint the living room. A good name for our dog or cat.

On the other side of the ledger, questions that reach deeply into our very souls, affecting our lives, are much harder to answer. Painful and absolute. Like, who gets the breaks we all pray for ... and who doesn't. Who stays healthy and who gets sick. Who lives and who dies. Too often, we learn this lesson at too young an age. The reasons are always confusing and never seem to have a simple answer.

Ed Lowndes would always say, "Nothing, nothing is simple or easy."

In the late 1980s, I was on my way home from a consulting project in Florida. It was a Thursday. I was waiting in Charlotte for a connecting flight to Baltimore. I ran into Doug Dianis. We were surprised to see each other.

During our brief time together, I learned that Doug had come to feel disdain towards baseball. He had played as a young boy in his Simsbury backyard. Through Little League. Babe Ruth League, high school, American Legion, and then college ball at North Carolina State. A game that he loved.

Every day, every night, he would practice his game while

growing up. Driven by his dad, who worked to improve Doug's pitching. Enhance his windup, leg kick, and delivery. How to better throw a four-seam fastball. A downward and sidearm curveball, hard slider, or a changeup. How to toe the rubber and hold runners on base.

For years. Every day. Every night. No matter the weather.

Doug's words reminded me of a quote I had read from Dr. Benjamin Spock on why Little League should be abolished. "Little League and its associated activities take all the fun out of athletics at a young age."

"I just didn't want to do it anymore," remembered Doug. He smiled and remembered our times playing against each other. "Hey, you always hit me pretty good." I had to laugh. He was right. I just seemed to have had his number, and over the years, I had hit Doug for about a .300 average. I didn't know how to respond and didn't want to be offensive, so I offered, "Yeah, I guess that I figured out your dad's system." Doug nodded. He didn't laugh. We shook hands and parted ways.

Years passed, and I learned Doug, a good family man, had died in Louisiana from one of life's awful illnesses. During ensuing years, we'd also lose Jimmy Gagnon and Ricky Burr, a Vietnam vet, to illness. All at much too young an age.

On the Rockville side of the scorebook, Alan Putz went on to have an eleven-year pro career playing mostly in the St. Louis Cardinals minor league system. Jim Martello attended Wesleyan University. He set pitching records that he still holds to this day. He had a successful career pitching in Hartford's Twilight League.

Rockville's first baseman Whit Ferguson, serving in the 1st Cavalry, died in Vietnam on March 11, 1969, from frag wounds near Nui Ba in the dangerous triangle of Tay Ninh Province. His name appears on the Vietnam Veterans Memorial in Washington, DC. One of 616 from Connecticut who died in Vietnam.

Dick McGill, a slick-fielding shortstop for Rockville with a good bat, earned a major league tryout with the Minnesota

Twins. After a short stint in baseball, he began a career as a construction specialist. He died in Bridgeport, CT, at 1:36 PM on April 23, 1987. One of 28 killed in the infamous L'Ambiance Plaza building collapse.

It was May 2013, and I was on a consulting project in Puerto Rico. One evening, I was sitting in an outdoor restaurant along San Juan's Condado, working on notes for what would become my first published book, *The Monsters That Never Die.* One of the story's bullet points was an occurrence from 1963. I immediately remembered the state championship baseball team from that year.

And, of course, I remembered Easy Ed Lowndes.

I used a few online search engines and found that Lowndes, listed as living in Liberty Township, Ohio, had recently died at age 74. I sighed deeply. Further research uncovered a warm and wonderful tribute written about Ed as part of his obituary.

As I sipped a cold beer on a sultry evening, I suddenly remembered a memory from 1963. It had happened on a Saturday. One of those chilly, raw days in early April. To my surprise, Ed Lowndes pulled into our driveway. I was the only one home and greeted him as I always did, "Hiya, Coach." He greeted me as if I were close family.

He had a varsity baseball uniform in the front seat of his car. He wanted me to have it. Be a part of the 1963 team. He had always liked me from our first meeting when I was in eighth grade and my playing leftfield for his 1961 JV team. He knew I was battling hepatitis and hobbling around with other injuries and most likely would not be able to play in any games. But his offer, wow, it was so touching that I had to turn away for fear I might cry.

With humility, I thanked him for his wonderful and thoughtful offer. I said no. Somebody else needed to wear that

Springfield College Photo
Ed Lowndes
Weaver High School
Springfield College

uniform. Somebody who'd contribute on the field. Not a good luck charm sitting on the bench. I chose not to play that role.

Ed smiled. He admitted, "Every time I look down the bench, I see you."

I went to an early season home game, and Ed sat on the high back railing of the bench. Beside him, folded neatly, sat the uniform he had offered to me.

I guess we learn from just about everyone we meet in our lives.

For me, it's all those people I've met during the journey. Those many experiences we've lived and re-lived. Always, I'd take away a little of what's learned. I'd give back a little of what I've learned to others in hopes that it will be helpful. And I always ended up leaving a little bit of myself behind. For some, it's critical to be remembered in a special way. For me, hell, just to be remembered at all is something special.

That day in Puerto Rico, I learned respect is not always a litany of words. It's also conveyed in thoughts and deeds. I remembered how Ed Lowndes asked me to be a part of something special. And even as I turned him down, Ed had found a way to show respect to me without saying a word. Now, over 60 years later, I'm still thrilled and humbled.

Perhaps one of the most wonderful lessons I have ever learned.

I thought of Ed's passing. That a tragedy of life is not necessarily death. The real tragedy, well, it's letting all those good and wonderful things we have inside us die ... while we're still alive. With Ed's help, I made sure I didn't let that happen to me.

Ed Lowndes didn't let it happen. And he didn't ask for anyone's respect. That just came his way naturally because he led by example. Everyone gave freely of themselves and followed his script. We all learned that nothing in our lives comes easy, and we simply found a way to get it done. Ed's way, with simplicity, pathos, repetition, and knowing our roles and responsibilities. Yeah, he won a state championship. But his legacy was in what he taught us along the way.

For "Easy Ed Lowndes," that's just the way he would have wanted it!

3

RIDING THE BONEYARD

A LESSON IN TRYING TO MAKE STUPIDITY A VIRTUE

At first glance, it really didn't appear to be much of a hill. Just another path that wound its way down through the woods behind Central Grammar School. One of those alluring places kids always seem to find. Places that don't appear to be dangerous.

We were so wrong.

That hill became a place where we learned about pain and broken body parts. Because there was a time in our lives when a bunch of us kids found a winter toboggan run. Then, for years, we went out of our way attempting to make stupidity a sacred virtue. Nobody really saw it for the monster that it became. And it ended up scaring the living shit out of every one of us.

We called it *"riding the Boneyard."*

During those cold winter months from 1955 until 1959, it was the most terrifying toboggan run in town. Forty-five of the scariest seconds any kid would experience during those early years of their lives. Childhood exhilarations and fear, real piss-in-your-pants fear.

Hurtling down a blind path while warding off low-hanging

64

branches. Zig-zagging through twists and turns and over jag-ged branches and sharp rocks. Sometimes going airborne. On every run, we had to negotiate an almost impossible ninety-degree turn. Knowing all the while, you're probably not going to make it to the end of the ride without being in a painful crash.

And, on some days, traveling faster than 40 miles per hour.

I first saw the path in the spring of 1954, when I was eight years old. It was used by high school students. Many had classes in the old building attached to the newer Central Grammar School atop the hill on Massaco Street. After fin-ishing one class, they'd make the five-minute walk down the path to the main high school building on Hopmeadow Street for their next class. Grammar school students weren't allowed in that part of the grounds behind our school. It wasn't until fourth grade that a few of us began sneaking away to investi-gate that section of forbidden woods.

Rob Penfield Photo
The Boneyard Today

As with most paths, it was ordinary, about five to six feet wide. The path itself was made up of hardened dirt, pebbles, and small stones. Glass from broken bottles was scattered along the way with small bits of trash and litter. It was a heavily wooded area. The sun's rays hardly ever got through the thickness and heavy overhangs of the pine and oak tree branches.

When we needed a little money, we could always find a few bottles along the path, each with a two-cent deposit upon return. Quart bottles brought in four cents. We'd use an old burlap sack and fill it with as many bottles as we could carry. We'd turn them in for cash to the manager at the First National Grocery Store or the morning bartender at the Maple Tree Bar. On a good day, we could make over a dollar and change.

With my share, I'd usually get a soda from the machine at Mainville's Gulf Station at the bottom of Seminary Road. And always, I would invest in a couple of wax packs of Topps bubble gum baseball cards from Leader Department Store in the old First National Grocery Store building that once stood at the bottom of Plank Hill Road.

The path was, for most, a shortcut of sorts. A quicker route for getting to or from the high school or getting to the downtown Hopmeadow Street area. It was heavily used, yet, ironically, I ran into very few people during my times walking it, up or down.

For other folks, it was that secret, wonderful place where their first amorous engagements of ambrosia were realized. Holding hands, a first kiss, touch, or something more. When looking for bottles, we often found used male contraceptives. Rubbers amid the trash. "Lubricated Trojan Specials" advertised on the wrapper.

Those finds would later become the bane of jokes for our being drawn to this spot. For taking our punishment and not being able to resist. Year by year, as we got a little older, with or without a "Lubricated Trojan Special," we kinda knew what the hill was doing to us. If you wanted to play on that hill, you were going to have to pay for the pains associated with that hill.

Pain, no matter how administered, became the lubricated user fees that we all came to understand and accept.

A toboggan, unlike a sled, has no runners. It has a flat bottom designed to carry heavier loads over snow. It's long and narrow. Made from thin strips of ash, birch, oak, or maple wood. The wood strips are fitted together, like a tongue-and-groove floor, and then sealed with heavy glue and many coats of epoxy.

The standard toboggan was nine feet long. Usually, 30 to 36 inches in width. The word "toboggan" is an Algonquian word for a cargo sled and transportation. They were first identified in Western Canada in the early 1800s and were made from bark, whalebone, or buffalo hide.

Typically made from wood strips six to eight inches wide, a distinguishable mark of twentieth-century toboggans was the black-painted slats. The two outside pieces and the center piece were often painted black. It's said the black slats were used as measurement points, balance, and weight guides.

The wood in the front of most toboggans is curled up like a winter sleigh. Riders hold onto a hemp-like rope strung through leather eyelets along the toboggan's outer edges. The rope went up through the curled wood of the front sleigh and was used by the driver to help with steering.

We owned a toboggan. We named it *Woody*.

It had come from my aunts' home in Old Wethersfield, CT. Stored in the upper rafters of the old garage and shed since the late 1920s. When we moved to Simsbury, my dad brought it home for the family to ride the gentle runs at the back of the potato fields behind our house on Seminary Road.

Nobody had any idea of the fate that awaited Woody. During its last years, our beloved 50-year-old toboggan would spend its final days barreling down a brazen backwoods trail we called the Boneyard.

You didn't just put four people on a toboggan and ride down a hill. You had to plan for each run. It didn't stop you from crashing. It did give you a better chance of not being hurt or limiting injuries during a crash.

My first run down the hill came on a Tuesday in February 1955. I was nine years old. From my grammar school classroom windows on the backside of the school, I could see junior high kids near the top of the run. When the bell rang to end school, instead of going home, I went straight to the hill.

An older boy asked, "Whadaya want, shithead?" I answered, "I want to take a ride down the hill."

He said, "You're stupid if you want to."

I shot back, "Well, so are you, shithead." My answer earned me a ride on the next shuttle.

First, I had to understand there are positions on a toboggan. And each rider had responsibilities. Always on this hill, there would be four riders. You needed that weight, about 400 pounds, to keep the toboggan from bouncing too much or going airborne. And each of the four riders had to know their responsibilities during the ride.

The lead, or driver, was usually a bigger kid. His responsibilities were to control the slight degree of steering available to toboggans by pulling or pushing on the front ropes attached to the sleigh-like curled wood. If, during a run, he leaned left or right, the three riders behind him would also lean in that direction to aid in steering.

He would sometimes shout out instructions. Like use your right or left hand as a drag link. This could pull the moving toboggan left or right. Like being in a rowboat and putting one oar in the water. He would shout out, "*DUCK*," for what quickly would become obvious. Low-hanging branches.

The last rider was known as the anchor. He, too, was usually bigger in size. His job was to make the ride on his knees, his feet near the back of the wood. That way, he could stretch either foot onto the trail, acting as a dragline or a brake to slow the ride. He, too, would often call out instructions.

The two middle riders, smallish in size, were ballast. Our job was to sit together like stacked chairs, or piled spoons, to add stability while hanging on to the ropes. Ballast was a blind position. It was best to keep your head down instead of trying to watch the world go by at a scary rate of speed.

I boarded and took ballast position three. In position two was a girl I didn't know, though I did hear someone call her Kit. The toboggan was being pushed out of the staging point. Soon, we were riding downhill through the darkened trail.

My first trip down the Boneyard ended badly. Both the girl in front of me and I didn't duck low enough at the halfway point. We felt the wrath of low-handing pine tree branches. Large, whiskbroom-like branches swept us out of our seats and took us down like deadwood in a candle-pin bowling alley.

It felt like being punched by an extraordinarily strong person. And it hurt.

The driver had been able to fend off the branches with his shoulders. Steering off the trail and avoided crashing into trees. The anchor kid had bailed at the right second, avoiding any injuries. The girl and I took the brunt of the hit.

I sat up. Saw the driver looking at us. He stood up, shaking his head. He screamed at the two of us, "WHEN I SAY DUCK, I MEAN FUCKIN' DUCK! GOT IT?" The girl was on the verge of crying. But she didn't. She said, "Yeah, got it." Rubbing my head, all I could do was nod.

The Boneyard would become a five-year learning curve that included our toboggan, "Woody." I would learn about actions and reactions and the by-products of those actions. It's a little like screwing around with a hornet's nest. It doesn't get interesting until you've poked it with a stick. You quickly learn you're going to have to pay for those actions, one way or another.

From that first ride in 1955, when I was nine years old,

until January of 1959, when I was 13, I would make 107 runs down that hill. I kept a tally. I would make it successfully to the end of the ride without crashing just six times. It became my hornet's nest. And payment, well, every time I rode that toboggan, those hornets came back to sting me in the ass.

Yet, I will always remember that first run with pride, honor, and fear.

During the second and third years on the hill, I learned about reading conditions and sensing pending doom. Yes, I feared the hill. And I respected it, too.

Real learning started with being able to read the day itself. Whether it was gray and cloudy or sunny and slightly warmer because that would affect the trail. You could tell if the run was going to be a little slower. Or if it was to be a very fast track. You learned when to steer off the path and scuttle the run, minimizing the effect of what became an eventual crash.

You became more aware of the trail. More aware because we all began seeing it as a living and breathing thing. Like a brutal football game or a survival competition. Against something that seemed to be alive. It became a battle of us against the hill.

I knew the trees and how they behaved. Where all the small dead tree stumps were located. I knew the locations of the dangerous rocks covered with snow and ice, their sharp edges exposed, where many kids ended up with cuts on their arms and legs. We knew the areas where the toboggan's front would bounce uncontrollably, zig-zagging through a rough patch.

I learned about the critical drop-off points along the run. Places we referred to as getaways or gully-whompers. Places where, because of your speed and the drop off in land, you'd go airborne for 10 feet or more. Those places affected every ride we took down that hill.

It was physical and usually scared all of us. Because of

those runs, when many of us got home, we just took off the underwear we were wearing. Threw 'em in the trash can. They had become soiled, unwearable!

And we all learned about "Dead Man's Curve."

The California singing and surfing duo of Jan and Dean told us in a 1964 song that folks usually didn't come back from "Dead Man's Curve." We were learning that lesson almost seven years before their song reached number eight on the Billboard Hot 100 Chart.

By 1958, not many who rode the Boneyard came back from Dead Man's Curve without a body part broken, sprained, cut, or swollen. I recall when I was 18, I ran into Dr. James Stretch at the local drugstore. He shared with me a story from years before. One weekend, five kids with various toboggan injuries were brought into his office by their parents. All said they had been hurt riding the Boneyard, with most of the injuries occurring at Dead Man's Curve.

The physical pains were more than enough. It was those mental injuries that lingered in your mind, always creating doubt and second-guessing your decisions and courage. Like a voice speaking to you from inside that hill.

Dean Man's Curve was plain ole fucking scary.

The "Curve" wasn't like the other parts of the hill. It came upon you quickly during the last ten seconds of the ride and had its own personality. Its own physics with little tolerance for error. Some days it had no tolerance for physics, or for us.

In fact, 99% percent of all runs down that hill ended violently at the "Curve."

Reaching Dead Man's Curve, the toboggan was required to

perform an almost impossible ninety-degree turn to the right. Why we even tried to make this turn is a question I will never be able to answer. Riders would have just exited the last wooded area and would now be in an open-air section with a few trees on either side of the trail. The toboggan would have been airborne before flying through an open-air area known as the glacier.

When entering the open-air area, riders would clearly see the back side of old Simsbury High School. Because of double sessions until 5 PM to handle the growing enrollment, students taking classes would have been able to see the toboggan and its riders exiting the woods into the curve with riders screaming in terror.

Dead Man's Curve was really a two-sided canyon. The east, or terror, side was taller. Scary even to look at. If you stood on the trail, you couldn't touch the top of the east side as it was over seven feet high. It was about 25 to 30 feet long.

The wall of the curve's east side was concave. Like if you laid a stalk of celery on its side. Exposed in that area were a menagerie of rocks and intertwined roots, like tentacles on an octopus, sharp, pointy, and often filled with rocks and ice.

Atop the east side were large pine trees. All were dying, and each had low-hanging branches. We had tried to remove as many of the dead branches with sharp points as we could so we wouldn't get skewered if we crashed into them.

When entering the curve, the driver had to make a quick decision. Whether to take the low track or the high track. It really depended on weather conditions and the speed of the toboggan coming off the glacier.

It came down to the decision of picking your own poison.

Drivers who felt they had control of the toboggan took the low road. Riders had to understand their responsibilities down low were to ensure the ride didn't slingshot out of control and climb up the east bank. That always ended in a nasty crash.

When you hit the curve's east side bank, the toboggan would ricochet off the wall and snap quickly to the right. Now airborne, it would dive towards the west wall of the curve that was not as tall but a bit more forgiving. It was usually covered with soft snow and a row of low-level bushes. If luck was riding with you, the rebound off the west side would be somewhat easy, allowing you to complete the ride. The low-road crashes were typically ones where the toboggan, upon hitting the ground, slid out of control, with folks falling off along the way. As bad as that may sound, it was the best way to crash.

If you took the high road on Dead Man's Curve, oh baby, you were on your own.

The high road meant you were entering the curve at speeds near or above 40 MPH. It also meant the riders were unable to slow the toboggan down before hitting the glacier. All on board would now be screaming. Like making an emotional 911 call before there was such a thing. At the very second you were about to hit the east wall, you squeezed your ass muscles so hard your butt was probably watertight.

The high-road driver was granted little tolerance for error. He had only two to three seconds to make the decision to ride it out. The other option was to just let go and allow the inertia of speed and gravity to take over. When riding the high road, both decisions were usually catastrophic.

The toboggan would go along the top edge of the curve, usually falling away upside down with riders strewn like trash throughout the bottom of the curve. The degree of injury was determined by how the rider landed. Land on your ass, and you were OK. Land on your head or back, not so good. This was dangerous, very dangerous, and always, when riding the high road, there were injuries.

Most kids brought extra clothes, Band-Aids, gauze, and mercurochrome. We'd clean wounds with cold, fresh snow and bandage the cuts, bruises, and swellings. Often, we'd sit with a kid until he stopped crying, with us hoping to hell nothing was seriously broken.

Before making the trudge back up the hill for the next run, we'd sit together quietly as a group. Each kid alone with his own thoughts catching his breath. Nobody said a word. After a few minutes, someone would rise, grab the toboggan rope, and head up the hill. One at a time, we'd get up and begin the prep for the next ride. I remember hearing kids say, "Why do we do this?"

"Because the hill wants us to," was an anonymous reply.

There was always doubt with lots of other kids that such a toboggan run really existed. Or if it was really as thrilling and dangerous as the kids said it was. Those doubts came from those who lived outside the Central Grammar School area.

They didn't know about the Boneyard and its legacy.

One day, Steve Pileski, talking with another who didn't believe stories about the hill, invited him to come visit. Take a ride down the Boneyard. Like most who visited, he made a big mistake and accepted the challenge. My memories of the events are somewhat comical, in a respectful way.

His name was Chris Watson. Everyone called him Topper. He was a nice kid. Tall, sharp features with bright red hair. Had a nice smile and an infectious laugh. Just about everyone liked Topper. He brought along a friend I didn't know. My only thought about both was "Fresh meat for the Boneyard."

Topper stood at the beginning of the run. He seemed amused as he walked down the trail about 50 feet with Steve. "This is it?" he asked of everyone near him. "The terrifying hill," he added in a sardonic tone.

"It'll grow on ya," replied Steve.

"Or it'll grow over you," said a serious Davey Davis, one of the neighborhood kids.

"I ain't afraid," said Watson, who took the first position as the driver.

"Well, you should be," said Pileski, who had said no to Watson when Stevie was invited to join him on the ride.

Said Stevie, "Nope, not this run."

The run was doomed from the start. Watson, his friend, and Davis boarded the toboggan. When the fourth rider, needed for ballast, started to get on, Watson waved him away, saying he wanted just the three to make the run. Watson's run started slowly. We pushed the toboggan almost 50 feet before it picked up speed and disappeared into the pine trees.

Steve looked at me, saying, "He's doomed. Boy, is he in for a surprise."

About 30 seconds into the run, we began hearing hollering coming from the riders. Then, it was screaming.

Rob Penfield Photo
The Glacier Today

Next, it was louder screaming. We knew they had reached Dead Man's Curve. There was silence. I mean dead silence for a long time. We waited two … three minutes. No word from below. So, Steve and I headed down the path on foot, which I would like to emphasize was no easy task.

We reached the bottom and found Davey Davis rubbing his shoulder. We asked the observers at the bottom of the hill what happened. Oh yeah, they had crashed all right. A nasty one. They had gone high into Dead Man's Curve, wildly out of control. They said Watson's eyes were as large as boiled eggs, and he was screaming the loudest of all. Then, they hit the east wall of the canyon. Careened off the top of the curve and flew upside-down across the abyss into the west side hill.

The kids at the bottom of the run said Watson "just sat motionless in the snow for a few moments. He seemed stunned. Every few seconds, he uttered a few sounds." His friend had injured his right arm. He had cuts on his arms and neck and a look on his face like he'd just seen the Frankenstein Monster.

Watson got up and began walking, stumbling away from the crash scene. Then, he broke into a brisk walk away from the area with his friend in tow. He was out of sight in a few seconds.

Steve didn't see him in school the next day. Days later, when they'd see each other in the school hallways, Watson seemed to be avoiding him. They didn't talk for weeks. Topper Watson never came back for a second run down the Boneyard.

He'd experienced the monster inside the mountain. It scared him off.

🏁

I remember a Thursday in early January 1959. It was a cold, snowy day. The runs down the trail were a bit slower, but the hill seemed to have its own agenda for the day. There would be pain for all who would test its soul.

I dislocated two fingers. Surprisingly, the high school nurse, Mae Passini, was standing near Dead Man's Curve. When we crashed, I came up hollering, holding up my right hand. Two fingers were pointing in the wrong direction. The nurse grabbed my hand and yanked on each finger. Each popped back into its socket like it was attached to a rubber band. She reached into her pocket, pulled out adhesive tape, and taped both fingers together. She said they'd heal in a couple of days.

On the next run, Robby Elliott got a huge bump on his head. Passini put a few drops from a bottle on the bump and covered it with Band-Aids. Every run that day ended with a crash that produced cuts and bruises. Passini stayed and attended to each injury. After about six or seven runs, we shut it down for the day. The tally was seven kids injured.

Just before stopping for the day, Police Officer Lester Tuller arrived. He saw the walking wounded. Asked Passini about the injuries. She didn't mince words. "Les, this goddammed thing needs to be shut down. One day, somebody's really going to get hurt."

Tuller said he'd take it to his chief and to the fire department.

Why Mae Passini had chosen to come out of the school on that day and stand at the bottom of Dead Man's Curve, we'll never know. Perhaps she had heard enough from the teachers in the classes along the backside of the school. The ones who saw the everyday crashes. Perhaps she sensed there was going to be a bad crash.

Then, there came one day. There was a crash. A very bad crash.

I was then in junior high school, so I got to the hill earlier than some of the younger grammar school kids who didn't get out of school until 3 PM. I was on board the first run of the day. It was an unusually fast track. Fortunately, we crashed before hitting Dead Man's Curve. I jammed a finger and hurt my elbow, so I decided to head home and not take any more chances with the hill. I had no way of knowing that I had just taken my last ride down the Boneyard.

I left my toboggan, "Woody." Many kids had to pass my

house, and I asked if one of them would bring it back to my house on their way home.

I was home and had started writing an essay assignment from my English Comp class. I remember my assignment. I had to write about the feeling I got when, during summer, I walked over the sands of Cape Cod's Yarmouth Beaches.

There was a knock at the door. I was greeted by Davey Davis and Bobby Bagshaw. They were sullen and quiet. Davy said I should come outside and see something, and I did. My toboggan, "Woody," was in pieces. The front sleigh-like curl was half gone. The other side cracked. The main body had been split in two places, and along the left side, a huge chunk of wood was gone. The boys had used two small pieces of rope to hold the toboggan together so they could pull it to my house.

"Woody" was, in a word, totaled.

I noticed there was blood on the boards. Lots of blood.

"Steve Pileski's blood," said Davey before I even asked.

"It was a bad crash," said Bagshaw, who was noticeably shaking. They said Stevie had been taken away in an ambulance.

Davey and I walked up my street to the Pileski house. Mrs. Pileski answered the door. She was crying. Before either one of us could say anything, she said she knew what happened. The police had called. She thanked us for stopping and closed the door. As we turned to leave, we could hear her sobbing behind the door.

I learned that many in the high school's upper floors saw the crash. Pileski was hung upside down in one of the pine trees along the top rim of Dead Man's Curve. A sharp branch had punctured his leg. He was not moving. He'd been knocked unconscious. Teachers came running out. Basketball practice ended with Russ Sholes also coming to help. School nurse Mae Passini was there. The police were called.

The new Simsbury ambulance was summoned. Pileski was transported to Hartford Hospital. I learned that he was unconscious for most of the ride and disoriented for most of his time while being processed into the hospital. He would go into surgery that evening to repair his leg, hip, shoulder, and arm. It was that serious.

My dad took one look at the toboggan. "Looks like a bad one," he said. I told him the story and what had happened to Steve. My dad called the Pileski house that evening and talked with Steve's dad, Alex Pileski. No news as yet; Steve was still in surgery.

I wouldn't find out about his injuries for almost a week.

The day after the crash, the town shut down the toboggan run. It was the end of the line for the Boneyard. That evening, First Selectman Russ Shaw made a call to the police department. He wanted to know what occurred. The police department made their report to Shaw's office first thing the next morning. Shaw didn't hesitate. "Shut the damn thing down," was his order.

Makeshift signs were made at the town's Highway Department and posted at the site. Simple signs reading, "**KEEP OUT**" and "**TRAIL CLOSED.**" Another said, "**Trespassers Will Be Prosecuted.**" And there was my personal favorite: "**PLEASE STAY AWAY FROM THIS HILL!**"

Highway Department personnel arrived. So did a few of us, to watch the activities we called "the death of the Boneyard." Trees were cut down, felled across the trail in about a half-dozen locations. Large boulders were loosened and rolled into the middle of the trail.

Holes were dug, and eight-foot telephone-pole-sized plugs were sunk into the hardened ground at points near Dead Man's Curve. Those large pine trees atop Dead Man's Curve were cut down. A bulldozer and payloader dismantled a size-able portion of what had been the high east wall of the curve. That terrifying, seven-foot-high concaved wall of sharp ice, rocks, and menacing roots. A huge stump was then placed in the middle of the trail at the end of the curve. Like an exclamation mark highlighting an obituary.

There was an irony of sorts that came from two highway department workers. It wasn't lost on us. One worker nastily said, "Git outta here, ya little shits. You're the cause of all this."

Another man came up to us and said in a softer tone, "Sorry we have to do this. My kid tells me this here hill was a real whopper." We all gave a sarcastic laugh and just nodded.

One of the kids in our group made a remark, "The spirits is dead."

He was corrected when someone said, "You mean are dead."

His comeback: "Yeah, that too."

Another kid said the Boneyard is gone.

I spoke up. "Oh no, it's not gone. It's still there. Laughing at us."

The walking trail would reopen to foot traffic eight months later in the fall of 1959. I would walk down the newer makeshift trail on a few occasions. At times, I could swear I heard the voice in that hill laughing at me.

Maybe it was just in my head, or perhaps my heart beating loudly in my chest.

Steve's injuries were serious. He'd broken his left leg and foot and cracked a kneecap and his hip. He dislocated his shoulder and had a broken hand and three broken fingers. He underwent two operations. He remained in the hospital for three weeks. During the ensuing three months, he had to make return visits to the OR for additional procedures.

At Stevie's home, an adjustable bed was set up in the living room. The medicine table next to his bed looked like a pill shelf for prescription pickup at Doyles Drugstore. Due to his numerous injuries, he was attended to by both Drs. Stretch and Cannon. The Simsbury Visiting Nurses provided the everyday support. In-home rehab began in March and continued into May.

Beginning in March, Steve's teachers would give class homework assignments that I would deliver to him. I would pick up his completed work assignments on my way to school, dropping them off with his teachers. I'd update each teacher on his physical and mental status. His return to everyday school classes was scheduled for late April.

Steve and I stayed close for another year or so. Fished local streams and ponds together and skinny dipped in Eno's Brook. We played baseball in the Simsbury Alumni League, a pre-curser to the Babe Ruth League that began in 1960. In high school, we just started to drift apart. He was a year older and began hanging out with the others in his own class. As often happens with teenagers, we just faded out of each other's lives.

I left town after high school for junior college in Massachusetts and three years in the US Army. Another three years of college followed. I did return to town for five years, from 1973 to 1978, working as the sports editor for the local paper, *The Farmington Valley Herald*. In late 1978, I left Simsbury and moved to Baltimore.

Steve became a barber. A good one. He worked around town for a few chop shops. Earned the reputation for having a "good book" and running a "clean chair." For many years, he ran his own business, *The Razor's Edge*. Located in the center of Simsbury, just a few hundred yards south of the old Boneyard.

Whenever I'd be in town for visits or events, I'd try to stop and say hello. I stopped at his shop to talk in July 2016. It was a quiet day. We reminisced, lots of memories from our days as kids. Catching brown trout in local streams. Playing Little League, Babe Ruth League, and YMCA basketball. Getting chased by the wild bulls in the orchards near Eno's Pond.

We made small talk. Always recalling those terrific lessons

learned and all our times together. We said little about how we both grew up so quickly and drifted apart. Avoided talking about those painful things that became a part of being an adult. Those transformational times that bring unwanted personal challenges and changes into lives.

We didn't talk much about the Boneyard.

Towards the end of our conversation, our tongues got tired, and we just ran out of words. I thanked him for his time. Said that I'd stop again during my next visit. I remember his parting words to me: "Until we meet again."

Steve was dead less than three weeks later. A stroke and heart attack.

I found his obituary in the *Hartford Courant* Newspaper. Nice words about him and his family. Yet I felt something was missing from the announcement. Like when a military veteran's achievements are noted, like that he was a WWII or Vietnam vet.

Perhaps I was looking for, "He was a survivor of the Boneyard."

We often look back in our lives, breaking the years into phases. Like being a kid, a teen, or a young adult. Our years as a mature adult, then our senior years. I'm not sure why we do it. Maybe that way the passage of time, the memories and regrets we have, are easier to digest or justify.

Easier, perhaps, but not easy.

We look back not for joy or entertainment. We do it because we're concerned, ashamed, or embarrassed about something. Perhaps looking for an unencumbered avenue to set the record straight. To improve something or make right in our lives what we believe is a wrong. Something we did that we're not proud to admit. A mistake we made, an error in judgment. A second chance at redemption before we begin to hear the chipping away of our epitaph on a tombstone.

Maybe we just want to talk about something that's hard to discuss. Looking for somebody to just listen in a non-judgmental way to what we need to say.

For me, the Boneyard is, has always been, one of those monsters that never die. It's a living entity inside all of us who fell under its spell. That haunting voice from deep inside the hill beckoned us to come test our courage and stupidity. To come and beat the hill. Challenging us to find our own thresholds of pain. When the chances of beating that hill were less than the odds of our memorizing a telephone directory.

What that hill did, it taught us, taught me, the value of having a plan.

With a plan, you didn't necessarily win any more than usual. A plan gave me a better chance at survival, then, and in life's later years. Using a designated plan, a procedural roadmap of sorts, became a part of my everyday survival.

Having a plan as a sportswriter covering major events like the World Series or Super Bowl. A plan as a worldwide management consultant making decisions affecting millions of dollars. Or my having a plan when I was one of four kids on a toboggan, hurtling out-of-control down a hill, when the odds were always against us.

A plan didn't guarantee success, but it did offer me precious options.

On a visit to Simsbury in 2019, I made a trip to the hill. Sixty years had passed. The trail was almost indistinguishable. Near the bottom, close to the old high school now serving as town offices, I heard a voice calling out to me. It was a Simsbury policeman. He wanted to know what I was doing roaming through his woods.

I answered, "I'm searching for a little piece of my history, my childhood." He frowned a bit, saying he wanted a more definitive answer. I told him about the toboggan run. I was trying to see if I could find it hidden within over 60 years of change.

He had one of those so-what looks on his face and told me I was trespassing. I asked who owned the land. He said it belonged to the town of Simsbury. I asked, "Do you really think every person in town will mind me being here?" Again, the officer frowned and rubbed his forehead. Then he smiled, laughed, and said, "OK, be careful. Please don't get hurt."

I turned away to hide my face. My anger and frustrations. Afraid his words and my memories of the hill would bring tears. Or I'd made a snarky statement to him. I looked up the hill through the now thinned-out woods with memories running wild in my head and said softly to myself, "Hurt, officer, you have no idea, no fucking clue what this place was." I told him I'd be careful.

No, I wasn't going to get hurt on the hill. Not anymore. Because I was wiser and had a plan. And the courage to use it in my life. To admit my mistakes because I was not afraid to come back and deal with those challenges. Those childhood fears. My adult fears, too. I roamed around the hill for another 30 minutes. Just remembering. I sat down on an old stump. Closed my eyes and listened. Soaked up the surrounding sounds like a sponge. Yeah, I could swear that I heard the hill laughing at me.

Then again, that hill, the Boneyard. That place for our virtuous stupidity. That place for the birth of my future living plan I would take with me into my adult life.

Did it ever really stop laughing at me?

4

THOSE EARLY DAYS WHEN THE ELECTRIC PILGRIMS ROCKED

WE LEARNED BECAUSE THE TIMES KEPT ON A-CHANGIN'

Change! Every day we live our lives within change.

It may gently come to us in a transformational manner. Or dramatically, in quick and sharp transitional waves. We're all given two choices for how to exist within its impact. You can become an agent of change. Or you can become a victim of change.

Whatever you choose, there are no guarantees for safe passage.

In the 1960s, change surged into our lives like poison ivy growing along a wooded tree line. You didn't see it until you were standing knee-deep in it. Often without a clue how you got there.

Change came in the form of a national recession in 1958. The post-WWII decay of inter-cities and its urban fringes. Ramped racism and widening gaps in the human classes. The breakdown of the two-parent family. Disrespect and mistrust for authority and government. The assassinations of a president and others involved with politics and racial change.

The change was a stark new wave of guns, drugs, and attitudes. The revivals of gangs, street warfare, the mystical silent majorities. There remained an ongoing beatnik movement. A new hippie movement and a sexual revolution. A war in Vietnam that violently split the country in half.

We were a country being torn apart. At war with itself and bleeding our precious resources. A young generation was teetering on the slippery edge of falling into a lifetime of self-induced mediocrity. Searching for a lifeline to grab onto.

Young people were busting out, riding a movement. Changing how we talked and walked. How we dressed and how we thought. Challenging what we had been taught. Rejecting the ways from the "Establishment." We were becoming a new and very different generation with an attitude.

And then, in the nick of time, there was music.

I was a high school senior in the fall of 1963. Henry James Memorial High School in Simsbury, Connecticut. Good school, good people. Classic old-style Southern New England town right out of a Currier and Ives painting. Now, like other towns in the area, in the painful midst of dramatic change from a long-time farming community to an expanding bedroom town. Beautiful pasture lands now adorned with new, upscale housing, their residents working in nearby cities and industrial areas.

Every night, I listened to music on my RCA Victor radio. Tuned into the new style DJs on AM stations WDRC and WPOP in Hartford, along with WHYN and WSPR in Springfield, MA. I liked rock 'n roll, doo-wop, big band, and beach music. I could handle a little folk music and early folk rock.

In October, the junior class held its annual dance. Called it the "Harvest Hoe-Down." A DJ spun his rock 'n roll records, and there was live music. A local high school trio known as The Mariners.

They played a folksy sound, hootenanny-ish. Folk and hootenanny, known as truth music, were still riding a strong wave throughout the high school and college scenes. Robbie Brainard was the group's leader, singing alongside fellow classmates Janet Stacey and Jackie Waters. Robbie was a self-taught guitar player and had become known as a good picker.

The group finished its set. I spied Robbie alone in the hallway and said hello. I told him the group sounded good. I liked hootenanny-like folk sounds, but too much became too boorish for me. I liked rock 'n roll with a strong beat. Robbie laughed, got a serious look, and said, "Rob, change in music is coming. I've seen the signs, and it's coming soon."

Oh my, Robbie Brainard was dead center on target.

Within ten months, hootenanny disappeared in the rear-view mirror faster than the use of Mercury Dimes. By the summer of 1964, Robbie Brainard was now playing British invasion sounds from the Beatles, the Rolling Stones, the Dave Clark Five, The Searchers, Them, and Gerry and the Pacemakers. He picked at his guitar strings, playing the new, imported electronic riffs as if they'd been written for him. His friend Jack Waters pounded away on a set of Ludwig drums. Steve Allen cradled his Fender guitar, picking the strings and playing lead. And Hughie Stacey sang the words to the many songs from those bands in the British Invasion to the large crowd of girls who swooned over his throaty voice and good looks.

The group became known as "The Defiants."

In the Farmington Valley and surrounding towns, they quickly became stars. Music-making darlings shilling for the state's most famous rock DJ, Dick Robinson of WDRC. The Big D in Hartford, 1360 on your AM radio dial.

Band-wise and music-wise, "The Defiants" became the musical gold standard.

During the winter of my senior year, I was fending off the lasting effects of a year-long battle with hepatitis. Instead of sitting in study halls, Russ Sholes, longtime gym teacher and athletic director, asked if I would like to come to the gym and help him with the sixth and seventh-period gym classes.

He said I would be a huge help. Showing underclass kids how to dribble a basketball. How to shoot free throws or a jump shot. Make a bounce pass, do a pick-and-roll. And in the spring, show them softball skills.

Ever since I was a little kid, I wanted to be a gym teacher. Go to Springfield College and be a Phys. Ed. Major. Then reality, along with the academics of my high school grades, set in. I knew that wasn't going to happen.

I jumped at the opportunity. It would be my time as a phys. ed. instructor.

One afternoon, I ran basketball layup drills. One kid didn't want anything to do with the activity. He was also the target of some cutting insults by bullies in the class. Called him "Dumbo-Jumbo. Fatso. Fat ass. Big lips." It hurt just to hear some of the things being said to him.

His name was Larry Sotis.

At a young age, he was a surprisingly big kid. Large barrel chest with huge hands. He was awkward and kinda disheveled. Much too overweight for his age. Not very athletic, but strong.

"You don't want any part of this, do you?" I asked.

His answer: "Nope!"

I suggested he go to the back of the line each time he got close to the front. That way, it would appear he did the exercise and would get a checkmark next to his name that he completed the activity.

He said, "OK, thanks."

Class ended, and all headed for the locker room. I felt a strong tap on my shoulder. It was Larry Sotis. He again thanked me for my kindness. Said he knew who I was and wouldn't forget me. Said he was planning to quit high school in the coming weeks. I asked what he would be doing after quitting. He smiled a smile that seemed to take up most of his entire large face.

"Play music," said Larry. "Good rock 'n roll music people want to hear. On my bass guitar and with my own band." He walked into the locker room; I figured that would be the last time I'd ever see Larry Sotis.

But as Robbie Brainard had promised, times were a-chang'in.

I completed my freshman year of college, returning home in June 1965. I would be working another summer as a counselor for Jack Wilson at the Simsbury Day Camp. A fun job I enjoyed.

Beginning in late June, Wednesday nights had become music night at the Simsbury Bowling Lanes. Bands set up on the large front steps of the sprawling building at the urging of its owner, Ambrose "Amy" Puia. They played rock music. Lots of songs from the British Invasion. Crowds often swelled to over 500 and music played until 11 PM.

One evening, I ran into a friend of mine named Howie Krogh. We both liked the English sounds and listened to a new group from Simsbury named The Chapparells. It was an odd spelling for the true definition of a chaparral, an impenetrable thicket of shrubs and small trees. They had a good sound and a strong driving beat. Their lead singer appeared to be singing flat. And struggling with the words to the songs.

I said to Howie, "Geez, even I could do better than that."

It was just past 10 PM. I felt a strong tap on my shoulder. When I turned, I was surprised to see a very large face. It was Larry Sotis, the leader of The Chapparells.

Larry got right to the point. "I remember you. From gym class. So, you think you can do better singing songs?" I figured Larry had talked with Howie Krogh.

I responded, "Well, I dunno. Better than the person who was singing for you tonight."

"You're gonna get your chance," said Sotis. "Saturday, 11 AM. My garage, Shingle Mill Road. Be there." I assured him I would be there at the appointed hour.

Saturday morning, I met the group. Larry's leadership formula was simple. He was the leader, and if you didn't like it, he'd just beat the crap out of you. Jim Oberg played rhythm guitar. He had an ear for music, played a good and steady sound, and had an appealing voice when called upon to sing. His younger brother, Davey, was the drummer. He was 14 and still learning how to play. He was a fast learner. In those early days of British rock, learning was like drinking from a fire hose. Davey's beat was solid and easy to follow.

Rusty Stone played lead guitar. He had long, shaggy hair, much like band members from the British invasion groups. When he spoke, he'd mimic the language as if he came from a rough blue-collar area, like Stepney in East London. He held and smoked his cigarettes like the Rolling Stones' Keith Richard. His guitar leads were hard, loud, and creative. Often, he'd make up leads as he played while hollering out words nobody could understand. I liked all the guys from the first minute I met them.

Larry played a strong driving bass. His huge chest and large hands made his instrument seemingly disappear into his body. His strong fingers made the large Fender bass guitar shout out like a giant whose huge feet were thundering across a wood floor wearing cowboy boots. Collectively, the group had a penetrating sound that could easily pour into every corner of a room.

Larry reminded everyone that if I was to be a part of the group, the decision had to be unanimous. All agreed. I, too, nodded. Dared not do anything else.

We went through five or six songs. I did OK. Jimmy said, "Let's pick one song and play it like we're earning money." Jim always had concerns about money. All nodded. The song chosen, "Little Latin Lupe Lu," was a hard-driving and fun song by the Kingsmen. I knew the song well and put every ounce of energy into my vocal output. When finished, Oberg looked to the others and said, "Now that's a money sound." Larry nodded. Stoney spoke a line like he was in London. Davey banged a rimshot on the snare drum. I took a deep breath, trying to relax.

We did two more songs, "It's All Over Now" by the Rolling Stones and "Ticket to Ride" by the Beatles. They must have sounded pretty good. When we finished, there was a small crowd standing at the bottom of the Sotis driveway, waving at us with thumbs up. Larry made the deciding vote. "You're In!"

Larry said we'd practice again Wednesday night. The other guys laughed. I was confused and asked, "Practice, Wednesday night. Where?" Larry looked me straight in the eyes, saying, "On the steps of the bowling alley."

Rusty Stone said, "And we're gonna sound great, mate."

And on Wednesday night, we did!

Another new local band was called The Misfits. Randy and The Misfits.

Randy Faraar was small in physical stature, somewhat homunculus. He had a monster ego, quick fingers on the strings of his guitar, and a huge heart and soul to play music. And when he and The Misfits played, their sound was crisp and large. They played it loud. Their motto was, "Turn it up!"

The crowds liked their sound.

Randy and Jim Cooke were friends. Like so many teens of the times, they felt out of place and were searching for their own paths during these changing times. A lot like misfits. They wanted to play music and impress the girls. The Misfits were formed.

Randy would play lead guitar because that's what Randy

did. Jim Cooke played bass guitar in the classic style. He stood straight and erect. The neck of his bass guitar pointed at 11 o'clock like Bill Wyman of the Rolling Stones. Art Lane attended Westminster School and played rhythm guitar. Bobby Bagshaw, a neighbor of mine who lived on Northfield Road, became the drummer. Occasionally, others would perform with the group, most notably Brian Falk on saxophone.

Remembered Bagshaw, "We all came from different lives. We were Misfits."

One evening, WDRC's Dick Robinson put in a plug for The Misfits, who would be playing in a local Battle of the Bands. Robinson urged folks to come listen because "They're fun to watch, especially the little guy out front. They play good music."

Robinson added one more thought. "They're Misfits and they play loud!"

WDRC Archives Photo
Dick Robinson (circa 1965) Poolside at the WDRC Mic

The British Invasion impacted local kids who were forming bands and playing that new imported sound. Picking strings as far back on the guitar's bridge to get that sharp, almost off-key sound. That rough Stepney part of London or

Liverpool sound. The English echo and the Mersey beat.

Kids grew their hair longer. Bands dressed in coordinated outfits, wild colors like what the British kids along London's Carnaby Street were wearing. They smoked unfiltered cigarettes like Pall Mall Longs in the distinctive red package. Bands standardized their approach to a lead guitar, rhythm, and bass guitar. A full set of drums, lead singer, and occasional accouterments such as an organ, piano, sax, or other brass.

Influences came from outside our Farmington Valley. The one standard bearer of fame was an opportunity to play the K of C Hall in Windsor Locks. It didn't sound luxurious, but one Friday night at "the Hall" would put a band on a fast track throughout Connecticut and western Massachusetts. Especially with the support of DJs Dick Robinson at WDRC and Phil Dee at the Springfield, MA, station WHYN, 560 on the AM dial.

Robinson was something of an enigma. He could be friendly, or he could be aloof. He knew the Rolling Stones and the Beatles and was on a first-name basis with many rock 'n roll and doo-wop performers around the country. Dick Clark would call him at home. Robinson had input to the infamous 1964 documentary, *T.A.M.I. Show* in California. He could make or break a band with just a few words on his nightly show, *Poolside with Dickie Robinson*. He was the host DJ for those infamous nights at the Windsor Locks K of C Hall.

Three groups had a monster impact on our local area. Monty and the Specialties came out of western Massachusetts. They were involved in multi-music activities and backed up groups cutting records. They made TV appearances and were the house band on the stage in the mammoth ballroom at Mt. Tom's Mountain Park in Holyoke, Massachusetts. They featured a teenage sensation on saxophone, Barry Dill, who could belt out rock 'n roll, do-wop, gospel, and rhythm and blues. Dill had that throaty, raspy voice that oozed passion. Thousands showed up at the ballroom every Saturday night.

When they played at the K of C, the crowds were so large

that many wrapped around the building for hours waiting to get in had to be turned away.

Another Springfield, MA, group was The Northern Lights. It was 1964, and I saw them perform at a Springfield College dance. A local TV station director cut a deal with them right there on the stage. That next morning, they played live on Springfield TV station WWLP, Channel 22. They did a song called "All Alone."

They, too, would play the K of C in Windsor Locks to large crowds. Many were turned away at the door. Their popularity would grow. They would change their name to the Busters and have a regional hit, "Bust Out."

A hometown group from Windsor, CT, The Six Packs, would also make its mark in a very large way at the K of C. Led by a creative music writer, Al Anderson. Dick Robinson would hear them play. Start them on a series of gigs with nationally named bands. They'd play throughout Connecticut, including a local sixteenth birthday party in East Granby with the popular girl's group The Angels, who three years earlier had a national number-one hit with "My Boyfriend's Back."

They, too, changed their name, becoming The Wild Weeds, and would have a national hit with "No Good to Cry." "Big Al" Anderson would go on to become a prolific music writer and earn worldwide honors as BMI's Songwriter of the Year in 2000.

The Defiants' Robbie Brainard, at the urging of Dick Robinson, went to the K of C to hear these groups. Randy Faraar from The Misfits made the 25-mile journey to Windsor Locks to see and learn from the groups. Other emerging groups would make a pilgrimage to the K of C in Windsor Locks. The Esquires from Western Massachusetts. Connecticut bands The Ravens, The Shags from North Haven, Burgandy Sunset, and Davey and the Dolphins, The Del-Tones, Blue Echoes, The Ascots from Westminster School, and the Young Alley Cats.

National artist and Woodstock performer Taj Mahal

was seen in the K of C crowd. So was Jay Black of Jay and the Americans, Ronnie Dove from Baltimore, and George McCannon III from Winsted. Phil Spector, with his infamous "Wall of Sound," was seen taking notes. Moulty, the drummer from the Barbarians, made a visit, as did female singers from the Angels, The Ronettes, The Shangri Las, and national number one soloist Lesley Gore.

Robbie Brainard would say, "Play the K of C, and you made it."

In Granby, a new band formed. They became The Shadows.

Mysterious name. Kinda cool. The group didn't, as yet, have a sound or songs. So, they worked on a name. There was a British band known as The Shadows. Back-ups for English singer Cliff Richard and writers of a well-known and still used musical standard, "Apache."

A local high school student, Bruce Unger, was a band member. "We liked the name and just wanted to play a little music, impress girls, and make a few bucks." During their time together, The Shadows from Granby certainly accomplished those goals.

There was also a group in Chicago known as The Shadows of Knight. Their 1966 national hit was "G L O R I A ... Gloria."

Once established, The Shadows from Granby would use "Gloria" as a lead-in song on many nights.

During the early days, they worked on building their sound. Ralph and Roger Kemp were the unofficial leaders of the band. Longtime friend Bruce Unger was the group's lead guitarist. Perhaps the only one in the early days who's a true musician. Another student, Rich Linell, became the drummer.

Unger recalled the early days: "I think we first did a talent show at high school. Then, got a paying gig at the congregational church. Maybe $40. We hadn't practiced much. Had only six or seven songs we could play. But, like the times, somehow, we got through it."

Ralph Kemp played rhythm guitar. At times, he tried to use his instrument as a bass guitar. They'd loosen the strings, toning the instrument to a dull, soft sound. It didn't work, but these were the tasks used during the early years. Eventually, Ralph got a bass guitar, and often, other bass guitarists would sit in with the group.

During their ensuing years, the group would have an ensemble of folks who would help hone their sound and song repertoire, like Brian Fogerty on guitar and Dan Beaman with vocals. Bob Forte's keyboard would add a full-bodied sound, and crowds took notice. Larry Sotis from the Chapparells would play a dynamic bass for the band on many nights, and their sound would drive people to the dance floor. They would play British invasion sounds. Straight rock n roll and hard blues. Soft ballads.

The Shadows' name became known. From the stages at Granby's Kerns and Kelly Lane Schools and Granby Rec Center to those rock 'n roll nights at the old East Granby Firehouse. Throughout Connecticut and reaching into northern Maine. Drummer Rich Linell remembered: "One day, we're just trying to get through a few songs in the church basement. The guys yelling at me, 'DON'T SING.' Even though I had a mike set up next to my drums, I didn't have a singing voice. Then, in what seemed like a short time, we're playing huge dorm dances at UConn. It was exciting. And the guys were still yelling at me not to sing. It was lots of fun and a wonderful time in our lives."

The band and its sounds would grow. As would their shadows.

It was known as The "Battle of the Bands." Every week, beginning in late June 1965, the three Simsbury bands would come together and battle it out for ego satisfaction and prize money.

I used to refer to those events as "The nights the dogs barked."

Dick Robinson, from his WDRC AM 1360 "Pool Side Show," once used my dogs barking moniker to describe the competition.

Wednesday nights, it was the front steps at Simsbury Bowling Lanes. Usually, two, sometimes three, groups would vie for the money. The winner was determined by the lanes' owner, Amy Puia, and his son Vic, who would later become the first selectman of Windsor Locks. The winning band was awarded $150.

Thursday nights, it was the Barn in West Simsbury. Smaller crowds, but the music was loud and lively. The winners were picked by the town's rec people assigned to that evening's events, along with a member of the Marshman family, who owned the property. Often, a local policeman who was on duty helped make a choice, along with a volunteer fireman and a horse trainer. It was a little like West Simsbury's early onset version of the Village People. The night's band winner was given $100.

Saturday nights were special on the stage at the Ensign Parish House. Today, it's Metro Bis restaurant. Everything about that evening got ramped up a few notches. The competition, trash talk, insults, and intensity. It was a dance sponsored by the town and the church. But it was all about the battle of the bands. And everybody in that room knew it.

It was a big room with crowds of over 400. Bands played from 7 to 10:30 PM, and the acoustics were terrific. Typically, it was three bands: The Defiants, Randy and The Misfits, and The Chapparells. Each was to be paid $75. It was no secret that The Defiants were paid more. You drew for your spot in the lineup. Every band wanted the second spot. If you went on stage first, at 7 PM, the room was almost empty. If you played last, sometime around 10 PM, crowds were thinning. Band number two played during prime time, or what was called money time.

Determining a winner was unique. One member from each band had a vote and had to use that vote on one of the other two bands. Two or three attendees from that evening's crowd also voted for the winner. Typically, one of the Parks and Rec managers in attendance was also given a vote. The winner was awarded $200. Some nights, it was $300.

The Defiants, with one exception, won every Saturday night competition. The only night they failed to win outright, they ended up in a tie with The Misfits. Funny how that all worked out. Dick Robinson just smiled and continued working his magic.

Despite the complaints, The Defiants were the best band. Yeah, we all had our own self-imposed styles, but we all wanted to be The Defiants. The type of band we all tried to be. Hands down, they were the gold standard for the emerging music scene throughout the Valley.

There was an amusing occurrence associated with those Saturday night battles. It spoke to the politics of the times and the power of the media, in this case, Radio Station WDRC. One of those lessons learned. It taught me that despite everything I've been told, elephants do have long memories.

The Defiants had a relationship with WDRC's Dick Robinson. They often visited him while he was on the air. One night, Robinson began a promo for Saturday's Battle of the Bands. In the background, you heard the Defiants horsing around in the studio. They even answered phones. Robinson would muffle the sound. Laughing, he'd say, "NO, you can't do that." You'd hear Hugh Stacey say, "Good evening from WDRC. Hugh of The Defiants here. What can we play for you?"

During Robinson's on-air delivery, he talked up the Defiants and their stylish music. He mentioned Randy's Misfits and their turn-it-up sound. Then he stumbled a bit, not remembering the name of our band. You could hear Robbie Brainard say to Robinson, "The Chapparells."

Robinson let go a zinger, "Oh, yeah, tubby and the boys." A very unprofessional reference to Larry Sotis' physical appearance. My immediate thought: "Fuck you, Dick Robinson."

A few minutes later, my phone rang. It was Larry. Yes, he, too, had heard it, and yes, he was pissed off enough to say, "Tubby, huh? Maybe he'd like Tubby to kick his ass." Make no mistake, people. Larry Sotis would have kicked Dick Robinson's ass into next week's broadcast.

Searching for something to say, I mumbled words to calm him down. Said he could be the bigger man just letting it go. Sometimes, the most powerful words are the ones not spoken. Be the smarter elephant.

Larry was quiet, then said, "Thanks," and hung up.

Saturday night, I saw Robbie Brainard arrive. I went up to him and said, "We heard what Robinson said. That was pretty shitty, unprofessional. He talks you guys up, then says that shit on the air about people he doesn't even know. He's never talked to us." To my surprise, Robbie agreed.

Robinson wasn't expected to be in Simsbury. Yet, to everyone's surprise, there he was, standing in the doorway, talking with Hugh Stacey. I told the guys in the group that I'd be right back. As I jumped down from the stage, I saw Larry take off his bass guitar and follow me.

I approached Robinson. Hugh saw me coming and walked away. I introduced myself and my association with The Chapparells. He had never taken the time to introduce himself to us. I said his "Tubby and the boys" pot-shot at Larry and us was unprofessional. And I didn't care how big a personality he thought he was; I certainly couldn't respect someone who acted like that.

And I added, "I certainly don't respect or want anything from you."

He was taken aback. People around us had heard my words. Suddenly, he was uncomfortable. Couldn't look me in the eyes. Stared down at his shoes and woefully attempted an apology. The man of the public airways with a microphone and radio station as an amplifier struggled to find the right words.

"Don't apologize to me," I shot back. "Have the balls and apologize to Larry."

Larry was the next to confront Robinson. He stood in front of him. I thought Larry was going to deck him. I heard Robinson say how sorry and ashamed he was. He would do what he could on air to make it right. Larry stared at Robinson and said nothing. Powerful! Then he turned and walked back to the stage.

Later that night, we stood outside having a cigarette. Larry smiled at me and said, "Silent words, very powerful. Thanks." I smiled.

That night, from every direction, you could hear the dogs barking.

About 10 years later, I was covering sports for the *Farmington Valley Herald*. I'd been at Farmington High School and was on my way back to Simsbury on a cold and miserable winter's night. Rain and snow with nasty driving conditions as I drove towards Unionville.

On a dark, desolate stretch, I came upon a car along the side of the road. It had a flat tire. The driver was standing next to his car, irritated and animated. I stopped and offered help. It took about 25 minutes for me to change the tire. I was soaked and cold. The driver offered his hand and what appeared to be $25.

It was then I recognized him. Dick Robinson.

I shook my head, saying no, I didn't want his money. He

begged me to take it. Of my many lessons learned, one is that sometimes there is money that, no matter the amount, you don't touch. Perhaps because of pride, self-respect, self-esteem, and principles.

Robinson asked, "Do I know you?" My answer was, "I don't believe so," which, in fact, was the truth. He said I looked familiar. Asked if I worked in radio or TV. I shook my head no. I opened the door and got into my car. He blurted out, "Wait, yeah. It's you. I do know you." He took a step closer.

"It's Rob, isn't it?" he said softly. He smiled as if proud of himself for remembering my name. He waited for my response.

I looked back at Dick Robinson. Said nothing. Powerful words. Closed the car door and drove away.

Oh yeah, the elephant remembered.

Randy and his Misfits played lots of local gigs. The Ensign Parish House and the Barn. High schools in the valley, including proms. Bobby Bagshaw recalled the nights at the Ensign House. "We had a good following. People liked our sound. We won one of those battles. Beat out The Defiants."

The Misfits' sound was loud yet fun to listen to. They covered lots of British songs from the Rolling Stones, Beatles, Dave Clark Five, and others. They easily shifted into steady rock from Gary Lewis and the Playboys and the McCoys. Bluesy rock from Ramsey Lewis.

Randy Faraar was the frontman and lead guitarist. He played it hard and loud. He would pick someone out of the crowd. Make eye contact and stare at them. Play his lead and make a series of odd faces. Then, start bouncing around the stage like a rubber ball.

Perhaps it's why they decided on the name The Misfits.

Jim Cooke would always be heard. The strong, steady undercurrent he played from his bass guitar. A continuous sound from the rhythm guitar of Art Lane and Bagshaw, though not spectacular as a drummer, played a steady, definitive beat, especially on his drum solos.

Bands may have exchanged lots of trash talk. But we always listened to each other. Out of respect, and often because we were using each other's equipment. Like Larry's Sotis' Sears Silvertone amps. Everybody wanted to use them, including The Misfits, The Shadows, and The Defiants.

Jim Cooke could pick a bass guitar and give it personality. I recall my discussions with him. I would ask questions about playing bass. He was a nice kid. Friendly, pleasant, and enjoyable to talk with. He would always say, "Hey, thanks for asking."

Fans of The Misfits stood on the floor in front of them, yelling, *"Turn it up!"*

Dick Robinson heard about The Shadows from a WDRC station stringer doing a dance at the East Granby Firehouse. The band was dressed in Nehru jackets. Clean cut, polite, and they played music that drove people to the dance floor.

The birddog gave Robinson a call while he was on air. Robinson made an immediate decision and announced the group would be appearing at the K of C before the offer was even made to the Shadows. When contacted, the group eagerly accepted. Hey, this was Dickie Robinson and the Windsor Locks K of C Hall calling. During their appearance at the K of C Hall, The Shadows played spectacularly.

Suddenly, these four guys from Granby were casting a much larger Shadow across the state. People liked their act and sound. Huge crowds showed up to see them perform. Their notoriety throughout the region, skyrocketed.

The phone started ringing. UConn dorm parties. They played to an eager audience. They were asked back, again and again. The gigs became a cash cow. They paid well, and with each visit, the crowds did not want them to stop playing at what was the witching hour.

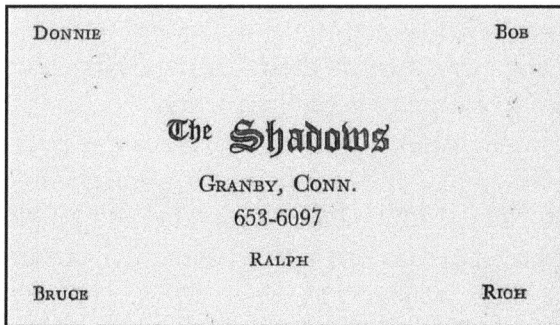

"The Shadows" 1966 Business Card

Bruce Unger laughed as he remembered how he'd open his guitar case and set it in front of the band. "We'll keep playing as long as you keep paying," was the message. Contributions flowed in, and the band played on. They would make more on the continuing donations than they were making on the original agreement costs. On some nights, the band would leave the dorm parties with over $700. Huge money for the times,

"Amazing and a little scary," remembered Unger. "We'd start playing a Stones song or an instrumental like 'Wipeout.' The money kept being tossed into my case."

"Yes, I remember that money," said Rich Linell. "And even though I had a mike, the guys wouldn't let me sing," remembered Linnell laughing. "The other guys kept yelling at me not to sing. I just kept banging my snare drum, keeping a solid beat, and watching the money being thrown into Brian's guitar case."

Unger recalled the time they were asked to perform at a town hall in Maine. "Big promotion for us. Good money," said Brian. "Local radio, TV, and newspaper coverage. When we arrived in the van, the folks promoting the show and the police had to make a path for us to get into the old town hall.

103

Girls were screaming and grabbing at us. Like we're a touring British rock band."

A local band got the night going. The Shadows then cast their aura over the large crowd and played a terrific show. "It was exciting," said Unger, "until we started to leave. The girls loved us. The guys, because their girlfriends liked us, they did not like us. It started to get a little scary."

There was pushing and shoving. Threats, a punch or two. Police had to step in and ensure the guys and their equipment made it to the van. "We didn't hang around," laughed Bruce. "We got the hell outta town. With some new memories. Our skins. And their money."

The group was also known to play many outside gigs. Most notably, those known as the "Comp Parties" in Winsted. Some of the last times, most of the original group played together. It was like the UConn dorm parties. The group was scheduled to play until 10 PM. The crowd called for more.

Once again, Bruce Unger opened his guitar case and announced, "Folks, the bank is open." They played well beyond 11 PM and had one of their most profitable nights ever. Often, Larry Sotis would join in with the group playing bass. Usually, because on those nights, The Shadows were using Larry's powerful Silvertone Amps. With Larry pulling bass strings, the band's sound got even better.

Rich Linnell recalled those times with sheer wonder. "What we accomplished. What I accomplished. Learned how to play drums on my own. Piano, too. Played in the marching band. Learned the drum riffs listening to old 45s. The Beatles, Stones, Beach Boys, Ventures. All those memories. And fun times with the guys."Unger's wife, Bonnie, and others from East Granby, like Merry Kimberly, when speaking indirectly about The Shadows, all agreed: "They played great music. All the best-looking guys came from Granby." The Shadows did play good music and developed a huge following.

Larry Sotis' Chapparells took to the road and began playing in places where, if you asked somebody where the people were from, the answer was always, "Everyone here is from someplace else."

We became nomads. The band nobody really knew, but they kept asking us to come back because those people from someplace else liked the British sounds we played. We played many times in western Massachusetts. In Northampton for the commercial college and Smith College. In Amherst at UMass and for Amherst College mixers.

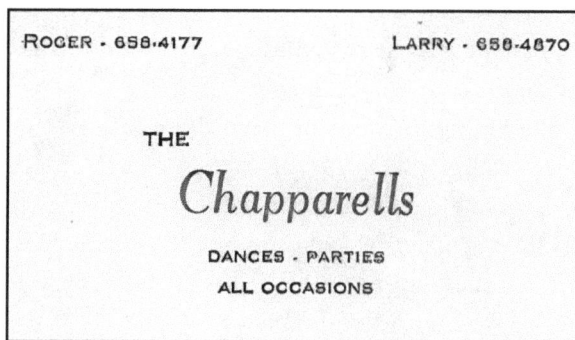

ROGER · 658·4177   LARRY · 658·4870

THE

Chapparells

DANCES · PARTIES
ALL OCCASIONS

"The Chapparells" of Simsbury 1965 Business Card

Springfield's WHYN Radio DJ Phil Dee heard our sound and invited us to perform on the stage at Holyoke's Mountain Park atop Mt. Tom with national bands like The Barbarians and Sam Sham and the Pharaohs. Both groups had performed on the popular teen shows *Hullabaloo* and *Shindig*. Sam the Sham had an appearance on *The Ed Sullivan Show*. The Barbarians had their big break appearing in the 1964 internationally produced *T.A.M.I. Show*, a production that has since become a cult documentary. A production that WDRC's Dick Robinson had a hand in producing.

We also would share the stage with the popular house band Monty and the Specialties, featuring their sax player and singer, Barry Dill. Barry and I sat next to each other in two classes at Northampton Commercial College. During class, we'd talk about baseball and music. Share answers on tests. Get the same grade. Somehow, that didn't get past the teacher. "I'm watching you two," said Professor Henry Trow, pointing at us with a scowl on his face.

We'd both answer, "OK," in unison, as if singing a duet. It drove Mr. Trow nuts.

Nights at Mountain Park drew over 2000, some nights as many as 3000 music fans from throughout western Massachusetts. It was a rough and rowdy crowd. We would play the Mt. Tom ballroom three times. One night, the house band's electric organ went down. Barry and I went to ask Sam the Sham if we could use his band's organ, which was the same brand and model.

Sam, whose name was Domingo Samudio, was a 27-year-old Vietnam vet. He was in the bar smoking cigarettes and drinking Scotch. He looked at both of us and said, "Sure, just don't put no cig-ga-retti burnies on it." Barry promised we would not. Sam smiled and doffed his turban at us. Drank his Scotch. We roared with laughter.

The Barbarians were a garage band from Cape Cod and during summer 1965 had a national song, "Are You a Boy or Are You a Girl." Their drummer was Victor "Moulty" Moulton. He had lost a hand in a childhood accident and played drums with a hook. During performances, he broke drumsticks. Yelled to me to toss him a few. I did; he caught them, inserted them into the hook, and played on. Occasionally looking over at me and nodding.

Following their set, Moulty searched me out. Tapped me on the shoulder with his hook. Told me our band had a nice sound, and he liked my voice. I said thanks. We went to shake hands. Yep, lefthanded, I shook his hook.

The Chapparells played fraternity parties for the University of Hartford and for the Hartford branch of UConn. There was a combo dance for St. Joseph's College and Hartford College

R.B Archives Photo
Robbie Brainard The Defiants
Six Decades Making Music

for Women. A Christmas party in Elmwood where the basement of the house resembled the deep hole of a ship. It paid well with free food.

On the ride home that evening, our discussion focused on the question, "How the hell do we end up in these places?" The second issue for discussion came from our young drummer, Davey. Earlier in the month, he had been looking for a piece of equipment and went into Larry's bedroom in Simsbury. When he returned, he had a strange look on his face.

Davey asked, "Why does Larry have an engine from a car on his bed?" In fact, it was a fully equipped 1953 Oldsmobile Rocket 88 motor. We never found out the answer to his question.

Nobody dared ask Larry.

The Defiants started with a name in 1964. Now, they needed a gig. Their first opportunity came from David Hogarth, who asked the group to play a small dance at Saint Albans Church in West Simsbury.

"I think we were paid $50," said Robbie Brainard. "And to do the dance, we had to borrow amps from Larry Sotis because we didn't have any."

Within a few months, they were in contact with Dick Robinson from WDRC. His *Pool Side* show was the most popular DJ show in the state. By mid-1965, the band was formed and putting out a sound people wanted to hear. With Brainard leading the group and Robinson pushing all the promo buttons, The Defiants' popularity skyrocketed.

Their sound became known at the K of C Hall in Windsor Locks. Robinson had them record songs. Sounds they had written and songs from others. They played shows emceed by Robinson in Hartford, West Hartford, Moosup, Bristol, Windsor, and New Britain. Wherever Robinson could find a paying audience.

Brainard was a good leader. He was one of the better guitar players and played within the controlled tolerances of sound and creativity. He had a good singing voice. Nice range, and the band's repertoire of songs performed was huge and diverse. It's why, almost 60 years later, he still has the energy and desire and occasionally performs his music in the Farmington Valley.

Jack Waters played the drums with passion. He'd lean in as he attacked the snare drum. Shift to his right with a rush of sticks over the tom-toms. His foot pumping up-and-down like a piston as the big bass drum boomed in a syncopated serendipity. He'd look out over the crowd, head nodding. A smile on his face. Yelling out, *"Yeah, Yeah,"* loudly.

Steve Allen was a reluctant star and lead guitarist. He liked to play and play he could. He'd walk out front and play a chorus and lead riff. His mannerisms were quiet and low-key. And when he was done and had played flawlessly, he'd just smile and take two steps back. He was a quiet and powerful personality.

They would open a show with crowds howling as they bounced through a spirited version of the Beatles song "Slow Down." They would do "Unchain My Heart" by Ray Charles. Folk rock songs from the Byrds. They would captivate you with their sound.

Hugh Stacey, his long hair falling in his face, would sing and raise the temperature in the room. And when Stacey, wearing a snug red sweater, would sing "Please Don't Wear Red Tonight," a Beatles song. Girls, rubber-legged and hanging on to each other in front of the stage, would swoon.

Oh yeah. When The Defiants had their sound smoking, things happened. Crowds formed. People sang along with the group, and temperatures in the room would rise. The music mixture was enjoyable, satisfying, and intoxicating. Dick Robinson pandered. And a few girls fell over, passed out on the floor.

And the music continued until the clock struck midnight.

Change. I've often said that nothing good ever lasts.

Eventually, we all come face-to-face with the great equalizer. Time. Because in so many ways affecting lives, the beat goes on. As agents of that never-ending change, we must adapt. Using the lessons learned, like from those experiences we had as a member of an emerging rock 'n roll band.

Albeit even if for just a few years or a few months.

The Shadows' Bruce Unger remembered, "Just knew when it was time to move on." He had enjoyed his time in the group. The fun, experiences, the money, and the memories. Like a perfectly timed extracurricular activity from high school. But now it was time. "Life's responsibilities beckoned," said Unger with no remorse. It was time to move on, time to grow and time for change.

Bandmate Rich Linnell agreed. "We went from a high school talent show to being known as a good band, The Shadows. Just a bunch of us guys from Granby who played good music. Wonderful memories. I'm proud of what we accomplished. We made our mark. But we all knew when it was time to move on."

In Simsbury, Randy and The Misfits drifted apart. Art Lane graduated from private school and went on to college.

Despite a lifetime heart condition, he stayed involved with music. He lost his battle with heart disease in 2021. Drummer Bobby Bagshaw moved downstate, eventually ending up in California.

Randy Faraar continued with music, playing with numerous local bands for years. He battled illnesses and afflictions and died in his early sixties. Jim Cooke settled in Vermont as a world-class artisan and maker of high-quality bass guitars. He would begin building his first bass the day after John Lennon was assassinated. He's stayed close to music and fondly remembers his days in Simsbury as bass guitarist of The Misfits.

You could hear the warmth and sincerity in Cooke's voice as he explained, "I don't think my words can adequately describe those wonderful, terrific times we had together. I cherish those memories. Thanks for asking me about them."

My time with The Chapparells ended in January 1966 after just seven months with the group. I was co-captain of my junior college's basketball team, and the schedule for practices and games made it impossible for me to continue with the group.

We did a final show in West Hartford. I thanked Larry and the others for allowing me to be a part of the band. I really wasn't much of a lead singer. I could hold a tune, and when my voice melded with other voices, mixed with the electric sounds of a rhythm and lead guitar, I sounded OK. And I knew all the words to the songs.

By late 1966, I was in the US Army. A year later, I was in Vietnam. Time...it's relentless and has no empathy. By summer 1966, each band member had gone his own way. To new bands, new music, and, for others, new endeavors in their lives.

Rusty Stone distinguished himself and his music style with many bands. He would continue to play an innovative, creative, and hard-driving style. His mom would move the family to Maryland. Perhaps to escape old memories or for a fresh start with new lives. He would stay involved with music during the ensuing years.

The Oberg family moved to Virginia. Davey eventually went to South Carolina because, as often happens when traveling life's roads, brothers become estranged from each other for any number of reasons. Jim would serve in Vietnam. And like me, he would struggle with horrible memories of those times in another world.

He would use his music to fight back against those horrible memories of death. What I have come to refer to as *"the Bastard."* He would write music about Vietnam. You can find his song and poignant words in a haunting melody on Google titled *"A Place We Called Vietnam."* You'll hear his hard emotions and what Vietnam does to a person as it lives on inside us. Memories that never go away.

We talked about those memories. About trying to forget. We agreed, you never forget what happened there. Probably because, if we did forget, it just wouldn't be worth continuing on. Wondering why we made it. Others didn't. That the real challenge is to continue on. Live a productive life, despite what you don't want to remember. Continue on because, with each new day, there's always hope.

Larry Sotis battled a lifetime of illnesses and physical conditions. He would play his bass guitar whenever he was able to do so. Often with The Shadows, then with the newer local bands that had formed. Most bands

Oberg Archives Photo
Jim Oberg
"A Place We Called Vietnam"

wanted his bass-playing skills and to use his wonderful Sears Silvertone Amps. His weight and circulatory problems, exacerbated by other existing childhood afflictions, would take their toll.

Larry would die before his 40th birthday.

I have good memories of Larry, that kid I met in gym class. More confident in his desires than those making fun of him would ever be able to comprehend. That kid who asked me to be a part of his band. And, of course, that sometimes strange individual who never answered Davey's question of why he had a car motor on his bed.

If asked, I'm sure his answer would have been, as I often suggested to him, an answer of silence. Powerful, just the way he played his bass guitar. When any one of us in any of the bands needed reassurance, we just looked over to the far corner of the stage. We'd see Larry's smiling face. His huge fingers pulling at the bass guitar strings. That large bass guitar almost lost as it rested against his giant torso. And we all felt a little safer and comfortable.

Another one of those signs of the times in our always-changing world.

Robbie Brainard is the last living member of The Defiants. A sad and strange epitaph to a local band that emerged during the British Invasion that seemed to have it all.

They had the good fortune to come together and play one more time about 20 years back for a two-night gig in Simsbury. They played their old music and wowed the audiences as they had done 40 years prior. Reminisced about their times together and played their favorite songs. Drank beer. Forgot a few of the words to their songs. Laughed heartedly and rekindled the gold standard. When they said goodbye, all in the group knew it would be for the final time.

Drummer Jack Waters died in 2020. I have fond memories of his driving style. Sweat glistening as it ran down from his mop of red hair. He had settled in Rhode Island. Was a painter, fisherman, and musician. He died because his body was just worn out by the enjoyment and indulgences during his life.

I recall a favorite saying of Jack's: "I just like having a blast."

Steve Allen was the group's lead guitarist. He was a strong, silent rocker. A football player, teacher, historian, and family man. He was reserved in his playing style, yet he could pick with the best of the lead guitarists. A nice, reputable person, kind with empathy. He died in 2020. Another victim of one of life's awful diseases.

Hugh Stacey joined the Marines and went to Vietnam. "Never was right after that," said Brainard. "He just wasn't Hughie anymore." I explained to Robbie that after what we saw over there, everyone is changed. I told Robbie, "None of us are ... well, nothing is ever the same."

Hughie died far too young, it was said, from a broken heart.

The times, yeah. They just kept on a-chang'in.

That first wave of electric pilgrims and local bands faded and blended into their next lives. A little of that early innocence died. Locally, new groups emerged, playing a more aggressive and cutting style of electric rock.

Vietnam took over the nightly news. The new army of defiant people seemed to grow precipitously. They and their music were angry. They ushered in psychedelic and acid rock, putting music into a different orbit. The Byrds took us "Eight Miles High." We romped through "Strawberry Fields" with the Beatles. The Doors challenged the world with "Light My Fire," and the Who said in a song, "I Can See for Miles."

From the grave, Otis Redding told us about "(Sittin' On) The Dock of the Bay." Steppenwolf said we were "Born to Be Wild." The crazy world of Arthur Brown regaled us with "Fire." Then we deteriorated to the lowest depths with bubblegum sounds from the Archies and the 1910 Fruitgum Co.

Mary Hopkin tried to reminisce and compartmentalize all the confusion with "Those Were the Days."

Even off-rock was like walking through a beckoning cemetery. "Abraham, Martin and John," from Dion DiMucci, chronicled the assassinations of three giants in the sociology of our history. Rhyming words heralding good and bad, right and wrong, black and white.

Simon and Garfinkel sang a chilling song, "Silent Night Seven O'Clock News." A song of Christmas overdubbed into a network news broadcast of disappearing mores, beliefs, and a breakdown of social support systems for law and order. Accelerating the decaying downward slide of our world's mental health.

It became a time of rebirth for philosopher and writer Ayn Rand's torturous novel *Atlas Shrugged*. The omnipresent omens for the coming apocalyptic referendums of life. The breakdown of the human class system, and the beginning of the end for what had been rational philosophy.

The con man Charles Manson's belief in the coming of "Helter Skelter." His planned war between the races. Choreographed to the music from the Beatles' *White Album* amid murder, mayhem, venereal disease, and mind-blowing drugs.

And we wondered. Had our world begun its irreversible swan dive into the final horrors of the ever-widening great abyss? The end, just as Jan and Dean had said so simply in song, "Won't Come Back from Deadman's Curve."

Fortunately, the answer was...maybe!

Maybe, because those early electric pilgrims, those kids I knew from the mid-sixties went on to live in the real world of adult roles and responsibilities. They used critical lessons learned about the need for love and hope. Surviving the daily challenges from life's Four Horsemen: Famine, Pestilence, Destruction, and Death. And survived because of those wonderful lessons learned about commitment and togetherness found in the words to their songs they once sang.

Fortunately, we all didn't get mired in Ayn Rand's philosophical world of manifestos that can dismantle our institutions for survival. Where the rich are allowed to do whatever they please. Or a world that allowed cold-blooded murderers to carry out conspiracies that are, in their minds, acceptable, above and beyond our laws.

Sadly, much like situations our world continues to deal with today.

We continued to fend off the ill winds because of the good that is still in so many of us. Those lessons learned. That the good in all of us will always win out over evil. There will always be hope as long as we keep trying.

We were the middle class and the early "Electronic Pilgrims of the British Invasion." Despite all, we're still the way of the world. Because sergeants, not generals, run the army. Because hourly workers and self-ownership of business, not management and its executives, are the reason businesses and corporations are successful. Because we still raise our own families and mow our own lawns. Belong to volunteer fire departments. Go to carnivals and holiday parades. Still shop in local stores and use local businesses. Have barbecues on the back deck. Fight for what we still believe in, because hope is still very much a part of our lives.

I came to understand that my time in a rock band wasn't just hollering words into a microphone. It was a time for learning about working together with others to build relationships and change. All the pieces needed that contributes to change. To give a little. To take a little. Understand, the trust we search for at every intersection is a positive decision we've all learned how to make. Not to be viewed or accepted as a compromise.

We did it because we wanted to. Not because we had to. Doing good deeds because, in fact, we're all "good-deed doers."

We grew up and became adults. Grew more confident with those words we once sang; only now, we sing those words in a different manner and on a much higher plane in our lives. Choosing to live and to be who we are. As opposed to an outdated and listless struggle of yesteryear, trying to be who we are not.

We were those early electric pilgrims, and we all remembered where we came from. Those critical lessons we learned. Because it's too damned important to forget what we learned traveling on those yesterday roads.

We were, among others, *The Misfits, The Chapparells, The Shadows,* and *The Defiants.* At a critical time in our lives, we all took a trip together and found opportunities and relationships through music and the times. We all learned lessons. And we all continue to learn today's life's lessons.

Because the times ... well, they just keep on a-chang'in.

5

WHEN THERE REALLY WERE CHIEFS

REMEMBERING THOSE WHO SAID THEY WOULD AND THEY DID

I love baseball.

It's been a part of my life since I began playing the game when I was four years old. Baseball is a game of trueness. Like the absolutes of math or the definitiveness of one of the sciences. But that's not what I want to talk about. I would like to tell you about some of the lessons learned because of that confusing and hard-to-understand love associated with the game of baseball.

The path the game is played on is defined in simplicity. They pitch it; you try to hit it. They hit it, and you try to catch it. There is a tolerance to how the game is played, with limitations. Like a well-rehearsed song and dance number. Like words used only within a special language. The game's specialized skills and abilities.

Like death and taxes. Because baseball is a game of honesty. You can cheat at it. But you can never cheat it. Its truths are less about the game itself and more about the people that you play it with.

The game will allow you to display your skills and strengths and experience the heights of its enjoyment. It will expose your weaknesses slowly in a painful decline or in the suddenness and heartbeat of an impassioned thought. It will humble the warmest of souls and cruelly break those with the coldest of hearts.

The game of baseball is commitment with honesty and without empathy.

I wasn't much of a ballplayer. Borderline OK. I was good enough to make the team at most levels that I played. I wasn't much of a hitter. I had a .231 lifetime batting average. I was a decent defensive player and made my share of errors. Yet, always, I was a very good, dependable teammate. Thrilled when I had those opportunities to play. Humbled by baseball's aura and its sheer power to give or to take away.

And I did not cheat at the game of baseball.

Throughout its history, baseball has been defined by the quality of the people who played the game. And for most, the little they got back besides the sheer enjoyment and satisfaction. And for all, the minimal time we have in our lives to do so as players.

At a young age, my dad told me, "In baseball, like in the business of living our lives, there are chiefs and there are Indians. If you want truth and honesty and to understand the complexity that goes along with baseball's give and take, then always trust the chiefs."

So, I did.

I remember the day the Chiefs came to my hometown, Simsbury, Connecticut. They were the Hartford Chiefs, a Class AA Eastern League minor league baseball team affiliated with the Boston Braves of the National League. As my dad had suggested, I couldn't wait to get out and see the honesty and power of the Chiefs.

Somehow, my dad, and others, had engineered a visit

from the team. A baseball clinic for our town's Little League on a Saturday, running from 9 AM until noon. Real professional baseball players in our town to show us how the game is played at their level.

I'll talk about how all that happened a little later in the story.

It was a Saturday morning in June 1952. When I woke, I could hear the rain hitting the window. My heart sank. I'd been anticipating the Chiefs' visit for weeks. Kept baseball cards in my back pocket. I'd memorized player stats. I slept with my old Spaulding leather glove. Now, there was a chance all would be washed away. Still, I got up at 7 AM and dressed for what I hoped would be a thrilling day of learning all about baseball.

Dad was having his coffee. I joined him and had a bowl of cereal topped with a banana and sprinkled with sugar. I asked about the rain and the Chiefs coming to town. Dad said, "Let's wait and see what happens." The phone rang, and Dad mumbled into the handset. Nodded a couple of times. Said OK two or three times. I held my breath. After the second call, he hung up. He wrote a couple of numbers down on a sheet of paper and looked at me.

"Let's go," he said. "The Chiefs are coming to town."

The first professional baseball games I attended were minor league games. Watching the Hartford Chiefs at old Bulkeley Stadium in the south end of Hartford. The old ballpark had been on that site since 1923 along the intersection of Hamner and George Streets. The Hamner Street name came from my dad's family, longtime residents of Wethersfield.

During most of the 1800s, it had been known as the Hamner Turnpike. Taxes first had to be paid for shiploads of goods coming up the Connecticut River. The entry point and tax house was then located at the Wethersfield Cove. A family member, John Hamner, was the first Cove Master. Once taxes were paid, horse-drawn wagons would then haul goods from the cove to purveyor distribution points in Hartford. One of the first drop points was a site next to where the ballpark was built in 1922.

My dad had played at Bulkeley Stadium for the Hartford Gas Company, Hamilton Standard, Pratt & Whitney Aircraft, Travelers Insurance Company, and the Savitt Gems. Even when the Chiefs were on the road in the Eastern League, the stadium was used. It also hosted football games, concerts, political rallies, and motorcycle races.

My uncle Steve was a West Hartford policeman. He was also good friends with the Chiefs' owner, Charlie Blossfield. He picked up extra income by providing security at the ballpark during weekend games. He'd let my dad bring my brother and me, along with other kids, to the games. We'd always get in for free. A hot dog and a soda cost us a quarter. If I came alone with my dad, we'd arrive before batting practice. I would go to the bullpen in the right field corner along Hamner Street, and I'd play catch with some of the ballplayers.

Many made it to the major leagues. George Crowe, an early Negro player known as the "Gentle Giant," would have productive years playing for the Milwaukee Braves and the Cincinnati Reds. He taught me how to protect my face on bad hop ground balls. Jack Daniels played for the Brooklyn Dodgers. Harry Hanebrink played in the 1958 World Series for Milwaukee.

And big 6'8" Gene Conley, an All-American College basketball player, would win 20 games for Hartford in 1951. He would show me how to hold a baseball. He would have a 12-year major league career with the Braves, Phillies, and Red Sox. He would also play pro basketball for the Boston Celtics and New York Knicks. Though always open to heated arguments, Conley is, perhaps, the most successful two-sport athlete in the modern era.

One day in the early season of 1952, I learned all about the truth and honesty of the game of baseball and the lives attached to it. Prior to a game against the Scranton Miners, I found a catch partner in the outfield. He was a Negro. His name was Leon Day. A longtime star from the "Negro leagues." Now, playing out his career in the integrated minor leagues. Too old and too late in his career, and outside the quota system for a spot on a major league roster.

Just as we were about to play catch, Day said, "George Crowe told me to look for you." I smiled and nodded my head. One of Day's tosses was low to the ground. Though I fumbled the ball, I did play the short hop correctly, protecting my face. Just the way Crowe had taught me. Said Day, "I'll tell George you did it right." I can't even begin to tell you the impression that made on an admiring seven-year-old kid.

In 1995, Leon Day was posthumously inducted into the Baseball Hall of Fame in Cooperstown.

Our game of catch ended. Day went in to take his turns in the batting cage. I stood alone, taking in all the wonderful baseball activity going on all around me. I heard a gentle voice say, "Would you like to have a game of catch with me?" A large, well-built man stood looking at me. Across his jersey were the scripted letters spelling *Chiefs*. He had a nice smile. He said, "You're pretty good." He tossed me the ball.

It was the day I met Dick Carmichael.

My uncle Steve was heavily involved in West Hartford's Little League baseball. Had been since its inception in 1947. He was also well-known throughout the Hartford Little Leagues. Preseason practice and post-season tournament games between the two towns were annual occurrences. Hundreds of quality players came out of those programs, dotting the rosters of high school, college, and industrial league semi-pro teams throughout the country. Many went on to play professionally.

Simsbury was in its second year of Little League, its first officially chartered year. Late in the 1951 Hartford Chiefs season, my uncle talked with Charlie Blossfield, asking if there was a chance his Chiefs would do a clinic in Simsbury. Some players were known to visit grand openings for grocery stores, car dealerships, and department stores.

Blossfield was engaged in legal battles with the parent Boston Braves' owners, the Perini family, and its executives, as well as local Hartford bankers over loans and lease protocols. His response to my uncle Steve: "Let's shoot for next year. I promise."

Blossfield was a man of his word. The Chiefs' players had done clinics in previous years. During WWII, to raise money for war bonds. In the late 1940s, they visited the Connecticut State Prison in Wethersfield at the request of its respected warden, Ralph Walker. The clinic was held outside the prison walls. Walker had allowed many inmates to work outside the walls as trustees on state projects.

And now it was the next year, 1952.

In May 1952, Blossfield asked his manager, Del Bissonette, how he felt about doing a clinic for the Little League in Simsbury. Bissonette wasn't committal, but as my uncle would say, "He didn't say no." Over the next two weeks, Bissonette talked with a few of the players, asking if they would be willing to travel to Simsbury for a clinic. Every player said yes. Bissonette then went to my uncle, whom he respected, and said, "Steve, if you're involved in this, just tell us the date, and we'll be there."

This was a time when a person gave his word and made a promise, then it meant something. All while the Hartford Chiefs were mired in seventh place in the eight-team Eastern Leagu standings.

Blossfield approved the date. Scheduled a couple of drivers he knew to drive the eight to ten players to and to-and-from Simsbury. This would happen after Hartford had played a Friday night game against Elmira. They would have to get up early on Saturday and get to the ballpark on their own. Travel to Simsbury and hold a local baseball clinic without compensation. Then, after holding the clinic, they'd return to Hartford for that evening's game against Elmira. The following day, they'd play a doubleheader on Sunday afternoon. Tell me if you see that happening in today's professional world.

The date was set for Saturday, June 28, at 9:30 AM.

We drove south on Hopmeadow Street through the center of town, arriving at South School's back parking lot at about 9 AM. There were about a dozen cars waiting in the light rain. At 9:15 AM, two late model 1940s four-door sedans arrived. I could feel the excitement in my chest. It was the Hartford Chiefs. They were here despite the early morning hour, the rain, and the aches and pains of playing the night before. A tough win over the Elmira Red Sox, 4–2. They had kept their promise. Like my dad had said. If you want truth and honesty, go with the Chiefs.

The idea of having pro players come to town had generated lots of interest. Over 50 kids had signed up for the event. Now it was raining. Most had stayed away, thinking it was canceled. My brother, Pete, decided not to come. He went to his Boy Scouts meeting at the central firehouse with his best friend, Orvie Winchell. Just 12 kids had shown up, along with six adults. First and foremost, my dad was there. My uncle Steve had driven from West Hartford. Elmo Comotti, manager of the Little League Braves and a former minor leaguer for Cincinnati, was there, along with other local coaches Lou Bourgeois, Bob Shaw, and Joe Pattison.

The players dressed in their cars. Baseball pants, sweat jerseys, and spikes. Some had their road uniform shirts that said *Hartford* across the front. We formed a group under the pine

123

trees at the bottom of the hill. Chiefs Manager Del Bissonette spoke to the crowd. "If you're not willing to learn or get wet, I suggest you go home." Nobody left.

We were broken into three groups. One would learn about hitting and pitching. One would be an infield group. Another group in the outfield. For the infield group, the instructors included Eddie McHugh from Bristol, Connecticut. He had just graduated from Yale University before being signed by Boston. Another was a young Joe Morgan from Walpole, Massachusetts. A Boston College grad who played both college baseball and hockey. He was then signed by his hometown Boston Braves to a minor league contract with a signing bonus.

They showed us how to position ourselves. Study a batter's habits. Be aware of the hitting count and the situation on the field. Know what pitch your pitcher was going to throw in that situation. Be ready to react before the play takes place.

We learned how to fade, or cheat a bit, by knowing which foot to push off from at the crack of the bat. How to turn the double play at each position. Wow, it was just like my dad had tried to teach his Giants players in Little League.

The outfielders learned positioning from fleet-footed Vince Pizzatola. He had just been recalled to Hartford from Hagerstown. He had just gotten back into town late Friday evening. He didn't have to come to Simsbury. He chose to do so. Alvin Aucoin, who was nearing the end of his professional career, showed kids how to read a fly ball. Veteran Ted Sepkowski taught kids how to throw to the right base and the importance of hitting the cutoff man to avoid a hitter or runners from taking an extra base.

The kids hitting were instructed by catcher Bob Roselli. They learned how to see a pitch. Pick up a pitcher's release point. Ray Crone showed them how to throw both a curve ball and a change-up. Charlie Bicknell, another pitcher, showed them how to pitch. To go through a windup and delivery. To know what pitch to throw on certain counts. How to hold runners on base, preventing them from stealing a base on you.

In the light rain, I executed the double play turn at second base, and I heard a voice say, "Way to go, Rob. That's how to turn it." When I looked up, it was Dick Carmichael. My catch partner from Bulkeley Stadium. I beamed with pride. Dick also showed us how to slide into bases. And when you were on base, how to read a hit to the outfield. How and when to run. How to touch the bases by cutting the inside of the bag with the right foot.

A magnificent opportunity for all. Learning the skills of baseball from real professional baseball players. From the Chiefs.

Each group rotated through the three sets of instructors. For over two hours, we learned and played baseball with real professional players. Nobody got mad at you for making an error. If you did err, you just got back in line and did it again and again. And you kept doing it as many times as you wanted to.

Even Manager Del Bissonette would step in. Show a kid how to choke up on a bat. How to go with a pitch and hit to right or left field. When to take a pitch. How to lay down a bunt. And when to swing away.

Not one of those Hartford Chiefs gave any indication they didn't want to be here. Early on this Saturday morning ... in the rain.

The clinic ended around 11:45 AM. My dad and Elmo Comotti had put up a tarp in the grove area of trees behind the school. It kept the rain out. The ladies' auxiliary had made sandwiches as a post-clinic snack: ham and cheese, liverwurst and bologna with mustard, and tuna fish. They also made lemonade. Elmo brought sodas and cookies from Kozloski's market in the south end, compliments of Walt Mitchell, your friendly Pontiac dealer at Weatogue Garage.

We all sat under the tarp. Clothes wet and clammy. The players didn't rush off. They sat among us and ate sandwiches. Talked baseball to and with anyone who had questions or just wanted to talk. Players signed autographs on Chiefs programs brought by Bissonette. I sat next to Dick Carmichael. Asked him about being a ballplayer. His answer to a seven-year-old was delivered gently and easy to understand.

"It's a dream come true," said the native of South Portland, Maine. "It's fun, but it's hard work. You'll learn that. Chances of making it to the major leagues are against you. Always know your surroundings. And know when it's time to move on."

"Amen," said Alvin Aucoin as he smiled and nodded at me. Aucoin, wrought with a career of injuries, would retire from baseball after just 10 more games playing for the Chiefs.

I took a bite of my sandwich. Washed it down with a swig of lemonade. Slowly panned the grove area, drinking in the scene of what was taking place. I couldn't help but think of how lucky we were to be a part of this. A memory for a lifetime. Yes, I was a Red Sox fan. But these guys, the Hartford Chiefs, they were the first professional games I had ever attended. They were major league to me.

I looked over at my dad. He adjusted his baseball cap adorned with a capital letter G for his Little League team, the Giants. He smiled at me and nodded. Said to me so softly I had to read his lips. "Chiefs. Always trust and go with the Chiefs."

The rain continued. The plain slices of white sandwich bread from the Bond Bakeries were now a little soggy. Still, it was the best damn liverwurst sandwich I ever ate.

That evening, the Chiefs would lose 4–2 to Elmira. Less than 500 fans would be on hand at Bulkeley Stadium. They would have a very bad, injury-laden second half of the season and finish in seventh place with a record of 59-79. *Hartford Courant* columnist Bill Lee wrote that if the Chiefs continued to play at this level unbecoming to professionals, the parent ownership in Boston would likely pull their franchise out of Hartford. At that time, the profundity of Bill Lee's words hadn't yet come into focus.

On August 29, a group of Chiefs' players headed out to spend the day at the racetrack and gambling casinos in Rhode Island. During the return trip, an ill-fated pass of a truck on a busy two-lane road in Killingly, CT, resulted in a bad accident. The convertible overturned. Burst into flames.

Charlie Bicknell was ejected and thrown about 25 feet. He righted himself and rushed back to the burning vehicle. Joe Morgan's legs were pinned by a collapsed dashboard. Bicknell, using his bare hands, bent the hot steel dashboard, pulling it away from Morgan's legs and dragging him to safety just before the vehicle was engulfed in flames.

Charlie Blossfield issued a statement saying the injured players would recover. Manager Del Bissonette told writer Ron Melcher from the *Hartford Courant* he was relieved and happy that everyone was OK. Due to their accident injuries, three of the four players were done for the season.

Then Bissonette fined all four of the players for their actions.

Years later, my uncle Steve told me a story that had been told to him by Charlie Bicknell. Unbeknown to Bissonette, the heavy fines he levied on each player were paid for by the team's owner, Blossfield. Bissonette never knew.

"Makes for good neighbors" was all Blossfield would ever say about the incident.

The Hartford Chiefs ended their 1952 season playing a doubleheader on Sunday, September 7, against the Philadelphia Phillies affiliate the Schenectady Blue Jays. I stayed for game one only. Two future major leaguers, Ray Crone for Hartford and Jack Sanford for Schenectady, engaged in a good pitcher's duel. Sanford would make the major leagues at 27 and go on to win 137 major league games.

Hartford hung on and won game one, 4–3. In the nightcap, hard-throwing Chiefs' righthander Don Schmidt, nearing the end of his career, scattered four hits for a 3–1 win and a sweep of the doubleheader. By the game's end, there remained in the stands fewer than 100 fans. An epitaph just waiting to be written.

It would be the last minor league in Hartford for 64 years.

About ten years back, while visiting my hometown of Simsbury, I took time and made a trip to that old ballfield behind South School where that memorable Saturday morning clinic with the Chiefs had been held so many years ago. The field was now an asphalt parking lot. Brightly painted spaces for cars and neatly manicured grass islands. It didn't take long for those long-ago memories to begin flowing into my head. Powerful memories of that day. Memories about Chiefs that persisted through the years.

I remembered every player from that day. When there really were Chiefs.

On Monday, after the 1952 season ended, manager Del Bissonette stopped at Bulkeley Stadium to pick up his final paycheck. The good-hitting outfielder for the Brooklyn Dodgers in the 1930s and longtime minor leaguer then headed home to Winthrop, Maine, never again to be involved in baseball. A story I was later told by a sportswriter from Maine pained me. I learned Bissonette pined away during his final years. Lonely for baseball, he died of a broken heart.

At the end of his career and playing just a dozen games for Hartford, Alvin Aucoin walked into Blossfield's office and tearfully retired before the season ended. He returned to his home, Port Authur, Texas, and ran a family business.

Joe Morgan would have a 16-year career. He would amass

over 1300 hits in the minor leagues. He would play in the major leagues for Milwaukee, Kansas City, Philadelphia, Cleveland, and St. Louis. The Walpole, Mass native would coach and manage many teams, including four years as skipper of his beloved Boston Red Sox, leading them into the playoffs twice. His success may have never happened had it not been for the heroics of Charlie Bicknell pulling him from that burning car on that hot August day in 1952.

He would continue to stay active into his late 80s, working for the State of Massachusetts. Driving a snowplow during winter months. Clearing off the state highways, he would earn the nickname "Turnpike Joe."

Ray Crone would make it to the majors and have winning seasons with Milwaukee and would also pitch for the Giants, both in New York and San Francisco. He would marry a local girl and reside in Windsor, CT, for many years. His Chief's catcher, Bob Roselli, would have a 10-year minor league career. He would play in the major leagues for Milwaukee and the Chicago White Sox.

Vince Pizzatola would battle injuries to ankles and knees. He would retire after his 23rd birthday, returning to work in his hometown, Birmingham, Alabama. The Yale All-American Eddie McHugh would have some early success with the Chiefs. During the ensuing years, he would get beaned, spiked, and injure an elbow. He would retire to the business world at age 27.

Early in his career, Charlie Bicknell would pitch in 30 major league games. He would continue to perform at the Triple-A level. Yet, never made it back to the majors. He would retire in 1958. Ted Sepkowski would have three brief stints in the majors before his 25th birthday. He would never make it back. During the final three years of his long minor league career, he would hit 100 home runs in the low minors. He retired to Baltimore in 1955 at 33 years old.

Dick Carmichael, my catch partner from Bulkeley Stadium, would call it a career after the 1955 season. His minor league pitching record is a stunning 50–29. The Milwaukee Braves wanted him to go to Triple-A Wichita for the 1956 season with a shot at making the Milwaukee Braves roster. He had a sore elbow, swollen knees, and an aching back. He wrote a letter to the Milwaukee owners officially announcing his retirement.

As he had said to me on that rainy Saturday morning, enjoy what you have for the time you have it. Always be thankful for the opportunity. Your chances of making the major leagues are slim. Be aware of your surroundings. Know when it's time to make your move. He would return to his hometown, South Portland, Maine, and live an active and full life with family and friends.

At 24 years old, Dick Carmichael chose life over baseball.

I never thought of those Chiefs players as being old. I just thought of myself as being younger.

They all reached the end of their baseball careers in their twenties and early thirties. At such a young age, their bodies had worn out and their skills had eroded. As if within each of their lives, a precious allotment of energy and time had been used up. Like a needed med that has no more refills. Now, they were starting over with new lives because the skills of their early years had turned against them before age 35.

In my late twenties and early thirties, I was just beginning to hone my life skills. In my sixties, I could be creative and continue to experience success in running my consulting business. Those Chiefs, my heroes, were struggling to deal with problematic issues in their late twenties and early thirties. Now, at a point in their life of skills, much too early in years, the proverbial fastball was already past them.

And I never forgot Dick Carmichael's profound words.

It was 2012. I asked a friend, Al Fick, if he would find Carmichael for me. Al had been a longtime employee of the

University of Maryland, Baltimore, and was now a transplanted Baltimorean living in Bath, Maine. He gladly accepted the challenge.

Over time, we learned that Dick's mom and dad were loggers in Maine. Dick hadn't learned how to read until he was almost ten. He became a good student and an outstanding athlete in every sport he played. Yale University wanted him. He couldn't afford the price tag. He became the Boston Braves' number-one pick in 1949. He served in the US Army during the Korean War. Whatever he chose to do, in sports or in business, he succeeded with an unbridled passion. He was a father, a grandfather, and a gentleman respected by all who ever knew him.

It took about two months. Al found Dick Carmichael living in South Portland, Maine. Same neighborhood where he grew up. He made visits to Dick's home and told him about me and the stories I had shared

SPHS Yearbook Photo
Dick Carmichael, 1949 First Round Pick of the Boston Braves

with Al about Dick and the Hartford Chiefs. Told Dick I was planning to visit Maine and wished to again meet with him.

Dick Carmichael laughed wholeheartedly and said, "Absolutely."

In the fall of 2014, Al Fick and I met Dick Carmichael for lunch in South Portland, Maine. It had been more than 62 years

131

since I last played catch with him at old Bulkeley Stadium at the corner of George and Hamner Streets in the south end of Hartford. We had lots to talk about.

We went to a restaurant in South Portland. All the folks there knew Dick. The waitress delivered our food to the table. Added an extra plate of food if we wanted a second helping. Left a bottle of wine. Pitchers of coke and water. She simply explained, saying, "I hear lots of serious baseball talk going on. I won't interrupt. Call out if you need me."

Three hours later, we were still engaged in serious baseball talk. Stories that should never be lost.

It was an afternoon of memories. Stories from yesteryear. About players and games. Stories the average fan never gets to hear. The stories that, when a player dies, so do all the wonderful memories die with him. It's why I have the need to search out those folks and hear their stories. To revisit and to write those stories before I, too, forget them. Because when they're gone ... they're gone!

It was an afternoon of welling up with tears and choking back lumps in our throats. It was wonderful. And I laughed until my stomach muscles ached.

As our time together ended, Carmichael was pensive. He wiped away some tears with his napkin. You could see the thought developing in his gaze. The memory he shared was emotional.

"You know, I remember something about that clinic we did in your hometown," said Dick. "A man sitting next to me. He said there are chiefs and Indians." Dick Carmichael would think about those words then and during the ensuing years.

"The man said that the truth was with the chiefs," said Dick softly. He looked into my eyes. "The man said if you wanted the truth, always go with the chiefs." There was a brief pause. "He's right, ya know," said Dick. He looked out of the windows overlooking the Fore River. At the buildings that were Portland, Maine, across the river.

132

"I always remembered those words," said Dick, smiling.

I choked back another lump in my throat and said, "Dick, that man was my dad."

He got wide-eyed. Smiled in that grandfatherly way and said to me, "Now I know where you get your wisdom and passions." Now, I was wiping away tears with my napkin.

I stayed in touch with Dick over the next six to seven years via letters and phone calls. He was pleasant on every call. He always answered every letter. He was a Chief in every sense of the word. And he knew when it was time to make his moves.

Dick Carmichael died in June 2022. He was 92 years old.

Yeah, I love baseball.

Thankful that in my life, I had the opportunity to play the game at numerous recreational levels. I experienced a modicum of success. Usually in the form of simple enjoyment. Always, it was a learning exercise. About wins and losses. Hits and errors. Honesty and truth. And with none of the political correctness that had anything to do with today's meanings of the words "Chiefs and Indians."

It didn't matter what age I was or how many years had passed or how far I had traveled. Wherever I went, I found a niche where the game served me as a positive in my life. Especially in my adult years where it was a benefit with clients. Going to games together, doing business over a hotdog and a beer. Sharing childhood stories of Fenway Park, the Polo Grounds, and Ebbets Field.

And watching the Hartford Chiefs play at old Bulkeley Stadium.

But I will always remember those years when I was young. A time when my dad was my primary teacher. I was fortunate to be in the right places at the right time. Learned from good people who care about your well-being. About honesty, like when someone made a promise to you. The comfort you felt knowing you could pretty much bet the farm on them keeping that promise.

It was a time when we wrote complete sentences because it was the respectful thing to do. When mail came to us, not by downloading it, but by walking to your mailbox to retrieve what had been sent. We knew what RFD meant and the importance of knowing the names of our state capitals.

When policemen really did serve and protect, like my Uncle Steve, who proudly walked a neighborhood beat. When we used a rotary dial telephone. When we knew how to count and give cash change back to customers. When farmers were respected. And, when we really knew how to say thank you.

When kindness in thought, word, and deeds was appreciated. When handshakes were as good as today's multi-page contracts. When WWII veterans saved our world.

And during those fleeting special times ... like when a group of professional baseball players came to my town. Not because they had to but because they wanted to. They held a clinic and taught a bunch of kids the skills of their trade. In the rain. Paid for with sandwiches and lemonade.

It was a time when there really were chiefs.

6

THE PRICE WE PAY
FOR ACCELERATION

THERE IS ALWAYS A COST
TO GO FASTER!

I was a Cub Scout in 1956. A member of Den 4, Pack 76. On April 28, our den went to Riverside Amusement Park in Agawam, MA. A chilly and damp evening. The kind of night when the cold just goes right through your coat, mittens, and wool cap. We attended that evening's stock car races. Riverside Park Speedway had opened its tenth season of racing. We ate cookies and drank free hot chocolate.

"Good evening, racing fans, and welcome to beautiful Riverside Park," were the warm words of the opening night's greetings from track announcer Tom Gallant. A full, strong voice. His every word sounded like the voice of God. As if he was talking directly to you.

I watched heats and semi-final races speed around the 1/5th mile asphalt oval. We watched the Class B and Consolation Race, known as the last chances to qualify for the main event. Then, I was transfixed by the 20 cars and their drivers packed together as they screeched around the smallish oval during the 25-lap main event.

Drivers' names were like legends etched in stone. Buddy Krebs and Gene Bergin. Jerry Humistin, Benny Germano, Art Roussau and Dick Dixon. The loveable old man, Jocko Maggiacommo, from Poughkeepsie, New York. There was Moe Gherzi, Phil Mitchell, "Big" Ed Patnode, "Steady" Eddie Flemke, and Ralph Boehm from my Simsbury, Connecticut hometown. They were gladiators.

En masse, the pack raced around the tight asphalt oval at a deafening roar. Multi-colored race cars with large numbers painted on their doors. Car bodies of dented metal from the 1930s. As leaders broke away from the tight pack, you could hear their motors winding up tight, accelerating down the backstretch. Stretching the motor's capacity to get that extra one or two miles per hour.

Backing off the gas as the cars entered the third turn. Loud explosions and blue-yellow flames emanating from the side-mounted exhaust pipes. The wind blowing in your face as the pack of cars passed the main grandstand. You had to wipe your eyes from the track dust that whipped across your face, along with the strong smell of burnt gasoline fumes.

Eddie Flemke Website Photo
**Eddie Flemke Wins the Riverside Park Main Event
Opening Night in April 1956**

That night's main event was won by Eddie Flemke in his gold-and-blue number 61 car. Trophies were handed out. The gladiators and their machines returned to the pits. The sound of the roaring motors ebbed. The racing oval became ghostly quiet. Another glorious night had come and gone. I sat in the stands with other Cub Scouts. All of us, wearing our blue Cub Scout uniforms with gold trim. Slowly, I panned the now empty and quiet asphalt oval, its sounds still echoing in my ears.

Oh yeah, I really liked short-track stock car racing.

These were the years when local stock car racing was still a sport. A fun activity on a Saturday night and a Sunday afternoon. When the search for acceleration was a conversation in the pit area over a cigarette and a cup of coffee.

The days when most drivers built, owned, and maintained their own cars. They went to the junk yards. Found a body and frame from a late 1930s Chevy or Ford. Dug through the debris for a straight axle. Spent their own money and lots of late nights aided by a few friends in a lonesome garage putting it all together. They borrowed and traded for parts. Tires, rims, transmissions, and rear ends. It was a close-knit society in and of itself.

Some private owners got a few operating dollars from a local gas station or an oil company. From an auto-wrecking group or local junkyard. They painted that company's name on the side of their car, along with the names of the pit crew. When completed, they had put a competitive racecar on the track. Often for less than $1000.

A few cars were now being powered by machine-shop-built and more powerful overhead V-8 motors. All had to be within the qualified specs of the racing association. Many cars had a standard flathead V-8 motor. When set up right and with a good driver behind the wheel, those old flathead motors were every bit as dangerous to win a main event as a car with a modified engine and a big-named driver.

For those times, the sheer involvement was the price of acceleration.

Flathead-powered cars were in a class referred to as "sportsman." Cars whose motors were of fewer cubic inches and less horsepower. Still, if your car was running and handling well, you could hold off even the most powerful of cars and drivers. Especially during the early weeks of the season when asphalt tracks were cold and slippery. The more powerful cars, still in need of tweaks, had a hard time establishing a warm outside groove. Sportsman cars owned the inside groove of the track.

Those early-season races often produced unexpected results. Running a cold track with a smaller engine, all you needed was enough speed in the stretches to get from corner to corner. Once there, you could hold off a pack of modified engines that were trying to ride you into a wall. The large crowds would be on their feet and screaming as each lap brought an underdog car closer to the checkered flag. Tensions, both on the track and in the grandstand, became palpable.

It truly was something to behold when it happened.

Many drivers wore t-shirts and half-helmets with ear flaps. This was before the days when small track drivers wore fireproof racing suits and full protective helmets. They smoked cigars amid open fuel lines and wafting fumes from the motors. The driver's side door was closed and tied with a common belt. Not with the large door-window openings for crawling in and out that would come in later years.

It was a time when they raced for sport. Most weren't professional drivers performing two, three, or four times a week. During the work week, you could find many drivers working their trades in machine shops. In lumber yards and for trucking companies. They sold insurance, did landscaping, or operated heavy equipment. They were husbands and fathers. And on Saturday, many worked with a friend or a mechanic to get the car ready for that night's racing. When needed, even family members were asked to help. It was, at the time, a hobby for most.

In the late afternoon, the car was loaded onto an open trailer or a flatbed truck along with toolboxes and extra tires.

The car headed out for the track. Some stopped along the way to buy special higher-octane fuel. Family members piled into the family car and headed out to the track about an hour later. It was a family affair. As much fun as any picnic in the park.

The simplicity of the times began to change in the spring of 1960.

In the beginning, it was just a few owners and cars who pioneered the changes. It was April 1960. What appeared that spring were the early seedlings to what, over the next 15 to 20 years, would be a dramatic change.

Like Dinah Washington singing her classic "What a Difference a Day Makes." In this case, it was the years 1959 to 1960. In just one year, a small handful of investors had created a whole new world. In actual numbers, about 10 cars. The omens of change had come calling. A handful of cars would emerge that spring and separate themselves from others in style and performance.

And the most prominent change was the cost of acceleration!

That 1960 season wasn't a complete or dramatic change in and by every driver or owner. That would come later, during the mid to late 1970s. What I would come to refer to as the "big bang." A time when the costs of short-track racing exploded. And began to put so many of those small local tracks and stock car racers out of business.

The 1960 season would see the emergence of the "premium" cars. Those that came to the track with a noticeably higher price tag and operating costs. It may have happened elsewhere, but for me, it was at Riverside Park Speedway in Agawam, MA, where I first saw it happen.

Traditionally, the first few weeks of racing at Riverside could produce rather unpredictable results. Usually due to the cold weather. Moisture in the asphalt from the track, which was located next to the Connecticut River. The power cars were always in need of additional tweaking in the form of motor and front-end adjustments. It took a few weeks before power cars began to establish their prominence.

That, too, became the script for those new "premium" cars in April 1960.

In 1960, the first premium car I noticed was new and utterly stark in appearance. It was the M-6 car. A 1937 Chevy body painted silver with car-length racing stripes. It oozed power. The state-of-the-art 283-cubic-inch and bored-out Chevy motor had a deep, powerful sound as it made its way around the oval during practice laps.

The car was from Walker Motor Sales in Palmer, Massachusetts. It had been built by longtime professionals in the local stock car scene. Most of the basics for the M-6 were as common as any other car. The differences were the customized machine-shop parts, full-time mechanic and pit crew, and available backup parts in case of an accident. Those types of amenities did not come cheap.

Gene Bergin, once a high school football star and a terrific local racer from East Hartford, CT, was hired to drive the mighty M-6.

The cost, well, nobody knew at that time. Two years later, in conversation with *Springfield Republican* writer John "Chevy" Chevalier, I learned the build cost for the M-6 was about $6000. Roughly between $4000 and $5000 more than the typical modifieds from previous years.

The "Flying Zero," one of the all-time great cars in Riverside Park history, also reappeared that spring, completely rebuilt. The car was owned and operated by the racing team of Jim Jorgensen and Dexter Burnham. In a very public promotion, they hired Buddy Krebs, one of the top drivers in the region, to drive their car for that season. In a very quiet, strategic move, they paid him a handsome bonus to be their driver.

The Flying Zero won many main events that season. Krebs teamed with the M-6 and Gene Bergin to win the Riverside 500 Lap Race. Krebs eventually captured the individual track championship. The owners also paid him a post-season bonus for his performance.

The cost for the rebuild, again, nobody really knows. About 15 years later, as Sports Editor for Simsbury's *Farmington Valley Herald*, I had a conversation with Red Burnham, Editor and Publisher for the *Enfield Press*. He admitted to me that during that winter of 1959–60, the owners of the car spent over $7000 rebuilding the Flying Zero for the 1960 season.

That amount did not include operating and maintenance costs to keep the car running and on the track every week.

🏁🏁

Early in the 1960 season, "Money-bags" Moe Gherzi survived a huge third lap crash involving a dozen cars and won the 25-lap main event on a cold and damp Saturday evening in April in front of a crowd of over 4000 who braved the weather.

The car receiving the most damage in the accident was the orange-and-black 101 driven by Ralph Boehm of Simsbury, CT.

Boehm Family Photo
Ralph Boehm Simsbury, CT

His racer was hung up high on the fourth turn wall, and when his car was removed to the infield, it was declared *"totaled."* Eddie Flemke, a longtime friend, learned of the accident. He called Boehm's house on Sunday morning. Asked if Ralph was interested in buying Eddie's 1937 Chevy, a blue-and-gold race car, the number 61. By Monday evening, Boehm owned a new car, Eddie's old 61, known as a good, solid racecar. The very stock car that I, as a Cub Scout, watched Eddie Flemke win that opening night main event race in 1956.

By Wednesday evening, a man known as "Pinney the Painter" had turned Flemke's old number 61 on the car to Boehm's new 101. It was made ready to make a few practice laps at Riverside Park on Saturday night. Albeit, the car still needed, in the words of mechanic Dave Monson, "a shitload of adjustments."

The cost for the car, the motor, and the paint job: $1500.

About 20 miles up the road from Simsbury in North Granby, brothers Dean and Frank Moulton put the finishing touches on their new stock car, a '37 Chevy Coupe atop a '36 standard frame. It had a homemade garage paint job, blue and white, with a hand-painted number 265. It was powered by the standard and slightly bored-out Chevy 283-cubic-inch motor and was now ready for a few laps at Riverside Speedway.

The cost for Moulton's car, financed by brother Dean's paving company: $1300.

In Southington, CT, a 17-year-old racing enthusiast spent hours working on his old jalopy purchased for $50. The driver prepared the car for that Saturday's racing program in the new 1960 Novice Division at Plainville Stadium's quarter-mile asphalt track owned and operated by multi-businessman Joe Tinty.

The late Don Moon was the young driver. He lied to racing officials about his age to get his car on the track. He qualified for that night's first-ever Novice main event, where he drives a spirited race, bouncing off others but keeping his car on the track and holding the lead going into the final two laps.

On the final lap, Moon lost traction in the second corner, allowing the car behind him to pass by on the inside. Max Cavallo, driving the well-built 00 Novice car, would go on to win the 25-lap Novice event, with Moon finishing a close and surprising second.

The cost for Moon to get his car on the track: about $100.

Gordon Ross from Rhinebeck, New York, owned the beautifully built red-and-cream number 19. Ross' driver was a hard-charging, cigar-smoking veteran of the local racing wars, Jerry Humiston of Springfield, MA. The number 19 car went through a partial rebuild during the winter months in preparation for Riverside's 1960 season.

The cost of the rebuild: $2500.

In June 1960, Humiston's number 19 car was involved in a fender-bender during a qualifying race. Following light maintenance in the pit area, Humiston took the car out for a test run. He told his mechanic, "Steering seems tight, and the front end is piling into the corners." Not the words an owner and mechanic want to hear. Repairs would be needed.

During the ensuing week, the front end of car 19 was rebuilt. Typically, that's a straight axle change and whatever additional parts that had been damaged are replaced. Repairs that would typically cost around $500 to complete.

Saturday evening, Ross was heard telling Race Director Harvey Tattersall that the cost for the front-end rebuild was $1800. Hearing that story, track photographer and writer for *Illustrated Speedway News* Shany Lorenzet searched out Ross to get confirmation of costs.

"Oh, about $1200," said Ross. "Then, we went ahead and fixed a few other things we thought could use upgrades. Yeah, about $1800 sounds right."

During the February and March mini-rebuild, along with a front-end repair from the damage in June, Gordon Ross had spent an estimated $4000 on his number 19 car.

On a mini-rebuild and minor repair, Ross would spend

more, collectively, than Ralph Boehm had spent buying Eddie Flemke's car and motor after his accident. What the Moulton brothers had spent to build a new car. And the amount a young Don Moon had spent to put a competitive novice race car on the track at Plainville.

Stories like this were already creeping into the racing environment.

A few premium car owners were even building backup cars. An additional investment of over $3000. If the primary car wasn't ready for a race, the backup is put on the trailer and taken to the track for that evening's races. Some owners started bringing a second motor to the track in case they blew a motor in warmups. A replacement can cost up to $2500 and can be swapped and installed into a race car and be operational in 90 minutes. Notes *Springfield Republican* writer John Chevalier, "It's becoming an exclusive club known as the O-Os, meaning Obnoxious Owners."

It was the beginning of the end for budget car owners.

Dick Dixon from nearby Warehouse Point, CT, was a well-known driver throughout the east coast. The epitome of a race car driver, with one huge exception. He can afford the hobby. In fact, he was one of those rare breeds who is the owner of multiple businesses. He owned multiple race cars and drove every one of them.

In April 1960, Dixon was readying for another season of racing. Only this time, he was not driving his self-identifiable 1940 Ford modified Coupe, "The Eight-Ball." He would be driving a brand-new race car. A 1940 Ford powered Coupe, compliments of the Garuti brothers, a family involved with racing. Not because he couldn't afford to do so. In fact, Dixon's businesses were doing so well he had no time to do his own car building, repairs, and maintenance. Truly, a painless problem.

Estimated costs to build the Garuti Brothers number 14 car were $4500. From deep in the pits, a voice could be heard saying, "Jesus, the damn thing's an Edsel."

Just down the line in the tight pit area is another newly built car. The number 29 car had just been completed by Camerata Auto Wrecking. It was to be driven by one of Riverside's all-time greats, Jocko Maggiacommo from Poughkeepsie, NY.

Scuttlebutt around the pits puts the cost of the Camerota 29 car at $4000.

Just a short distance from Riverside Park is Suffield, CT. Home to the Suffield Auto Center. They, too, had a new, high-powered modified in process for a summer launch. It would make its appearance in a flat black primer finish, pin-striped, with a large number 5 painted on the car. It would earn the nickname "The Black Beauty." Wild Bill Greco, a minuscule but hard-charging driver from the sportsman ranks, would be behind the wheel.

Springfield Republican writer Richard Osgood would report the car is built to Greco's requested specs. The cost is reported to be over $4000.

Leo Matte would build powerful racing motors for Fenton Chevy and Olds of Westfield, MA, and later for Labbee Chevrolet of West Hatfield, MA. The Fenton number 92 would be driven by big Ed Patnode, an experienced and well-known driver from Westfield, MA.

Matte's car would cost Fenton $4300.

An interesting race story emerged during that 1960 season. An independent investor and racing fan, Bill Brown of Farmington, CT, spread the word throughout the racing community. He was willing to fund a modified stock car build and invest $5000. His phone rang throughout the spring.

No commitments for a car build were made.

In 1962, Brown would fund and build his own fuel-injected modified racer for Plainville Stadium to be driven by Simsbury native Bob Pringle. It would be numbered and called the

"Roamin' V." Build costs exceed $4000. On its second night of competition, Pringle rolls the car over in a three-car pileup on the Plainville Stadium backstretch. It would never finish in the money during the remainder of the racing season. In October, the car will be sold at auction.

Brown and his car would disappear from the racing scene.

On the other side of the ledger were the standard bearers of what would quickly become known as the army of "Budget Cars." Those cars that would be put on the track for less than $1500. Most were privately owned. Others indulged various levels of sponsors who offered backing with petty cash and other sundry supports.

Many were well-built and competitive cars. They would lack the luxury and depth of backup cash and resources suddenly available in that small group of new, more expensive, "premier" cars. Surprisingly, many would be competitive.

Benny Germano would be behind the wheel for Springfield's Auto Wrecking number 5 car. The build cost was about $1200. Southampton's Johnny Lobo in the easily identifiable 760 and South Windsor's "Joltin" Joe Paleski in his silver-blue 99 would always be in the running with cars costing about $1000. Billy Heeber, Charlie Brayton, Sal Dee, Gene White, and Phil Mitchell would all drive what was known as "budget cars."

Then there were the true sportsman division cars. The specially designated cars with smaller-sized motors and drivers who raced in their own Tuesday night division. They chose to come to the track on Saturday nights and do battle with the bigger motors of the modified stock cars.

One was Bobby Bard from Westfield, who would drive the very recognizable number 33 car. An old and battered Ford from the late 1930s painted black and yellow. It looked like a junker that had seen better days. That is, until a modified car tried to get around it on a Saturday night when the track was cold and the outside groove too slippery to use.

Said veteran Jocko Maggiacommo, "Some nights when that 33 car is right and running on a cold track, you cannot get around him. Then the race ends; you're still behind him and can't understand why. He's finished eighth or ninth. Good money for a sportsman on a Saturday night."

A lesson in timing that I learned. One of those business decisions. Pick your spots and make it happen. But that type of finish for a true sportsman car was now becoming a rarity.

Maggiacommo's thoughts were shared by many modified drivers when it came to getting around a sportsman division car like Bard's, Sparky Belmont, Bobby Bishop, Don Barnes from Canton, CT, in the Hudson Hornet number 16 car, or the always competitive Bill Gurney from West Springfield. Good drivers in cars with smaller motors.

In the late 1950s, it was common to see one of the sportsman division cars finish the night's main event in the top five. Definitely, at least one sportsman car in the top ten. Beginning in the 1960s, with the arrival of the premium cars, a sportsman division car finishing in the top ten of a Saturday night modified main event race would become like collecting Indian Head pennies or Mercury dimes. Something pretty rare.

I recall a sportsman driver, Bobby Tausher of Holyoke, standing in the infield at night's end, panning the now quiet and darkened track. He had driven his sportsman car, "The U/2," to a sixth-place finish in the night's main event.

"It's fun to scare the shit out of those big boys," said Tausher, smiling.

It was a Saturday in early September of 1960. I was at Ralph Boehm's house on Bushy Hill Road in West Simsbury, spending the day with his two boys, Kurt and Ralph Jr. We spent the day as we often did. Speeding around the house hundreds of times, trying to set land-speed records on the homemade Go-Kart.

Mechanic Dave Monson had been working on Ralph's number 101 car in preparation for the Riverside 250 lapper Saturday night. He was not a happy mechanic. We asked him what was wrong. He shrugged. Shook his head. "Wish I knew," was his response.

He was working on two repairs. Trying to set a gas and air balance in the car's three carburetors. And he couldn't stop the grease and oil leaking from the driver's side rear hub. Dave was an ace mechanic. His struggles with a carburetor were surprising, even to our young minds who knew little about carburation.

For all I knew, Dave most likely had created the correct balance. But he was a perfectionist. Perhaps looking for a level of perfection that is beyond the physics we know. It was a little like a world-class musician trying to play a note on his instrument. A note that doesn't exist.

Kidding around, we asked Dave if we could take a shot at the carbs and the leaking hub. Dave looked amazed but handed us the wrench and screwdriver and said, "Have at it."

I had watched my brother work on a car. I knew a little, just enough to be dangerous. We knew the gas screw had to be turned slightly, and the air screw also needed a slight adjustment. That's what we did. We're not sure what we accomplished. It was to be one of those let's just wait 'n' see things.

With the hub, we removed the old patch covering that looked like a slab of cloth from an old mattress or pillowcase. I found a piece of cork. Cut it into a round shape and fit it into the hub like a gasket. We covered it all with a piece of round-shaped plastic. Spray-painted it black so it blended in with the hub. We cut holes for the bolts. Some of the plastic even went into the threaded area as we hand-tightened the bolts. Dave then put the rear racing slick back on the hub. Lowered the jack.

To Dave's surprise, the car started, and after a few revs of the motor, he had that, "What the hell did you do?" look on his face. Also, the rear hub wasn't leaking. Dave lit a cigarette and shook his head. The 101 car was ready to go.

That night, Ralph Boehm, known as "The High-Flyer out of Simsbury," driving his budget 101 car, took a fourth-place finish in the final leg of Riverside's Triple Crown, the season-ending 250 lapper. Even a fourth-place finish was good for over $400 prize money.

Rob Penfield Photo
Jo-An & Ralph Boehm 1960, Eastern States Exposition Races

When Ralph met us in the bleachers after the race, he said the car had run better than it had been running the previous few weeks. Dave Monson pointed to us and said, "Probably due to the carburetor adjustment." And the hub did not leak any grease or oil. Ralph was giddy and happy. He was known to be a tightwad with money. Yet he dug into his pocket, handed us kids a handful of small bills, and said, "Go get some hotdogs and sodas." We were hungry young kids. You didn't have to tell us twice.

A week later, we visited Franny Bristol's house in Canton. He was getting his number 202 car ready for that weekend's show at Plainville. Fran was a friendly man. He had heard the story from Ralph about what we did with the motor and hub. When he saw us, he handed us a wrench and screwdriver and said in a comical way, "Why not give my carburetor a quick once-over? You know, to make sure it's OK for the race."

We accepted the challenge and gave Franny's car the once-over.

That evening, Franny Bristol's 202 car hung in there amid rough riding and multiple restarts, finishing sixth in the main event. The best finish for Bristol for the entire season. To the glee of both owners, we never charged them a dime for our services.

But if you wanted to buy us a hotdog, that would be just fine.

The years 1961 and 1962 brought in more premier cars. Crowds at Riverside Park Speedway and Plainville Stadium kept getting larger as local stock car racing moved into what I would soon come to call "the golden era." New drivers and cars were making their debuts weekly. And many old drivers were making some life-changing decisions.

The true dichotomy is when each of those individual groups experiences its own highs and lows. Like when an expensive premier car performed well and finished in the money two and three weeks in a row. Only to fall out of money positions for a few weeks due to unexpected accidents or the failure of a part that cost five dollars.

For budget cars, the winning is not finishing first in a main event, or even in the top five prize money positions. Just earning an opportunity to compete and have your car on the track in the main event's field of 20 to 24 cars is a victory. Once there, you use your skills to find a spot and finish in the top ten. Or, for most, just to outlast other cars and finish in one piece with no costly damages.

That's the challenge to those longtime drivers in budget cars.

The large crowds of fans didn't pay money to see budget cards. They came to see the big-name drivers battle it out. Those nights and races when Buddy Krebs and Gene Bergin battled each other wheel to wheel. Those heated battles between Billy Greco, Ed Patnode, and Jerry Humiston as they bumped each other, sending sparks flying.

I remembered a night I was in the pits before the start of the evening's racing. A crowd of over 7000 had crammed their way into the bleachers. Simsbury's Ralph Boehm was heard to say, "They didn't pay their money to see me race."

Racing Director Harvey Tattersall, Jr. didn't confirm or deny what Boehm had said. Because there were just too many incidences that were all going in the favor of the premier cars and big-named drivers. That's what the fans had paid their money to see.

In 1961, Ralph Boehm, and many other budget owners, became the early victims of that growing institutional dichotomy.

In April 1961, the second half of a Saturday night show was rained out. The sanctioning club decided to run a double feature the following week. Finish the final five races from the previous week. Then, run a complete eight-race Saturday night show.

In the first 25-lap main event, Ralph Boehm had a good starting spot and rushed out into the lead on lap four. On lap 21, an accident caused a single file restart. Boehm got a good jump on the green flag, with Buddy Krebs hot on his tail in second. As Boehm went into the second turn, a car pulled out from the infield, right in front of Boehm, who had to brake or slam into the car.

Krebs easily sped by the slower cars on the backstretch and won the main event with Boehm finishing second.

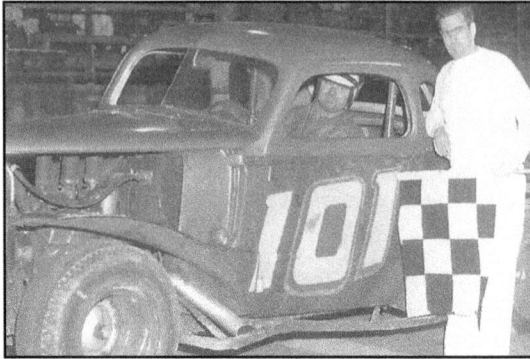

Shany Lorenzet Photo
Simsbury's Ralph Boehm Gets the Checkered Flag from Riverside Flagman, Al Parent, April 1961

Even to a young racing fan like me, it was obvious this was a sham job. A planned block. And that driver would be paid a small bonus by the Krebs' car's owners for his ability to get his car in the way of Boehm's car, allowing Krebs to win the main event and first place money. The race's finish smelled of conspiracy.

In the evening's second 25-lap main event, Boehm again got out quickly and grabbed the lead on the third lap. He never looked in his mirror. He ran away from the field and won the feature in his number 101 budget car. All finishers from second to tenth were premier cars and drivers, no budget or sportsman cars.

Ralph Boehm should have been a double feature winner that evening.

He had also won a semi-final race in each night's shows, and that meant a few extra dollars. His efforts paid off to a night's winnings of over $1200. As he was leaving for the evening, Director Tattersall came over to him. Offered his congratulations. As Tattersall shook hands with Ralph, I could see the money in his right palm. He said that Ralph had been robbed in the first main event. It should not have happened.

Ralph asked Tattersall just one question: "Harvey, why did it happen?" Tattersall did not answer Ralph's question. He looked down, then walked away.

In the truck, Ralph opened his hand and counted the bills. It was $400. He left the track that night with over $1600. Ralph laughed on the ride home, saying he was pretty sure those fans came to see Krebs win. Not to see Boehm win two main events, let alone even one of the features. I was learning lots of lessons, especially about the costs associated with change and its effects. With agendas. The politics.

For budget cars, it would only get worse as the season progressed.

Three weeks after Boehm's big payoff night at Riverside, his 101 car, bought from Eddie Flemke just a year before, was demolished in a six-car pileup on the front straightaway. Ralph's car hit the concrete wall. The collision bent the frame, cracked the motor, and caught fire. His car was totaled.

Ralph Boehm chose not to rebuild. He decided that night he would no longer privately own and operate a stock car. He would, wherever he could, find a ride elsewhere and drive for another owner. Just another crack in a slowly deteriorating wall that had once been a staple of existence for small-track racing.

What exacerbated the situation was the handling of guilt for the accident. Hard-charging and often out-of-control and aggressive driver Billy Greco had caused the accident. He was trailing a young Skip Barna from Southwick. Right on his tail and banging away at the bumper, trying to knock the youngster to the outside and into the fence so he could pass.

When the smoke cleared, Barna, his sportsman car badly

damaged, was given the black flag and disqualified. Greco would continue in the race, finishing in the money. Tensions ran high following the main event, and fights erupted in the pit area. A large contingent of Agawam Police had to be called to quell the tensions. It was becoming clear. The United Stock Car Racing Club was going to protect its prime assets. The assets those large paying crowds were coming to see.

Budget car owners, well, they began to see they were now racing at their own peril. No turning back now. As in that old saying, "That cow has left the barn."

It seemed that every week, I was learning a new lesson about the business of change. That the hobby of racing I had first watched had so quickly become a business for profits. The Riverside track was a 1/5th mile oval. Tiny, as tracks went. It had become much too small for the premier cars and the new speeds. It was becoming unsafe.

As Ralph Boehm said, "Too many people making too many promises that never came true." It was now the reason why so many old-timers began to migrate away from Riverside, because it seemed the rules didn't apply to a selected few.

Still, new budget cars made their debut to battle the premier cars. Don Smart from Monson. Paul Aselton, Walt Czepiel, and Jack Lecuyer. Dick Taylor, Dave Pelczar, Joe Bayck, Frank Tetro, and Steve Hoppi from the Farmington Valley. And 18-year-old Gary Barnes from Canton, CT, who began racing in the modified division before his high school graduation.

Another popular driver was Ernie Caruso from Bloomfield, the brother-in-law of my older brother and a former driver, Pete Penfield. He would win both short and long-lap main events at Riverside, driving his budget 14 car from 1967 to 1971. A car that would cost about $2500 to put on the Riverside track. Caruso would also be the winning car in the final modified race to be held at West Springfield's Eastern States Expo track in the fall of 1968.

Ralph Boehm continued to race for different car owners at

Riverside and Plainville with some modicum of success until the 1964 season. He would throw himself into the sport of flying small planes. Get involved in the world of competitive arial gliding.

Eastern States Archives Photo
The 14 Car, Ernie Caruso from Bloomfield
The Last Winner at Eastern States, 1968

Working as team chief for New Jersey native George Moffit, who would win both the US and World Gliding Championships. Their exploits would be documented in publications throughout the world, including a feature article in *Sports Illustrated*.

In 1971, Boehm, while en route from Virginia to Bradley Field in Windsor Locks, CT, he encountered engine failure and crashed a single-engine Cessna airplane onto Avon's Talcott Mountain. The story was reported by Simsbury resident and *Hartford Courant* writer Kirk Hatsian. Remembering, Ralph said, "I knew I was going in, going to buy a piece of the farm." A flyer's saying that means they know they're going to crash.

Boehm, the veteran pilot, knew his plane and the area. What actions to take in bringing the plane into an area to minimize a crash. He survived without injuries. Much the way he survived his many crashes during his stock racing days.

Four months later, another local pilot crashed in almost

the same location in heavy fog. That pilot died. Boehm was called in by the National Transportation Safety Board as a consultant to the crash investigation. It was learned that many of the actions taken by Boehm to minimize crash effects and save himself were not carried out by this plane's pilot.

As Boehm would say to reporters from the Hartford newspapers, "When you're going to crash, it helps to have a plan ready to use. It just might help you to survive."

I remember an old-time stocker from Connecticut. His name was Johnny Georgiades, known as the "Flying Greek." He once won four main events in a row at Plainville Stadium. To stop him, a group of drivers put up a bounty, or what is often called blood money. Gang up and stop him. Disable his car. Put him into a wall if need be.

Georgiades, a Hall-of-Fame racer, had a plan. He understood the costs of change and of his plan.

Instead of racing at Plainville against the bounty hunters, he took his $1400 budget stock car to the Waterford Speed Bowl. He won third-place money. His plan was simple. "When Joe Tinty, the owner of Plainville Stadium, and Moe Gherzi, the racing director, clean up their acts, maybe I'll go back."

That was Georgiades' plan of survival. It worked.

He did return because Georgiades, though he drove a budget car, was a fan favorite and a good crowd draw, and he knew it. Only after he was invited and paid a pre-race stipend by track owner Tinty did he commit to return. A wonderful way to beat the premier cars and the corporate system at its own game. Gherzi, afraid of a tight-knit group of drivers turning on him, refused to acknowledge Georgiades' presence. He started him at the tail end of a 24-car main event.

Georgiades shiftily moved through the large field, managed to evade the attempts to knock him off the track, and won the 50-lap main event and top prize money of $700. He had also negotiated a $300 bonus from Tinty if he won the main event.

Gherzi would not shake hands or have his picture taken

with Georgiades. The premier car owners and drivers stood watching as Tinty presented the winner with the first-place money prize and his bonus for winning. The owner of the stadium and the winner of the race did not shake hands.

Said Georgiades, "Doesn't bother me. I'm the one who gets to spend the money." As I would write in one of my *Farmington Valley Herald* columns about the incident, "What a premier way to strut your budget stuff."

Pick a lane and defend it. Another of those wonderful lessons I learned.

New cars appeared at Riverside Park Speedway. Some had price tags of over $5000. Many others continued to be competitive budget cars with a price tag of under $2500. Some under $1500. An endless list of wannabe drivers.

Gary Colturi became a crowd favorite along with Steve S.J. Evonsion from North Granby, CT. Ray Miller, a University of Bridgeport grad from East Granby, was competitive and a crowd favorite. Newcomers Reggie Ruggerio and Bob Polverari became two of Riverside's all-time greats.

In Plainville, many of the early 1960s novice drivers graduated into the modified ranks. Don Spazano, Skippy Ziegler and the Alkas brothers, Dave and Fred. Don Moon, Ronnie Wycoff, and Bart Rocco. Ronnie Berndt, George Hotchkiss, and Stan Gregor. Most of those racing guys would put competitive modified stock cars on the track for under $1000.

Oh yeah, you still went to the junkyard. Dug through the maze to find a frame and a body. A straight axle and whatever other parts you could find. You dealt with others and traded for parts and services. You swapped brake drums for a homemade gas tank and front-end parts. You bargained for tires, services, and paint jobs.

Don Moon said he put his first modified racecar on the

Plainville track for $700. And he was competitive and won main events with that car.

The late 1960s and early 1970s continued to be the golden era for local stock car racing. Costs seemed to be at a temporary standstill. It became a time for the Gremlin, Pinto, and Vega revolutions. Cheap cars with inexpensive repairs. A conglomerate of cars on the track. New boxcar type racers, late models, old style Chevy and Ford coupes both chopped and tallboys. Some days, the track looked like a junkyard that had come back to life.

But the handwriting was on the wall.

And that's how it went until the late 1970s. Then, prices for, well, just about everything went out of sight. By the 1980s, it became a moot point. If you wanted to be a modified stock car owner or driver, you entered the fray as a business and not a hobby.

It remains that way to this day.

It was early 1976. I was having coffee in Simsbury and ran into Ralph Boehm. I hadn't seen or talked to him in years. I introduced myself. At first, he didn't recognize me. When he did, he smiled and said that he enjoyed reading my sports stories in the *Farmington Valley Herald,* where I was the sports editor.

We talked a little about his days racing Riverside, Plainville, Eastern States, and other tracks in New England. I told him I thought he was one of the better drivers. He was a conservative race driver and seemed to have a plan. Was a bit more cautious. Not as hard-charging, but effective and more in control. He usually found a way to get around the track quickly and finish in the money.

He said it paid to have a plan and be prepared to use it. Know your track and the competition. Know your car. Stay within yourself and stick to the plan. Don't try to be something you're not. Whether racing or flying a plane. Crashing into a concrete wall or crashing into Talcott Mountain. He was able to stay competitive for many years against that tsunami of rising costs and cars that were better and faster than his.

Ralph wasn't a quitter. He made good business decisions. "Costs, yeah. But racing became a business. Even the small tracks. It stopped being fun," said Boehm.

For Ralph Boehm, those decisions became more important. Family, futures, flying, and other enjoyments. It became that simple business decision, knowing when to take that fork in the road. Cut your losses that are always waiting on the next lap, corner, or backstretch. Or mountain top. Find a different kind of track to race. Life's bigger decisions. Pick your spots to make your moves.

I listened intently and took heed to the lesson he was offering me.

⚑⚑

I worked as a business consultant from 1979 until my retirement in 2015. I did projects in 30 countries. I often made many decisions that affected people and costs that were in the millions of dollars. Decisions that affected my life, too.

I never raced stock cars. But I did listen to all who did during those wonder years. Including my brother, Pete, who was a winning race car driver past his 70th birthday. I learned about costs and about competition. Of having deep resources as opposed to not having a reserve pool.

To know when losing can often be perceived as a time of winning.

I learned when to cut one's losses. To understand that even when you still have the physical and mental skills, sometimes, you admit that the race is now often faster than your reaction times can endure. A case of losing even while winning. A lesson in decision making.

So, you find other avenues to test your skills.

Stock car racing in the 1950s and into the 1970s was a sport of people and driver enjoyment. Then, one cold winter day early in 1960, a few folks of commerce decided to make it a business.

No different than the management consulting business I was a part of for 37 years. Simply, if you wanted results, you lived that old saying, "You get what you pay for." Only here, you often paid and got nothing for your investment.

You could stand in the pit area at Riverside Park Speedway in 1960 and take in the business storefronts. There was Ralph Boehm's number 101 car. A toolbox and a few tires. A mechanic for those fixable things. Then, there was the Flying Zero car. The M-6. The Garuti Special 14. Gordon Ross' cream-and-red beauty 19. Deep resource pools.

It was like looking at a startup computer company, like Business Systems, Inc. Then, looking at Microsoft. It wasn't a case of picking your poison. Hell, as a budget car, you were already two car lengths behind and losing ground.

What I did learn from that situation. You pick your lane and spots. Just do your job as well as you can. Keep in the mix. Create opportunities. Somewhere along the line, your opponent will always make a mistake. Be ready to take advantage during that time because those opportunities won't be there for long.

Respect your opponents. But never fear them. And always remember that when it's time to make your calculated moves, pull the trigger.

During consulting projects, I went to a few stock car races

in the years 2000 to 2005. In places like Vermont, Virginia, Louisiana, Florida, and Ohio. I remember asking a Vermont driver who owned a tire company the cost of building his modified. He thought it to be around $12,000. Maybe more. I asked him if the cost was worth the investment. He said, "Hell, no!"

Talking to owners In Virginia, the same type of modified race car cost was between $10,000 and $15,000. In Ohio, about $8000 to $9000. In Louisiana, an estimated $2000, and the driver said he owned his own gas station and got all his needed parts and services from friends and relatives who owned businesses in town.

I was doing a project at an oil company in Oklahoma. Developing a training program. The billing cost for my company to develop that program was between $450,000 to $500,000. The projected return on investment to the company would be between four to eight million dollars. I learned the executive we were working with was a huge stock car fan. NASCAR and short-track racing.

The same program we were planning had been developed for these same folks twenty years earlier. At a cost to the oil company of $100,000 with projected returns to be around one million dollars.

One night, I had an epiphany. I decided to do the math of the times.

I contacted the man in Virginia. Asked what he believed would be the lowest cost he could build his modified stock car for and still be as competitive as he thought he was now. With reluctance he admitted he might be able to get by for a cost of $5000, maybe $6000. About half of what he had originally spent.

Over dinner with one of my company partners, I asked what minimum cost he believed we could develop the training programs, still providing a reasonable return on investment to our client. With reluctance, he said $250,000 to $300,000.

Half of what we had proposed as our development and implementation costs.

Our client, a maker of industrial, oil-based products, listened to our rationale. If we could do the project for less, would he offer a longer term of involvement with options for add-on projects. The client, impressed with our proposal, said yes.

I asked the stock car builder a similar question. What if the building of all cars within a certain division was limited, having a cost cap? Would that be a type of compliance commitment that might just create a whole new way with costs in which the cars were put on the track with little or no loss of performance. He, and others, said yes.

Yes, we did change our approach for our consulting client. And yes, our project was successful. And we enjoyed a three-year involvement with our client.

No, the racing community in Virginia, and the one in Ohio, did not accept the proposed changes to a cost cap. I didn't think they would. Just as I didn't believe those early makers of those premier cars from that 1960 season would have accepted.

But I learned a most important lesson. Business is business, even when you try to say it's not. And to always pick your spots when you want to make a business decision. And I learned that compromise is not a viable agreement.

And the costs for acceleration depended on what track you were racing on.

There will always be big track racing like the NASCAR circuits. And there will always be big business everyone competes against.

There will always be a smattering of small track racing that survives in small-town burgs throughout the country. Just like the small companies and mom-and-pop bodegas that remain as a backbone of how people live and exist.

There is a price to pay. When I moved to Maryland in 1978, there were 15 multi-type racetracks throughout the state and nearby in Virginia and Pennsylvania. Now, in Maryland, only Hagerstown Speedway remains. A script that has been rewritten in every US state.

The challenge for all has always been to find the balancing point. To pick our spots and create our own opportunities. Know when to make our moves. Like all those budget cars at Riverside Park Speedway that have forever competed against the premier modified cars. Always looking for that opportunity to make progress.

Little businesses in a big business-minded world.

It's a lifetime battle that has left a path soiled with a residue of design. But not failure. Just like every business venture I've entered. That lesson I learned. I didn't win many outright. But I didn't lose many, either. I didn't let those others win without a good battle. Fought them to the last lap. I survived and I didn't compromise.

I learned business deals, whatever the components, are arbitrary.

Yeah, I began learning in that summer of 1960 when I first started to make financial decisions. Ironically, my first classroom for big business was in an amusement park. At a stock car track. Not in school or working for a large business. I learned business watching budget race cars, within a self-imposed and handicapped environment, do battle with the epitome of premier race cars.

Kinda like bringing a Cub Scout knife to a gunfight.

The war between common race cars and racing machines. That small corner store against the corporations. That small wooden wall against the on-coming title wave. That cozy B&B versus the brand-named hotel on the boardwalk. The unwinnable war between weekly wage earners vs millionaires. Billionaires. The war against compromise. Knowing when it's time to send in the clowns.

As time passed, some of the people and those places of the sport that I knew had now become even bigger businesses survived. Sadly, many did not.

Yeah, big business will usually win out in the end. At Riverside Park Speedway, premier cars and their worth won all the battles, beating out the budget cars.

Time marched on. I learned another lesson in protocols. Big business not only won the battles, they won the war, too. The speedway closed in 1999. The land and its uses were worth more than the premier cars could ever hope to be. For the speedway, it became the last checkered flag.

Because … that's the price we all must pay for acceleration.

7

POMP AND MY CERTAIN STANCE

THE ETERNAL BATTLE BETWEEN "US AND THEM"

To the surprise of many, I was selected as a graduation speaker for my 1964 high school class at Henry James Memorial High School in Simsbury, Connecticut. My selection as a speaker was, in retrospect, no surprise to me. The only unusual activities were the rather unexpected occurrences I experienced in my journey to the graduation night podium.

Graduation nights typically have three, maybe four, speakers. The class president offers opening greetings. The valedictorian, the student with the highest four-year academic achievement, gives the valedictory, commonly known as the class's farewell to their four-year feathered nest. The salutatorian, the class's second-highest academic performer, offers another form of welcome. Sometimes, as in our graduation, there are two salutatorians. Often, a fourth speaker is named, typically an academic and scholarship winner politically selected by local businesses or a teacher's group.

Graduation night speakers are, academically, the best of the best. National Honor Society members, Mensa members, and recipients of multi-scholarship monies from local businesses and organizations. Under yearbook pictures, their

165

short bios are usually filled with accomplishments and group associations. Typically, graduation night speakers are en route to highly respected colleges and universities.

Yeah, well, that wasn't me.

I became graduation night speaker number five. A huge surprise to most in my class. But not to those who wanted and needed to be heard. A special group that needed to have a voice. And when the opportunity appeared, surprisingly, I was the one they wanted to be their spokesperson. Represent a certain class within our class. A class that exists within every class. Those groups known as "us and them."

Unbeknown to me at the time, I would become the voice for "us."

Two months earlier, I had no interest or intention for such a lofty achievement as being a graduation speaker. The only voice I was fighting for was my own. I was engaged in a battle just to graduate. Taking six classes, including a third year of business typing and an elevated math class, to reach the required academic credits and acceptance at a junior business college in Western Massachusetts.

It all began on a Wednesday in April. Providence came calling.

Reading the morning announcements over the school's intercom, Mrs. Coughlin's final item caught the attention of many. An opening for one additional graduation speaker had been created. Selection would be determined by tryouts in front of a panel of teachers and administrators.

I had no interest, and at first bell, I headed out to my history class. Little did I know that I was less than 24 hours away from being pulled into the competition.

Jimmy Dearden was the initial messenger. Jeez, Jimmy and I had known each other since kindergarten class. Played

HJMHS Yearbook Photo
Jim Dearden
Wednesday's Visitor

together in the fields and barn behind his house near Kelly's Corner. Fished local ponds and streams together. By high school, I had opted for general business studies. Jimmy was an industrial arts and shop guy. Thursday morning, he came into my homeroom before classes. He sat down next to me and looked me in the eyes. His words were straight and true and spoken like a seasoned politician.

"You need to be that graduation speaker," were his opening words. "Because we need a voice." He had hesitated after saying the word "we."

"We?" I asked slowly.

"Yeah, we," he shot back, then added, "You know what I'm talkin' 'bout. You've always known. It's us and them."

Yeah, I knew what Jimmy was talking about.

Jimmy pointed at me, got up to leave, and repeated his thoughts. Turned and left the room. That day, I ran into him a few times in the crowded hallways. He, and others, kinda gave me that look. You know the look. That one that screams out, "We're watching you."

Friday morning brought another plea. This time from another classmate I knew and respected. His name was John Supernaugh. He'd transferred to our school from Granby High School. We often ended up on the same teams in gym class. John was an easy kid to get along with. People liked him. He was friendly, easy-going, and had a nice smile. A little mischievous. And, like Jimmy Dearden, he had the same message for me.

"Penny," he said. A nickname of sorts he enjoyed using with me. "You need to be the graduation speaker. Speak for us. It's us against them. You need to be our voice. Because it will always be us against them." He quickly rose and left the room. My thoughts: Why me?

In typing class, Sharon Tetro, a girl I had known from my neighborhood since we were pe-schoolers, turned to me and asked, "You gonna do it?" referring to my trying out for graduation speaker. Well, it was now coming at me from many directions. Word was spreading fast. Made me nervous. Yeah, there was "us and them." It was real. But I knew many of "them." Kids I grew up with in my neigh-

HJMHS Yearbook Photo
John Supernaugh
Friday's Visitor

borhood. Schools, the playgrounds. People I liked. Others, of course, I knew nothing about.

Again, I asked, "Why me?" A question that would take me years to answer.

Look, I may not have been the sharpest pencil in the box. At times, we're all a little dumb with the things we do. I was smart enough to know that gaps existed throughout social environments, especially in high school. Kids with certain interests tended to group together with others who shared those same interests. Whether that meant one group sharing thoughts with other academics about physics or mathematical probabilities of changes in calculus. Or another group talking about the performances of fuel injection systems and ratios of a quick-change rear end in drag racing. Maybe the importance of tolerances for PH levels in skincare affecting health and beauty pros. Whoever the group, they stayed close to the people they were a part of. They discussed matters and materials they were comfortable with.

The true question was not "us and them." It was more about how one stands up for his or her beliefs. Decides to make one of those "tough decisions" we all make during our lives. Situations experienced by people in all groups.

There's an old saying in sports when the game is on the line and we need to make one of those tough decisions. It's an odd and amusing saying. Goes like this:

"Sometimes, in the heat of the battle, we don't know whether to shit or to steal second base." Now, I had this uncomfortable challenge and a tough decision to make. Whether I should shit. Or try and steal second base

Hell, I wasn't sure if I had even reached first base yet.

Along with almost 200 others, I entered seventh grade at Henry James Memorial Junior High in the fall of 1958. We were given our class designations. The seventh-grade classes would be of equal size, with class identification numbers from 71 to 76. Each number, though not identified, would have its own associated academic level of performance and expectation.

Nobody really knew what the designations were, with one exception. Class 73. Everybody knew that if you were in Class 73, you were tagged as an incoming student with low fifth and sixth-grade academic credentials. And your expectations for seventh-grade performance were lower than those of the other seventh-grade classes and students.

I was assigned to Class 73.

Other classes were offered advanced opportunities like algebra and geometry. We, in 73, took general math. Others took world history, advanced sciences with labs, and political civics. We, in 73, labored in simple American history, general sciences, and art classes. Where languages were offered, Latin, Spanish, and French, for other classes, we, in 73, struggled with basic English and composition. And, of course, we had many who were offered classes in home economics and shop classes in the service industries.

For every nerdy-looking pen pocket-holder, there was a dirty, oily-smelling rag hanging out from someone's back pocket. For every Latin or French language word conversion card, there was a laminated guide explaining the difference between a spatula and a cooking turner. For every manually operated slide rule, there was a concealed switchblade.

And I rued the comments from those other classes. We, in 73, were perceived as pigs with lipstick. A math problem that had no answer. Mice, lost in our own little mazes. Once, I had to deliver a note to the teacher's lounge. That smoke-filled sanctuary of unbridled personalities, foul language, and a disdain for anything and anybody who provided a whiff of non-compliance to outdated expectations.

I entered their room without being noticed. A teacher, their back to me, was pontificating on the challenges of educating today's students, especially "that 73 class. A real menagerie of fucking idiots. A roomful of potted plants."

I was noticed. The room went silent. I looked down, shook my head, breathed deeply, and stared at the teacher. I flipped the note into the air, letting it fall to the floor. For the ensuing six years, that teacher avoided me. Never said one word to me. Yeah, us and them!

I did feel like a fucking potted plant that nobody wanted to water.

It wasn't just teachers. A growing number of seventh-grade classmates avoided contact with us as if the number 73 was the plague. As the months passed, the gap widened. About the only time there wasn't a gap and classmates were interacting together was during gym classes.

When it came to interaction away from the gym between boys and girls from other classes and Class 73, that hill was much steeper and harder to climb. In fact, with limited exceptions, it was non-existent. We weren't dummies, idiots, or potted plants. We, "us," were a class of good kids. So were "them." Both groups were smart, friendly, caring, and worked hard to achieve personal goals. Too often, "them" were so smart that they were dumb. They just couldn't see who we were through their own self-imposed barriers. Unfortunately, "us" had the same feelings and perceptions about them.

If anything, oh yes, we were different. But always in a very positive way.

By mid-year, two of my teachers read me the riot act. They let me know, in no uncertain terms, I was being lazy. Not giving my schoolwork any effort. They said I was smart and that they believed I should be performing at a higher level. And they were about to make that happen.

My social studies teacher, Mr. Robert Amstutz, said he had engineered my being transferred. Elevated two levels into one of his classes. He said to get my ass in gear because I was as smart as any student he had in any of his classes.

Maggie Wade was my English composition teacher. She, too, had me reassigned to a next-level English writing class. She would tell me that I was "a good word writer," but I was much better as "a bad grammar word writer." Mrs. Wade could always turn a phrase. And I could always understand a lefthanded compliment.

Maggie Wade once said to me, "Robert, one day, you will write books."

Funny, classmates in those next levels hardly spoke with me during my time with them. I was still one of those from Class 73. I did pretty good in my new classes. Ironically, I struggled with everyday 73 classes. A little like a sports team that plays to the level of its competition. My math teacher, football coach Roland Morrison, called me into his room. He stared at me, shaking his head and saying, "Penfield, you confuse me. You're smart. Got a good head on your shoulders. Just wondering when you're going to decide to show it."

He had a good point. I didn't have an answer to his question.

I began eighth grade in Class 83. Which is 73, just a year

later. Another year in the wasteland of mediocrity and potted plants. Again, I was moved up a few levels in two classes. Few words were spoken to me by anyone in those classes, and I didn't speak with them. I struggled with my base 83 classes. It was really more my being aloof, lazy, and not interested. Four years of high school loomed ahead of me.

I wondered. Was I destined for Class 93?

With help from my mom, I chose a general business course curriculum entering my freshman year of high school, thinking maybe I'd do well enough for acceptance to a two-year business college. Other classmates picked from a variety of college courses, business classes, and skill courses for the service industries.

For my 73 and 83 classmates, girls chose secretarial, health, beauty, and home economics. Boys entered the industrial arts, machine, auto, and wood shops. If we thought there were social gaps in "us and them" during our junior high years, freshman year of high school drove that point home like a stake being driven through the heart of a vampire.

Not only were classes diverse in skill levels, but their learning locations would exacerbate an already widening abyss. For many in the shop and services fields, classes were held in learning areas on the backside of the school. Far away from the general school enrollment and frontal classrooms overlooking the main thoroughfare, Firetown Road. That part of the school was all crowded hallways that were social hotbeds, always packed with students.

Some even referred to it as "that other part of the school" or "the Island."

I played sports for two years until injuries ended hopes for any further involvement. A comeback in my junior year ended in disaster. More injuries and a new stark reality. Many were now far better in their athletic performance than me. While I stayed the same size, others grew bigger, faster, and stronger. While my skills rusted in non-use, theirs were elevated beyond the minimal varsity requirements.

I sank deeper into my own world of funk.

In the winter of my junior year, I was diagnosed with hepatitis. Couldn't shake it. Kept losing weight and feeling weak. Dr. Cannon, seeing no improvement in symptoms and my physiology, pulled me out of school for bed rest. Thoughts of a summer job or playing American Legion or JC Courant baseball were all now secondary thoughts. More serious thoughts were about my senior year and graduation. I was struggling and didn't know if I was going to move on to my senior year. I was embarrassed. Quite sure my mom and dad were embarrassed, too.

I really was a potted plant. Wilting on the vine.

Then, something unexpected and profound happened. It made me ashamed of how I'd been acting and my awful academic performance. For me, it was like finding a four-leaf clover amid the weeds in the leftfield grass. It would be a whole new ballgame.

Mr. Amstutz stopped by our home to drop off homework assignments. He didn't want me to fall too far behind. He had a message for me. It was disciplined and rather chilling. He tapped my shoulder in a rhythm with his every spoken word, emphasizing I'd better listen. "Robert, you will be moving on to your senior year with your classmates. Do you know why?" Sternly, he said to me, "Because, Robert, they, the entire class, need you."

It would take almost a year before I truly understood and appreciated just how powerful those words from Mr. Amstutz were to me and my life. How unexpected and ensuing actions would impact my senior year and with so many lifetime decisions, like my deciding to "steal second base."

All because, one day, I listened to Mr. Amstutz and decided to do my homework the way it was supposed to be done.

It was Thursday, the day before signup ended for the seniors' open graduation speaker tryouts. Before first period, a guidance counselor, Ed Batagowski, stopped me in the hallway. "Heard a rumor you might sign up for graduation speaker," said Bato as he was known to be called away from school. The best I could offer was a quick shrug of my shoulders. That safe way of saying, "I don't know."

Moving through the crowded hallways between classes, I ran into Miss Carol Cope, an English teacher. Walking briskly towards me, she lifted her left arm, index finger pointing up. Then she pointed it at me while nodding her head. I got her message loud and clear.

In typing class, Mrs. Ruth Schultz walked among the rows during a typing test. I was banging away on the keys, trying to better my words-per-minute from a previous test. While I was typing, she leaned in close and asked, "Robert, are you going to try out for graduation speaker?"

Not missing a beat, I finished my typing test. Did 43 words-per-minute with one mistake. When I looked around the room, the other 14 students in the class and my classmates from 73 and 83, all girls, were all staring at me, waiting for my answer.

Oh yeah, it was a conspiracy, all right. Alive, breathing, and growing.

Friday morning, I put my name on the signup sheet for graduation speaker tryouts. Mrs. Marion Coughlin, the mother of one of my senior classmates, Judy, witnessed my signature. She didn't say a word. Just smiled at me, nodding her head.

Monday morning, my homeroom teacher, Mrs. Ruth Hutchinson, called me up to her desk. Informed me my speaker tryout time would be Thursday at 3:15 PM. She gave me a short list of specs I needed to follow for the completion of my presentation. She wished me luck. I laughed, telling her I really didn't believe in luck.

John Supernaugh saw me in the hallway. Gave me a friendly punch in the chest. "Penny, I heard you signed up. Good going." I asked how he knew so quickly. He gave that wry smile of his and said, "Hey, I got people everywhere."

Jimmy Dearden saw me in the hallway and nodded. So did Sharon Tetro. And many others. It was a little scary. I even got looks from some of "them."

During study hall, I made a list of items I wanted to include in my talk. Items like opportunity, prejudice, corruption and graft, dirty politics, and truth. I fooled around with words as I penned what would be my intro. Did the same with a closing statement. Wrote a few paragraphs for each item I wanted to include using a few four-letter descriptives. I struggled to arrange words into a sequence, eventually putting together a five-minute talk that seemed to make sense to me.

During gym class, I shared my speaking intentions with a student, one whom Dearden and Supernaugh referred to as "one of them." Initially, the softball teammate was emotionless. Then uttered, "A graduation speaker. You! Are you shitting me?" I couldn't tell if he was going to laugh, puke, or congratulate me.

By Wednesday evening, I had edited and completed a handwritten speech I would take with me into the tryout room. I didn't care what the folks in that room thought about me. I did want the people in that room to listen to my words.

I hadn't yet told my mom or dad about the tryout.

I showed up for the speaker tryout at exactly 3:15 PM. There were about a dozen people in the room; most were teachers. I was dressed in blue jeans, sandals, and no socks. A light blue

Hawaiian-type beach shirt. Untucked and with a banded collar. My blonde hair was longer than most guys' hair in my class. Parted in the middle, ala hairdos for the early British bands of 1964. All eyed me with curiosity. I'm sure to many I was somewhat an enigma.

One teacher said, "You're late." Another glibly added, "Glad to see you dressed for the occasion." I said nothing. Walked to the podium at the front of the room. The moderator asked me for a copy of my speech, and I gave it to her. She asked if I had another copy for myself.

"Don't need it," was my response. She offered a friendly smile and nodded.

At first, I was a little nervous. I panned the room, staring into the face of every person. I began to speak in a moderate tone. As I addressed each issue, my intensity ebbed upwards, and I spoke a little louder. More quickly when inserting a thought. I showed them my passion.

I didn't stay at the front of the room. I moved, slowly and defiantly, among the rows of desks. Up and down aisles, staring at specific individuals. Pointing and speaking more loudly when driving home a complex thought. I kicked a few of the lightweight desks out of my way when walking. No halfway shit here. They were going to get the whole package.

Memories of those few tryout minutes are cloudy. I do recall the general thoughts and passion I felt inside while delivering my finishing salvo. I focused on learning opportunities, like this tryout for graduation speaker. I said one day, a member of the 73 and 83 classes would come back as president of a successful business. A politician making decisions for the town. Or, perhaps, a beloved member of this school's faculty. A beautiful potted plant. I finished, saying, "And won't that be a kick in the ass?"

My talk completed, I again stared at every face in the room. Then, quickly headed for the door and exited. A few steps outside the room, my heart beating wildly in my chest, I stopped to catch my breath. It was then, from inside the room, that I heard the voice of Carol Cope. Loud, succinct, and with emotion, she said to her colleagues, "Cancel the rest of the tryouts. We've got our graduation speaker."

I thought to myself, "Oh, shit. I just stole second base. What have I gotten myself into?"

Don Burnett was a science teacher. He knew of me. Didn't really know me, and I don't believe he disliked me. But over the years, he had no problem giving me a series of detentions for what I will refer to as a bunch of sundry and innocuous transgressions. Fun stuff for me. Pains in the ass for him.

Morning announcements were made over the intercom. The names of the senior class graduation speakers were announced. My name caught many by surprise. Including me. My homeroom teacher, Mrs. Hutchinson informed me I was to report to Mr. Burnett's room during my morning study hall. Honestly, I was expecting that he was going to hand me a detention for another now-forgotten activity. I figured he had a few on backlog for me. All written out, just needing a date and his signature.

Entering Mr. Burnett's room, we exchanged greetings. We sat at a table in the back of the science lab. He congratulated me on being "the chosen speaker." I thanked him. Admitted that I was a tad confused, not sure of my next steps and "all that other shit." He laughed and said that's why he had become involved.

Burnett got serious and said, "Rob, I've been ... we've all been waiting for you to show your potential. For six years. Amstutz, Wade, Mrs. Schultz, Miss McGrath, Mr. Sholes, Mimi Wells. We all know your talents. Your passions. Just didn't know when they'd appear." He had requested to be my speech coach. I guess that old saying is right. Sometimes you can't see the forest for the trees.

Burnett said I would have to write a new speech for graduation night. A lot more toned down than the one I had written for the tryout. Speech specs would be simple, a range of 1000 to 1400 words. Four to five minutes to verbally deliver. Mine would be the final speech of the evening. Or, as Burnett emphasized, "The only speech the crowd ever really listens to."

Burnett asked if I could memorize 1400 words. Then, he laughed, saying, "Yeah, you can. I've heard you know just about every major leaguer's batting average."

We sketched out three parts for the speech. An intro as an interest grabber. The base speech of two to three items. A closing epilogue. Something the folks would remember. I was adamant that two of my tryout speech points be included. The part about truth and about corruption in business. The growing gaps in the world of "haves and have-nots." Burnett agreed.

He wanted me to work with someone who was good with words and would help write a terrific speech. His name was Danny Mudgett. I had known Danny for many years. He was intelligent and insightful. And like me, mad at so many things in the world. Mad at life's things we hadn't yet, defined.

Both of us were angry at being angry.

For three days, Danny and I hunkered down in a small anti-room behind Bill Goralski's social studies classroom. Together, we created thoughts. Disagreed over critical points. Argued over words and tenses. Marveled over our combined work. Often admonished by Mr. Goralski for being too loud.

By Friday, we had a speech to be reviewed by Don Burnett. He had us change and rewrite one critical point and did wordsmithing in two other areas. He sent us back for two more days of work. On Wednesday of the following week, it was ready. Burnett read through it once. Looked at us and nodded.

We changed just one sentence. Said Burnett with a smile, "I had to. So we all won't go to jail." Burnett looked at the both of us. Said, pointing at me, "With your thoughts and direction," and then pointing at Danny, "and with your words," he felt we had combined to produce in his words, "one hell of a speech."

That evening, I told my mom and dad about my being

selected to be a graduation speaker. Mom cried. I think my dad did, too, but he turned away so I couldn't see it.

I remember Danny Mudgett's parting words. He smiled, punched me in my arm, and said to do a good job. Always the tough guy wanna-be, he said his speech would have been even more cutting. "I don't mind going to jail," said Mudgett.

"Yeah, well, after graduation, I'd rather go to a party," was my response.

I didn't attend my senior prom. That's not me. I did help a classmate move decorations that were to be used in the cafeteria for Saturday evening's event. She thanked me. Asked more questions. I had the feeling she wanted me to stay and talk. Her name was Wendy MacDonald. She, too, was not going to the prom. It was the first time in our six years together at school we had spoken to each other.

In that constantly changing world of pomp and my certain stance against, well, just about everything, Wendy was viewed as "one of them."

On senior prom night, Wendy and I went out on a date. Two people from each end of the class of '64's spectrum. Opposites attracting like moths to a night light.

We went to the stock car races at Riverside Park Speedway in Agawam, MA. Big Ed Patnode from Westfield, MA, won the 50-lap main event. Wendy and I talked a lot that evening. We learned about each other, our hopes, our fears. Tried to understand why it took us six years to talk to each other. We strolled through the evening at our own pace. Saluted only those flags that meant something to us. Danced to our own music. Ate junk food and drank beer. Held hands ... kissed.

It happened that way only because, one day, I wrote a graduation speech.

The gears of change were grinding. The final five months of my high school years surprised even me. I improved academically. Finally shook off that nagging case of hepatitis and started eating foods I had been denied for a year. Gained back a few pounds. For the first time in over a year, I felt sharper mentally and physically stronger.

After being chosen as a speaker, I found myself being asked questions by people I had not talked with in six years at school. Most of the people were "them." I didn't shun questions. I answered politely with words and answers I'm sure some of the folks were surprised to hear. I was, as I still am today, too brutally honest. I hadn't yet cultivated a soft, caring bedside manner. Still don't have one today.

It truly was pomp. And me searching for my certain stance.

I began to experience a wonderful feeling of indescribable solace and confidence in situations where I was comfortable with being slightly uncomfortable. A familiar Rubicon. I remember Don Burnett searching me out just before we would march into the gym on graduation night. He asked, "You are going to stick with the evening's script, aren't you?"

My confident answer was, "I rather think not."

Our class advisor, Mrs. Wells, was frustrated with me. She saw I was wearing a blue shirt under my gown instead of the required white.

My confident answer to her was, "I'm colorblind."

Wendy MacDonald found me just before we lined up to enter the gym. She hugged me and wished me luck. I laughed and told her, "Luck had nothing to do with it." She said that many in our class were blown away by my being one of that night's speakers. For years, they didn't know me, didn't care to know me. And now here I was, center stage. And tonight, they were going to get to know me.

My confident answer to Wendy was, "Yeah, no big deal."

That part was a lie. No matter how aloof I pretended to be or how I rationalized what was happening. As John

Supernaugh had said, "It had always been and will always be us and them."

Oh yeah, it was a very big deal. I should have been more honest with Wendy.

The evening's graduation activities seemed to pass quickly.

Together, our class marched into the gym in unison with a hitch step to the familiar sound of Edward Elgar's "Pomp and Circumstance." An Englishman, Elgar had written the music in the key of D as the first in a series of five march tunes. Featured at a British Coronation in 1901, the march was then adopted for graduations in the US beginning in 1902. As "The Star-Spangled Banner" had become America's anthem, Elgar's "Pomp and Circumstance" had become our country's gateway to and anthem for graduations.

Only a year earlier, I hadn't been sure if I'd be graduating with my class.

I sat in the bleachers, amid my classmates. Just one of the graduating mob of unknowns. Many were strangers to me. Snugly packed in, side-by-side, under the huge sign that hung from the wall behind us. Adorned with the 1964 class motto, "Seek the Truth Without Prejudice, Speak the Truth Without Fear."

I hoped the evening's audience, those controlling elders, would believe and support the words in that motto. My speech was about to test their boundaries of understanding and moral compliance. I wanted to paint my name on a wall for all to see. And I wanted to be heard.

As usual, graduation was taking place on a hot June night, but not uncomfortably warm. Just as I would do on a hot day playing baseball, I filtered out the thoughts of heat and focused on my responsibilities and the tasks at hand. I would close my eyes and drift to a place where I was alone. As I did on graduation night. To a place where I was comfortable with being slightly uncomfortable. My forever, lifetime Rubicon.

I could hear the goings-on all around me. The din of the audience. The opening ceremonies. Quiet and low-key chatter among graduates. Like a controlled environment that becomes nervous anticipation and soft noise that makes up the protocols for these events. A muted confidence and awareness of the oncoming expectations.

It was as if I was orchestrating everything to move at my chosen speed.

HJMHS Yearbook Photo
Suzanne Driscoll Eloquently Spoke of "Responsibilities"

The evening's welcoming address was given by Class President Joe Bonczek. I listened to his every spoken word. I'd grown up with Joe, and his voice was that of having a typical, everyday conversation with him. He was big, over six feet tall, weighing over two hundred pounds. Yet, his voice was soft and reassuring. When Joe spoke, you trusted in him.

Suzanne Driscoll spoke to the audience about "responsibilities," and with her every word, I kept rooting for her. Why not. She was pretty and smart. She'd always been friendly to me, going back to our days together at Central Grammar School.

The day before graduation, Suzanne had seen me in the hallway and asked if I had my speech memorized. I smiled and nodded. As she walked away, I spoke softly to the ghosts of the empty hallway, saying, "I don't need to memorize my talk. It's part of me. I've lived the words for the past six years."

I had admired Suzanne since fourth grade when I first had a crush on her. The time of being a youth is a challenging and confusing period. Despite being smallish in size and a little scared, I would fight a bully who was bigger, older, and tougher than me. Fearlessly, I'd take him on and give it my all. Usually got my ass beat up pretty good.

Yet, over many years together in school, not once could I find the courage to tell Suzanne Driscoll I had a crush on her. Yeah, life sure can be a funny old dog.

A talk about "prejudices" was given by Peter Fisher. I never knew him. Can't recall if we ever had a conversation during our school years. Peter had a brilliant mind, smart beyond my comprehension. I was told he built an atom smasher in his cellar for a science project. About the best I could do in my cellar was create a way to string my own baseball glove. Actually, a very hard and highly skilled task to complete.

Cynthia Radding was another brilliant academic who spoke about "flexibility and change." She would attend Smith College in Northampton, Massachusetts. I don't remember having any conversations with her during our years together as classmates. In the fall of 1964, I, too, was in Northampton, attending Commercial College. Just a short walk from the Smith campus.

One Sunday afternoon, I decided to visit her at Smith and say hello. We sat in the dorm's large living room, amid others. Our conversation seemed forced. I could tell she was uncomfortable with me. I wasn't from Amherst or Trinity College. I looked and spoke differently from those other guys in the room. I sensed that I was embarrassing her, so I left after 10 minutes.

During the speeches, I thought of Jimmy Dearden and John Supernaugh. Their pleas for wanting me to be a voice. To speak for those who typically did not have the opportunity to be heard. And many others who thought of me as being their spokesperson. I thought of the past seven weeks since I had been selected to be a graduation speaker. The previous five months. Six years. Yeah, we really did exist within a caste system. But only if we allowed it to happen.

My mind shifted into another gear.

I thought of Suzanne's talk on "responsibilities." Now, I had taken on the burden of being a voice for others. To talk about "us and them." It's not wrong to point that fact out to others. The world knows there are beautiful gardens and there are attractive potted plants. Both deserve the loving care and support they've earned.

I also learned a critical lesson. I had to be a voice for me, too.

Peter Fisher talked about "prejudices." In the past two months, I had conversations and social interactions with classmates I hadn't spoken with in all my years of school. I had overcome prejudices with some. Hope they felt the same.

I had worked with Danny Mudgett to write a graduation speech. If I were a betting man, I don't believe I would have taken on any odds of that successfully happening. Yet here I was. And Don Burnett, my speech teacher. I had expected detention. What I got was a teacher who, despite my perceptions, had been supporting me for years. I was too blind, too prejudiced, to see it.

Being "flexible to change," as spoken by Cynthia Radding. Well, I didn't see it as a thing, but more a living and an evolving process. Not just change for the sake of change. But positive, transformational change with definitive indicators of benefits and concerns. Learning about critical success factors. The change indicators for the measuring of performance, productivity, quality, and compliance. You could be an agent of positive change. Or you could fall behind and become a victim of that change. I was learning fast. Like drinking from a firehose.

Then, suddenly, it was my turn on the podium.

I rose from my seat. Carefully descended the steps of the bleachers. En route, I thought of my speech. It was about "truth." I knew the words in my speech would be a bit more biting than the previous speeches. As I arrived at the podium, I said softly, "Give 'em the truth, Rob."

I took a breath and slowly panned the audience. I picked out people and looked them in the eyes, gently nodding my head. I wanted them to have a few seconds to be quiet. Perhaps be a tad uneasy. I was the last speaker. I wanted them to see me and wanted them to hear every word I was about to say. This would be my time.

Just before speaking, I remembered Mr. Burnett saying, "You're the chosen speaker. The last one. The one everyone will listen to."

I opened with my greeting, thanking folks for their patience during the evening's activities. Going slightly off script, I said that they should listen to every word I was about to say because they needed to. I looked at Don Burnett, who was sitting in the first row to my left. He smiled.

"Truth," I said, "is today's big lie." Lots of heads looking down snapped up and looked at me. I talked about balancing points of truth that were no longer in the middle. That one could only hope to find those elusive points of balance usually after an exhaustive search. That "the honesty of truth was no longer an absolute."

I removed the mortarboard from my head. Placed it on the podium. Brushed a few wisps of hair from my eyes. I said, "Corruption and graft are now today's compromises." Explaining that it could start from the highest levels, cascading downwards. Or, in the lowest levels, "like right here in this auditorium, and work its way upwards."

Throughout the huge audience, including my classmates, there was dead silence in the building.

I spoke about "the truth within a truth." I emphasized that "it's never the wrong time to do the right thing. And no matter what your level of knowledge and intellect, a sign of a good person at any level was in knowing what not to do ... and when not to do it." I pounded my fist on the podium and added, "Sometimes, truth's most powerful words are the ones not spoken."

HJMHS Yearbook Photo
The Author Used Hard Cutting Words Speaking About "Truth"

I hesitated, like the pending truth within a truth. Like an epistle within a pause. What Don Burnett referred to as a pregnant pause. He said it would re-grab their attention. It did. I spoke about the world we were about to enter. The endless opportunities. From the highest levels of business and management. To the creative levels of the numerous support services and professions. Those flowering gardens. Those potted plants that every living person needs to have in their lives to survive.

Loudly, I said, "The truth is, we will, as a people, cease to exist unless all the multi-levels work together like a freshly shuffled deck of cards. And justice for all must be dispensed evenly and honestly, or it doesn't work." A lot like what we're dealing with today.

Again, I hesitated, then put my mortarboard back on my head. Panned the audience. Turned and looked at all the graduates behind me. I began my closing remarks.

Once again, I went off-script. Talked about challenges, responsibilities, prejudice, changes, and the truth. I lifted my right arm and pointed out over the audience, saying, "We better be ready, and you better be ready for us as we begin marching through tonight's gateways into the painful truths of our future."

I stayed at the podium for another 10 seconds. My head held high, I panned the audience with my eyes, taking a few seconds for a hard stare at the members of the Simsbury Board of Education sitting just below me in the second row. I saw my mom and dad. Both were smiling. My dad nodded, like he'd do when I turned a good double play or when I'd steal second base. God, inside my guts, I felt pride.

I left the podium and slowly climbed the steps to my seat.

I was told there was thunderous applause, a standing ovation, when I finished my talk. People hollering and yelling. Even my classmates stood and applauded. Truthfully, I never heard it and can't remember much about what happened during the remainder of the graduation activities. I do recall I received my diploma. Stood before Don Burnett. He had smelling salts for those who might be light-headed. I nodded that I was OK. I quietly asked, "You wouldn't have a cold beer, would you?" He smiled.

We marched out of the gym and broke ranks when we arrived in the hallway. There were lots of smiles, hugging, and noisy chatter. Pictures being taken. My mom took a picture of me in my cap and gown. My dad congratulated me and said I did a good job with my speech.

I felt a tap on my shoulder. It was Raymond Dry, chairman

of the Board of Education. He eyed me up and down, then chose his words carefully, saying that I had presented some "rather interesting and unusual thoughts." Prior to tonight, this man had no clue who I was. I nodded, smiled at him, and said, "Yeah, no shit."Superintendent of Schools Robert Lindauer then approached. He had known me since I was a toe-headed kindergarten kid at Central Grammar School, where he was the principal and often chased after me when I broke the rules. He spoke in that slow, methodical voice, looking down at me, his glasses slightly lower on his nose. "Robert, I am proud of you," he said in a machine-like manner. Carefully chronicling his quasi-praise by saying, "You've certainly experienced a colorful journey traveling through the Simsbury school system. Nice finish."

My response was, "Mr. Lindauer, I'm just getting started."

Mr. Amstutz approached, put his hand on my shoulder, and reminded me of his words from the year before. "Like I said. Your class ... they need you."

Don Burnett found me. Smiling, beaming, he shook my hand. He said he was both thrilled and very proud of me. I could tell he really meant what he said. He asked if I felt satisfaction for all the reasons I chose to try out and become a graduation speaker. I offered him what I would later come to refer to as "my vanilla answer." Yes, I could now put a checkmark next to the reasons others wanted me to be their voice.

For me, it went much deeper.

The real reason would always be that I had to do it. I needed to do it for myself. For the first time in my six years of junior-senior high school, I was pleased, proud, and even happy with what I had accomplished. It wasn't because of "us and them." Or the gap between what I came to see as a cultured garden and a potted plant.

Maybe, for the first time, I was beginning to learn why I was angry all the time and didn't know why. Probably scared of all that was happening around me. Afraid to step into the mainstream and give it a try. To take a chance on those other avenues of learning and challenges. I didn't, yet, know or have the confidence to clearly see and understand the triggers of my anger.

Always, it seemed, I knew what I needed to do. Yet, continued to make all the wrong decisions. Knowing they were wrong when I made them, thereby defeating the very goals and objectives I had set out to achieve. I was directionless. Just breathing while moving through time. I was a living paradox.

Cloudy waters sometimes have a wonderful way of suddenly clearing.

Now, I was curious with a new-found passion. I did care about my thoughts for others. My feelings about them. I wanted to know what others were thinking of me. What they had been thinking about me.

Then again, did I ever really not care what they were thinking?

It couldn't be because I was a speaker at graduation. That answer seemed just a bit too simple. Kinda like saying the shortest distance between two points is a straight line. Or, in baseball, you still have to swing the bat to get a base hit. Then again, Occam's Razor, or the simplest explanation, is the one used in the toughest of rationalizations.

Simple results. What is the residue of positive change? Well, it's truth!

And occasionally, that decision really is to "Shit, or steal second base."

It's been more than 60 years since that graduation night in 1964. The world has changed in many ways. Some positive, some negative. Others, destructive and irreversible.

Throughout the years, our class has distinguished itself in many professional endeavors. Company presidents in insurance, banking and financial services, plumbing, electrical, and landscaping. Real estate and investments.

In politics, medicine, and the military. Self-employed consultants. A wide range of musical and entertainment services. Small boutique businesses like bakeries, specialty shops, and delivery services. Teachers and professors. Scientists and building trades.

There are those who gave their life in service to our country and freedom. The many others we've lost over the years. A very impressive list of people.

I have not stayed in close touch with classmates, even those who were my best friends from those years. I did attend the 50th reunion and, in recent years, have attended small reunion get-togethers. They've been enjoyable and free of expectations. No "us and them" now. Just a bunch of friendly folks in our late seventies managing our way through the twilight of the journey.

It's taken most of my life to understand and appreciate just how much I learned during my last months of high school. More than my words could ever explain. I learned how to build bridges. Some worked well. Others collapsed and folded like cheap suits. Learning comes in many ways. Often leaving us with more questions than answers.

For me, those long-ago, embarrassing class numbers of 73 and 83, once viewed as punishment, I now accept as station stops along the journey. A chance to restart my life. Like Rob 2.0 or 3.0. Because I learned how to accept and manage that list of perceptions and commitments to all those changing and never-ending responsibilities.

I understood the enormity of the task from those classmates who asked me to speak for them on a huge platform. Also, I learned from a handful of teachers who believed I had so much more to offer during troubled times.

I learned this from my toughest critic. Me!

I learned how to walk into a maze of confusion. And, with the help and support of others, find the confidence to take a few chances with no guarantees. Accept the positive change that was just waiting to be discovered. To find my way out of that confusing maze with trust and confidence. Feelings and skills I didn't have when I entered that maze. Now, I cherish them.

Us and them, yeah, it's real. Always has been, always will be. Yet, at a critical time in my life, I was fortunate to find and be surrounded by resources who offered help. Showed me how to understand and manage the perceptions of confidence and fear. How to make better decisions.

They showed me how to stop cheating with the game of life.

I came to understand the trust a group of people put in me. Asking me to speak for them. Eventually, I learned that I was speaking for a much larger population. One that went far beyond the walls and realm of our high school gymnasium.

Learned how to admit my prejudices and that not-so-easy task of telling folks when I was wrong. And I learned about flexibility. Being able to give folks a little wiggle room in relationships and decision-making.

I learned about the honesty that I took with me to the podium that graduation night so long ago. Yesterday. And the message I wanted to share. A message that came from my heart. A message that lives on inside me today.

I learned about pomp and all its perceptions amid my own certain stance. I came to better understand and appreciate "us and them."

And to all, well ... that's the truth.

8

ENFIELD BEATS SIMSBURY 20–12
THE FOOTBALL FIX AND
THE LOSS OF INNOCENCE

A LESSON IN CHEATING AND ITS LIFETIME IMPACT ON ME

During the fall of 1959, I was a 13-year-old eighth grader. I thought of myself as a typical junior high school student in Connecticut. I was an avid sports fan, and in early November, I went to a high school football game. Simsbury High School, the mighty Trojans, my hometown high school, played an away game at Enfield High School.

Simsbury had recently been elevated from the small-school rank, Class S, into the heavily populated and very strong Class M. Simsbury was a good team in the fall of '59. They went into the season finale with a record of 6–0. They did hold a high ranking in the state's Class M. Enfield was designated as a Class L, or large school in Connecticut. Their record was 3–1. Despite being a Connecticut school, they were associated with and had played in conferences located in Western Massachusetts dating back to the 1940s.

Enfield won the game, 20–12.

Over the ensuing 40 years, I came into curious bits and

pieces of information about that game. Some a little odd, unusual. Circumstantial wedges of evidence. Most folks wouldn't have given it a second glance. Well, that's not me. Not that curious sports fan that I have always been. Especially because some of the information I came across cried out for questions to be asked.

The information came from many sources. College students I knew. A stranger I met on a train. A motorcycle policeman. A few sports-writing peers. A medic in Vietnam. And from a lonely alcoholic at a nowhere bar who begged for absolution. Each person contributed a stitch of information that eventually sewed together a story that I would come to believe is a true epitaph for that high school football game played on an overcast Monday, a late fall afternoon in November 1959.

For on that day, that game. I believe I witnessed my first "fix."

Let's be clear what is meant by a "fix." This is when outside influences are used to impact the outcome of an event, like a football game. The goal is to ensure one team either wins the game, beats a bookmaker's created point spread, or is put into a position where their chances of winning have been dramatically, albeit surreptitiously, enhanced.

Simply put, they have pre-placed advantages and influences that the other team does not have. And money has been paid to those who have been put into the position to affect that outcome. Put there by the people who have created the advantage so they, too, will make money.

Viva Las Vegas. Or, in this case, the Springfield, Massachusetts, mafia.

Outside advantages and influences can wear many disguises. Often, personnel in the form of illegal or ineligible players. A tactic used by high schools and colleges going back to the beginning of the 20th Century. More so, of late, it can be the use of synthetic, banned, and/or dangerous chemical enhancements. Especially in the drugs used for muscle strengthening or accelerated healing of any human physiological system.

A team's home playing surface is another form of fixing. Fields or courts that have been altered or doctored to benefit the home team. That can include the poor quality of playing surfaces and less than adequate facilities used by visiting teams, like locker rooms. There are also the psychological scheduling advantages, like playing on odd days. Thursdays, Mondays, and at unusual starting times.

And, of course, the one advantage that has persisted since, well, forever in sports or any competition. Tainted officials. Those folks, like in football, often have the final word in decisions. And years ago, they were not questioned. They can dramatically sway outcomes of any game with a questionable call, or a no-call. Easily in 1959.

Following the NFL's officials' strike in 2022, ESPN did an exhaustive study of game endings at multi-levels of competition. The study identified an estimated 19% of games played every week, where the outcomes of those games were affected by an official's questionable, bad, or no-call. Just think for a moment how many football games are played each weekend. In high school, college, and in the NFL. The number is in the thousands.

In Connecticut alone, almost 200 sanctioned games are played. The number of games that may possibly be in question by an official's call: almost 40 games.

Perhaps on that November afternoon in 1959, the game officials, those checkers and maintainers of the game's integrity, may have been Simsbury's toughest opponent.

For, on that day, nobody was checking the checkers.

When the battle had ended, it really wasn't too hard to determine the true combatants. Nor was it very challenging to identify the unscrupulous and manipulating villains of the day. Just as those villains whose handprints were all over what Lord Byron would pen in his 1815 poem, "The Destruction of Sennacherib."

More on Lord Byron's poem later in the story.

For all the right reasons that were not heeded and all the wrong reasons that found their way to fruition, this game should not have been played. From its curious birth right up to its ugly, painful-to-watch death.

Both schools, Simsbury and Enfield, are located in the state of Connecticut. Still a farm town in 1959, Simsbury was changing. Growing. Becoming a bedroom town for higher-priced homes being built on those once pristine pasture lands. For those who worked in Hartford, its surrounding communities and the few who commuted daily to New Haven and New York City on the old New York–New Haven & Hartford Railroad.

The school nickname was the Trojans. Had a good tradition of playing competitive high school sports at the Class S level dating back to the late 1920s. They had no conference affiliation in 1959, though they did play in a triumvirate with Canton and Farmington High Schools called the *Little Three*. Traditional opponents also included Rockville, Plainville, and Berlin. They also played high schools in the state's northwest quadrant, such as Gilbert of Winsted and Housatonic Regional in Falls Village.

Enfield was a large school. Located in North-Central Connecticut along the banks of the Connecticut River. Just south of the western Massachusetts border. It was, for many years, an industrial town with mills and factories along the river. Machine shops and small businesses. Many folks worked in Springfield and West Springfield, MA. The high school educated kids from Enfield, Thompsonville, Hazardville, and many surrounding communities.

By Connecticut high school standards, Enfield's Green Raiders were a large Class A school. But, since before the war years, they had not been in competition with Connecticut high schools. They had been affiliated with conferences in Western Massachusetts. The Pioneer Conference and the Inter-County League. Later, in the Western Massachusetts Suburban League. Traditional games versus Longmeadow and West Springfield, MA. They played Massachusetts schools Palmer, Agawam, and Ludlow and games against the Springfield city schools the High School of Commerce, Classical High, and Springfield Trade.

So, how did they end up playing each other? Simple answer. Because of two coaches. Old friends always make great enemies. It happened in the summer of 1958 at a coaches' clinic at Central Connecticut State College in New Britain, Connecticut. Enfield's football coach was Carl Angelica. He was known around the coaching ranks as a good man and a good coach.

A longtime friend of Angelica's was Russ Sholes from Simsbury. He had just resigned as football coach to focus on basketball, giving way to the new head coach, Roland Morrison. Sholes and Angelica had known each other for years. Angelica had a few open dates on both his 1958 and 1959 football schedules after possible games with powerful Cathedral High in Springfield could not be scheduled. Sholes knew the Simsbury team would most likely be over-matched. Over a few drinks, they agreed to play a home-and-home series. The dates were set.

In the fall of 1958, a young, inexperienced Simsbury squad upset a good Enfield team at Memorial Field in Simsbury by the score of 20–12.

In the fall of 1959, a tough and gritty Enfield team beat an improved and ranked Simsbury team at home by the same score from the previous year, 20–12.

With the short, two-year series now over, this story should

have been at its end.

But it was not. Not even close.

The 1959 game was scheduled for Saturday, November 7, at 1:30 PM. It began raining on Friday night. Hard, pelting rain. Over three inches. It was still raining early Saturday morning. Coach Angelica checked the field at 6 AM. It was unplayable. One corner of the south endzone had washed away. The field was a quagmire. He went into his office. Notified Pete Staszko, the faculty manager, and his assistant coach, Don Flebotte. Then, he called Russ Sholes. The game was postponed and eventually rescheduled for Monday afternoon.

Early morning hours were spent notifying players and others who had multiple responsibilities for supporting the event. The four officials assigned to the game were called. Two of the officials said they would not be available if the game was rescheduled for the coming week, due to work responsibilities. One was a VP for Massachusetts Mutual Insurance Company in Springfield. The other, a VP for Western Massachusetts Electric, would be traveling.

There were no bookmaking odds or point spreads for this game. What is commonly referred to as "action." Pretty rare for a high school game. The only exceptions were a few of the traditional Thanksgiving Day games. There was already enough action for the Springfield, MA, "Families." The Mafia. Who, according to police reports, were responsible for running the local betting and numbers rackets throughout Western Massachusetts.

There were betting cards for local and national college football games. Minor league hockey right in town with the Springfield Indians of the American Hockey League. Saturdays offered betting lines for NHL and NBA games. And Sundays, well, that was the mother lode for betting with a full slate of

National Football League games. Especially the usual heavy betting lines in the Northeast for the now-successful New York Football Giants.

Said a Springfield police detective, "If there's a payday for the local Mafia, it's Sundays in the fall. Pro football. Even detectives I know on the force play the cards."

So, a 1959 regular season high school football game between high school teams that had no affinity to Springfield's betting folks. Who would waste their time on a game that was, at best, very small potatoes?

Well, we were about to find out.

The game was played on Monday, November 9th. Daylight Savings Time ended Saturday night. It would get darker sooner. Just after 5 PM. Kickoff was set for 1 PM. The Simsbury team's bus from Salters Express Company on West Street would leave around 11 AM to make the 40-mile trip to Enfield during school hours. Bump Curtiss, a former First Selectman in town, would be behind the wheel of the team bus.

Early school releases for two additional buses, one from the high school and another from the junior high, would leave at noon for students who had signed up to attend the game. I was on the junior high school bus with about 50 other students.

It was a mostly cloudy day. Temps in the high 40s. Chilly with a steady breeze. The sun peeked in and out at times. A typical November day in New England. You knew how to dress for the weather. Both activity buses with students arrived at Enfield High School, located near the town's historic district on Route 5, about 10 minutes before kickoff. The field behind the high school was in terrible shape. If I'd been in charge, this game would not have been played on that field.

Simsbury came into the game with a record of 6–0. They had a good offense, averaging 34 points per game. An All-

State quarterback in Jim Bidwell. A breakaway runner in Bobby Holloway, who had gained over 1000 yards and scored 15 touchdowns. The linemen on offense and defense were big and tough. Their weakness was in the deep defensive secondary. Corner backs and free safety positions were not good tacklers, and they had been burned by opponents' TD passes.

EHS Yearbook Photo
Mike Bromage
Enfield's Senior QB

Enfield, with a record of 3–1, averaged 18 points per game, led by their smallish quarterback, Mike Bromage. They could run the ball. Didn't throw much. Defensively, they were tough as nails. Overall, Enfield's competition level and its opponents were at a higher level than Simsbury's. Folks who were casual followers of football called this an even game. What is referred to as a "you pick 'em." Folks I knew, those in the know, said Enfield was a much stronger team and favored.

It was Monday. Real football weather. But something just didn't feel right.

On the game's second play from scrimmage, Simsbury co-captain Mel Ollestad was called for a major penalty. When he attempted to ask the official what he had done, he was told, "One more word, and it'll be another fifteen yards." Ollestad backed off.

Something else was amiss. High school football games always had four officials. On this day, there were five uniformed officials on the field. Or, somewhat uniformed.

A true omen of things to come.

Simsbury managed to take a 6–0 lead in the first quarter. Bob Holloway got loose for a 65-yard TD jaunt on a broken play. It was to be a pass play, with Bidwell tossing a short pass to split end Ray Mildren. Protection broke down. Bidwell ended up running right, handing off to Holloway, who zigzagged through a gang of Enfield defenders going untouched into the endzone. Or what was left of it after the rain.

SHS Yearbook Photo
Simsbury Co-Captain Mel Ollestad
Penalized on Game's Second Play

Enfield's Lenny Lavalette remembered: "Coach wrote Holloway's name on the blackboard. That's the guy you have to stop. Holloway, their All-State halfback."

Ironically, during Enfield's pre-week practice, there was no mention of Jim Bidwell. Following the 1959 season, the Simsbury signal-caller would be named Connecticut's first team's All-State quarterback. Holloway, a second team halfback.

A footnote to that touchdown. On the play preceding Holloway's TD run, offensive tackle Beanie Pattison was penalized for holding. The Trojans had been assessed a 15-yard penalty. Years later, Pattison shared with me, "Penalty on me?

Hell, I was grabbed from behind like a horse collar and pulled to the ground. Didn't touch an Enfield player. I didn't figure in the play in any way."

Enfield tied the game at 6–6, with Bromage going over from two yards out. They then took the lead by doing what they rarely did. Throw the ball. Bromage engineered a ten-play drive of bootlegs and deceptions. Culminating with a 44-yard TD heave to Dee Warner for a 12–6 Enfield lead.

Remembered Bromage, "I ran to my right, thinking I'd pitch the ball to my trailing halfback. Just as I was about to make my move, I saw the wide receiver to my left. He was wide open, waving his arms. I threw it as far as I could. When Warner caught the high-arching pass, there wasn't a Simsbury player within 10 yards of him." Simsbury cornerback Bill White had bitten on the running play, thinking Bromage was going to cut back to the center of the line. White figured he beat him to the spot. He abandoned his coverage of the wide receiver. He got burned.

On the ensuing possession, Simsbury's fullback Hank Plona caught a short pass and rumbled for 10 years. The ball was knocked free by Enfield's Biff Landry and recovered by Len Lavallette at the Trojans 40-yard line. Three plays later, Bromage again went off script, tossing another TD pass. A 22-yarder to Rich Korona, who was uncovered and went untouched into the endzone. Another play of blown coverage by Simsbury's secondary. A pass to Enfield halfback Carm Ravenola for the two-point conversion gave the home team a 20–6 lead. Simsbury's players and its large following of fans stood in stunned silence.

And it was about to get worse. In so many disturbing ways.

In the waning minutes of the first half, Jimmy Bidwell led an eleven-play drive featuring two gutsy runs from Holloway that put Simsbury on Enfield's 3-yard line. On third down,

Bidwell ran a quarterback sneak, going over the goal line and into the endzone behind the blocking of center Tom Hayes and linemen Dick Eckhart and Ed Spear for a touchdown. Or so everyone thought.

An official, not the referee or the linesman, hollered out, "No score ... No score. His feet didn't cross the goal line." This was after Bidwell had been dragged out of the endzone by Enfield linemen.

From my right, I heard a voice scream out from a man in a suit and tie, "What the fuck ya talking about? What kinda fucking call is that? There's no such thing as his feet crossing the line. It's the ball. THE BALL! How much you git'n' paid to make these asshole calls?"

Also, the situation had just worsened in a way that could not be repaired. As the play ended, two Enfield linemen fell across Bidwell's legs. He cried out in pain.

There was Bidwell on the ground at the goal line, where he had been dragged back out of the endzone. Football clutched tightly under his arm. Crying out in pain as two linemen lay across his stretched-out legs. The oddly dressed official standing along the sidelines was pointing at the Simsbury crowd and yelling, "That's going to cost you another fifteen yards." He was assessing a penalty because fans yelled at him.

A well-dressed man in a suit stood next to me near the endzone. He said his son played on the Enfield team. The man seemed to know football and its rules. He shook his head and pointed to the field, saying, "That's not right. Something is not, well, that's not right."

Almost as a whisper, I said, "This game is fixed."

Simsbury was assessed 30 yards in penalties on a play where they did not commit any violations and had a touchdown called back. Enfield took over the ball on the 34-yard line and ran out the first half's clock, leading with 20–6.

Along the sideline, Russ Sholes stood staring at Enfield's coach and his longtime friend, Carl Angelica. Sholes hollered out, "Carl, what the hell is going on." The coach saw Sholes' glare. Heard him call out. Angelica pulled the bill of his cap over his eyes and walked away with his team to their halftime digs.

Sholes stood firm. Staring at his friend, who was walking away from him.

At halftime, the team found refuge between the Simsbury school buses. It was a quiet and sullen group.

"We were a beaten team at halftime," remembered senior co-captain Dick Eckhart, who recalled details as if the game had been played yesterday. Not over 65 years ago. "We let them [Enfield] and the refs get into our heads. We were not going to win this game, and most of us knew it."

I walked over near the buses to hear what was going on. Coach Morrison walked slowly through the area. At first, he spoke softly. Then, his voice rose in volume, and his words quickened. His message was not for the dinner table.

SHS Yearbook Photo
**Dick Eckhart Senior
Co-Captain**

He was embarrassed by his team's performance, saying, "You should be ashamed." He was accusatory and hard on individuals. It was his next outburst that made me take notice of the vitriolic assessment of his team's efforts.

"You are letting down your teammates. The coaches. Me. Your school. Your mothers and fathers. You're letting down your God."

Letting down God! Whoa, that was a bit too much for me. There was no need for that type of language. At a football game. Not to teenagers who are supposed to trust, respect, and look up to you. Busting their asses, and that's how they're talked to. Motivated. They're letting down God!

Roland Morrison was my math teacher. On Wednesday, after that game, I went into his room. I didn't mince words. I told him how sorry I felt for the team. Especially the way he'd addressed them during his halftime tirade. His comments about letting down God.

I recall he said something to the effect, "That's football."

I responded, "Call it what you want. I'm not very religious. But that's wrong." Turned and walked out of the room.

Years later, before I was to graduate, Mr. Morrison asked me to stay after class. He wanted to wish me luck in my endeavors after graduation. He wanted to tell me how much he admired me for the day I came into his room and spoke my opinion about his halftime talk about God five years earlier.

I thanked him. Said I stood by my words.

Defensively, Simsbury came alive in the second half. They played tougher. Meaner. Perhaps as dirty as a few of the Enfield linemen had been doing in the first half.

But offensively, they sputtered. Jack Demsky had replaced Bidwell as quarterback. He could call signals and hand the ball off to running backs. He could not throw a pass. But he was a senior, and Morrison said to his assistants, "We'll stick with a senior."

I thought junior Phil Lambert would have been a better choice. Smaller in size than Demsky, Lambert could run the offense effectively. And he could pass. Not a strong arm. But a good passer when throwing quick out-patterns. He threw a nice arching ball with a tight spiral that was easy to catch.

By the fourth quarter, Simsbury's defense had taken control of the game. Finally, the offense put together a solid drive. Holloway ripped off a pair of 15-yard runs behind the vicious blocking of fullback Hank Plona. A 10-yard TD run from Holloway was called back by a backfield-in-motion penalty. It was a good call. Perhaps the only one of the day.

What happened next pretty much sealed Simsbury's fate. And my belief that I was watching my first fix. Holloway, running behind Plona, ripped off his patented play, "the 923 Quick," off tackle. He scored on a 5-yard run. Or so everyone in the vicinity of the field thought.

The back judge was standing on the endzone's backline. He held his hands up, signaling a touchdown. Holloway handed him the ball. He reached out for it, then pulled his arms away. The ball dropped to the ground. An Enfield defensive back picked it up. The back judge began waving his arms. Blew his whistle and yelled, "Fumble recovered by Enfield. Touchback." No TD for Simsbury.

Holloway stood motionless. He took his helmet off. He had that look of utter amazement. He looked to his sideline for help from coaches. Teammates. Anybody. We all had just witnessed perhaps the worst football call any of us had ever seen.

It took about 30 seconds before fans from both sides began spilling out onto the field. Players began pushing each other around.

Russ Sholes again walked to midfield. Called out Angelica: "Carl, what the hell is going on?"

This time, he got a response. With a look of confusion on his face, the Enfield coach said, "Russ, honestly, I don't know what's going on."

It was then that, for the first time, I noticed local police and a few state policemen along the sidelines. Two officers stepped in to break up the minor melees. I then heard another officer say he was heading out to his cruiser and make a call to Bradley NGU for a riot team. Bradley was Bradley Field, the major airport between Hartford and Springfield. The NGU was the military's National Guard unit on duty at the airport.

The man standing next to me, whose son played for

Enfield, lamented, "No, no, this should not be happening."

Simsbury scored its second touchdown with four minutes remaining. Holloway exploded into the endzone from six yards out to make the score 20–12. The score came after a TD run two downs earlier had been called back on a penalty by one of the replacement officials. A phantom penalty that was not explained to anyone. Including no explanations to any of the other officials. A penalty that had again been called by the oddly dressed back judge who had no responsibility to make calls along the line.

I say, "oddly dressed" because of his uniform. It just didn't look like the uniform of a football official. More like he should be getting out from the back of a clown car at the center ring during a Ringling Bros. and Barnum & Bailey Circus.

It was the fourth Simsbury touchdown that had been called back.

Again, the defense stopped Enfield, and Simsbury had one more chance to tie the game. They drove inside the Enfield 20-yard line. A penalty was called on a Simsbury player, moving the ball back to the 35-yard line. Once again, the unexplained penalty had been called by the official dressed in the clown uniform. A penalty called on a player who wasn't even in the game.

Two minutes remained to be played. When asked, an official refused to tell the Simsbury coaches which official was now holding the game watch that served as the clock. Actually, a Timex wristwatch. These were days before most schools had electronic scoreboards.

Plays were being sent in by the Simsbury sideline. Demsky called the play. Center Tom Hayes broke the huddle first, as he usually did, before the rest of the team joined him. As he put his hands on the ball, he was jumped by two Enfield linemen. The instigator was Enfield's middle guard, number 32, whom I came to know as Butch Fiore. They began punching him. A

SHS Yearbook Photo
Center Tom Hayes
Jumped by Enfield Players

third player joined in.

All hell broke loose. The referees lost control.

Hayes was now under a pile of Enfield jerseys. Tiger Jones entered the fray going after Fiore. Yanked him off the pile. Mel Ollestad and Biff Landry began grappling. Eddie Spear went after Enfield's Vinny Marino. Fans from both sides spilled onto the field. Big lineman Benie Pattison disappeared under a wave of players and fans. Ray Mildren and Hank Plona defended themselves against rowdy fans that had encircled them.

More players disappeared into the sea of craziness that was happening all around them. Simsbury coach Perry DeAngelis had to be pulled off an adult by his own players and restrained. Fullback Hank Plona was pushed out of the way by a fan who then punched a referee. Dick Eckhart fought with an Enfield player and a fan who was swinging a hunk of wood. He was punched. Lost a tooth. Swallowed it. Fought side-by-side with Ed Spear and Mel Ollestad against a nasty bunch of players and fans that had surrounded them.

The growing crowd just kept getting angrier. The fights intensified. Among adults, too.

A second official was punched and knocked to the ground. What was a little puzzling was that the local police did nothing. They did not try to break up any fights. In fact, most just stood with their hands on their hips, watching, laughing at the mayhem in front of them. One watching the melee while calmly smoking a cigarette.

Coach Angelica tried to restrain his players. Pull them back to the sideline. Coach Sholes stood at midfield. Staring at his friend. His hands spread out in front of him in that position that asks, "Why?"

The man next to me, from Enfield, nudged me. Pointed to the far endzone. One of the officials, the one who had made many bad calls, was being ushered off the field by two men in black suit coats. To a waiting car parked on King Street.

On the far side of the field, another official, the one dressed in the odd-looking clown uniform, was being taken away by another man in a black suit coat. Towards a car parked on Garden Street. The three remaining officials were lost in the sea of madness that had been the football field just a few minutes earlier. One had been knocked down and was on his back with fans on top of him. The mayhem continued for about five minutes. Then dissipated. With lots of nasty language being hollered back and forth between groups.

The game was never officially completed. I felt ashamed. Just being there. Being a part of what I had just seen.

It was Christmas Day, 1968. I spent the first early morning hours at the 9th Infantry Division's base hospital at Dong Tam, deep in the Mekong Delta. The Viet Cong had lobbed in hundreds of mortars during the night. I had been hit with shrapnel the day before, blown out of a truck en route from Saigon.

The ward medic was nice. He brought me a plate of scrambled eggs, bacon, toast, and coffee. Asked me where I was from. "Simsbury, Connecticut," I answered. He said he was from Springfield, Massachusetts. Went to the High School of Commerce on State Street. Also, a semester at American International College before being drafted into the Army.

I told him that I planned to attend AIC in the fall of 1969 when I completed my active duties upon my return to the States, or what we referred to as "the World." Said I wanted to be assigned to Fort Devens, MA. I would be applying for a 90 day-early out from active duty so I could return to school.

"Simsbury, huh?" he said. "You guys lost a football game that was fixed, didn't ya? Enfield. About eight, ten years ago." Boy, did he ever grab my attention.

"How do you know that?" I asked.

His answer was matter of fact: "My brother. He played for Commerce. A week after the fixed game, Enfield beat Commerce pretty good. Like forty to nothing." The actual score of their game was 22–0.

"We all heard about it in Springfield," he said. He added it was the Springfield Mafia that fixed the game. "Hell, it was no secret; everybody knew that."

On Wednesday, two days after the Simsbury–Enfield game, Coach Morrison ran into Dick Eckhart, who was cleaning out his locker. Eckhart didn't say much until he was heading for the door. "Coach, if we played them again tomorrow, we'd beat the crap out of them."

Morrison nodded and said, "Yes, Richard, I believe you would."

Jim Bidwell went to the doctor's office, then on to the hospital to get his legs checked out. Both had been injured on that second-quarter non-TD play when he was dragged out of the endzone and then jumped on by Enfield's number 32, Butch Fiore.

Bob Holloway finished his one-year football career as a starter with almost 1200 rushing yards and 17 touchdowns. All that offense in just seven games. He averaged over nine yards per carry. Perhaps the greatest performance ever by a Simsbury High School running back. He gained 154 yards in his final game versus Enfield and scored both TDs.

Simsbury High School was penalized 190 yards against Enfield. The *Farmington Valley Herald* would report that the number was 90. What they failed to inform the reader of was that's the first half total only. Enfield was penalized 50 yards. Simsbury would have four touchdowns called back due to penalties.

Coach Morrison would run into Russ Sholes in the junior high school hallway. Sholes would share with Morrison that he has made many attempts to contact his friend, Enfield Coach Carl Angelica. His calls had not been returned.

Sholes had also made calls to the Massachusetts Secondary Schools Principals Association, known as the MSSAPA. The sanctioning body for high school sports in Western Massachusetts. They had an office in Springfield. Not surprisingly, it seemed nobody could locate the officials' log assignments or the post-game reports from officials for the Simsbury–Enfield game. These were usually submitted by the host school following a game. In 1978, the MSSAPA split into two sanctioning organizations. Many of the pre-1970 records were destroyed or lost in the moving of boxed-up records.

Once more, at this point, this story should be over. And, once again, not even close.

It was early October 1970. A beautiful Friday afternoon. I was in my junior year at college, sitting on the campus center steps in the quad at American International College in Springfield, MA. Right on schedule, he arrived to collect the weekly football gaming cards and associated bets.

His name was George Sergienko.

He was a junior. A lineman on the AIC football team. He'd been an All-Western Massachusetts player at football power Cathedral High School. His father had been a little All-American at AIC and played professionally for the Brooklyn Dodgers and Boston Yanks during the 1940s in the old American Football Conference. Young George's college football career had suffered. His performance was below expectations. He played overweight and battled a series of nagging injuries.

It was a case of his really not wanting to play football.

But he made everybody's All-Star team when it came to being a bagman running numbers for the local bookmakers. He quickly collected all the football game cards to be played and the cash bets. He noted the money collected from each in a small notebook. He sat down alongside me on the campus center steps and totaled the day's tally, saying, "Another good day at college."

"How much do you make?" was my question, knowing that George made many stops for pickups on Thursday and Friday. He looked over his shoulder to ensure we were alone. Nobody was listening. "On a good weekend, I can make $300 to $400. Pocket money. Small change compared to what the big boys make every weekend."

Well, now, for a college student in 1970, that amount of pocket money for a few hours' work was a huge haul. "Just for college football?" I asked incredulously.

As he made his entries into his book, he said, "Nah, every sport. And a big payday on Sundays with the NFL games."

It's what he said next that grabbed my attention, like being slapped in the face.

"These people can get a betting line on anything. The weather, traffic jams. People hired or fired. Somebody getting knocked off. Hell, they even fixed a high school football game about ten years ago. Got fake refs to do the game. Just because they wanted to show they could get some action on that, too."

He punched me in the arm, saying that he hoped I would win a few bucks. Said he still had two more stops before going to football practice. AIC had a game the following day against Amherst College. George got up and walked to the access road in front of the dining commons. A black, late-model sedan picked him up at the corner of State Street.

George Sergienko's career would be marred. Over the ensuing years, he would exist on the fringes of organized crime, be disgraced, and be fired from two Western Massachusetts police forces, eventually ending up in prison.

I sat on the campus center steps. Thinking about that high school football game from about 10 years ago. Phony referees. That would put a timeline around 1959.

Holy Shit! The 1959 Simsbury–Enfield game!

It was Wednesday, November 11, 1959. Veterans Day. Russ Sholes, varsity basketball coach, was getting ready to head to practice at the junior high school. He ran into Principal Eliot P Dodge. Sholes, referring to the Enfield football game, asked if Dodge would make a few phone calls. Ask a few questions. Dodge agreed to do so.

Dodge's first call went to Charles Rice, a lawyer. He explained the reasons for his call asking Rice for possible opportunities and next steps. Rice knew about the football game and its outcome from locals. He asked Dodge to send him an outline of the game's actions. List goals and objectives and what the school wanted to achieve from any future administrative or legal actions.

Rice said he would investigate policy, procedures, and statutes for both Connecticut and Massachusetts. Any possible opportunities for a legal protest. Said he would do the work pro bono.

Eliot Dodge's second call went to the local Circuit and Probate Court Judge Charles Hall, Jr. He, too, was aware of the game's outcome and knew a few details. Like any good judge who wants the wheels of justice to grind smoothly, his suggested recommendations to Dodge were expected and absolute. "Eliot, you need to bring me some evidence."

The justice system works. Only when all the parts fit together.

I spied the motorcycle policeman in my rearview mirror. Red lights flashing. He was waving for me to pull over. I uttered a typical response, "Aw, shit."

It was February 1976. I was scheduled to cover a girls' basketball game. Simsbury at Enrico Fermi of Enfield. I would be just 15 minutes south of Springfield, MA. I needed some of my personal college info for a job application I was working on to do some freelance writing for *Sports Illustrated*. Figured I'd leave early for the game. Make a quick run to Springfield for my documentation needs. Still have lots of time to find my way to the game in Enfield.

Well, sometimes, a little irritation can turn into a golden nugget.

Leaving the American International College campus area en route to State Street, I was pulled over on Wilbraham Road. Figured another blast of doom and gloom. Instead, the officer was pretty cool. He liked my car. Commented on the color of my '67 Chevy Camero, Candy Apple Red. I asked, "Did I do something wrong?"

"Na," said the officer. "You've got a brake light out. Thought you needed to know." When he read my license, he let out a quick "huh." He was tall and had to bend down to talk. He leaned in closer to me. "Penfield. Are you the Penfield who's a sportswriter in Simsbury?"

Well, I'll be damned and muttered, "Ya, that's me." He said he knew my paper. He'd recently read a story I'd written in my weekly column, "The Hot Corner," about a high school football game that had been fixed in 1959. He especially enjoyed that story, my views, and the details I was able to provide.

Admittedly, I was a bit perplexed. Here I was in Springfield, Massachusetts, pulled over by a local motorcycle cop. And he knows about me and a story I'd written in a Connecticut weekly newspaper. "How did you end up reading a story in our paper?" I asked.

He responded, "My sister lives in North Granby. She reads

your paper and will often give me editions with stories she believes I will enjoy."

OK, good answer. We shared a little small talk. I promised I would fix the brake light tomorrow morning. I pushed my questions further: "Why did you like that specific story about the high school football game?"

His answer floored me: "My dad was one of the honest officials. He, too, believes that game was fixed."

Roland Morrison ran about, yelling for his team to clear the field and get onto the buses. Players Mel Ollestad, Jack Demsky, and Bob "Tiger" Jones had to hold back coach Perry DeAngelis from fighting with fans. Coach Nils Ahlin grabbed players and directed them toward the buses.

It turned out to be a long, slow, and painful ride home to Simsbury. Players helped Jim Bidwell elevate his injured legs. His injuries would not be serious. He would complete a successful high school sports career. Become an All-American while pitching for Holy Cross. And pitch in the New York Yankees farm system for four years.

Bill White sat quietly during the ride home. On defense, he had been burned twice for long touchdown passes from Enfield quarterback Mike Bromage. He had missed tackles. It was not a good game for White, who would go on to attend the Air Force Academy.

Mel Ollestad spoke quietly with teammates sitting near him. Along with his co-captain, Dick Eckhart, they had been good team leaders. All conference players. Ollestad would go on to Hamilton College, where he would play varsity baseball.

Dick Eckhart would fume. With a game he knew they could not win. His ride home would be frustrating. He would remain angry. Knowing he had just done battle in football for the last time in his high school career. He can't decide which opponent, Enfield High or the officials, he should rail against.

Beanie Pattison would sob for most of the bus ride home.

Hank Plona would think about the game. The young sophomore would feel the pressure of trying to go through a season undefeated. He would mull over his play in the game. His blocking for Bobby Holloway and the running of his fullback play known as the "238 smash" off tackle. He would rethink the games' final minutes. The crazy ending. The fights. The officials. That creeping feeling that something about this wasn't right. Hank would go on to complete two more successful seasons of varsity football and baseball. He would graduate from Providence College.

Bobby Holloway would say he didn't really see the ways of the game officials, though he would say Simsbury did seem to be targeted with some very bad calls. He admits, "I'm pretty sure I was in the endzone at least two more times. And neither time ended up being a touchdown."

Ray Mildren, a University of Pittsburgh grad, would remember the game as "nasty." He would think of the game and the Enfield players as playing dirty. Especially their interior lineman. Simsbury linemen were being targeted on certain plays. Ray recalled, "Enfield played with a little more, well, let's call it enthusiasm. But, if you want to call it dirty, that's OK, too. Me, I played the game the way I was taught to play."

Like Dick Eckhart had said. The officials made sure this game was over by halftime.

I was assigned to a business consulting project in Chicago. It was fall 1984. Instead of battling the crowds at O'Hare Airport, I decided to take Amtrak's Capitol Limited to DC. Then, catch an early morning MARC train from DC to Baltimore. That way, I wouldn't be in a middle seat on a Boeing 727. Typically, sitting next to some overweight slob who most likely hadn't showered in three days. His head lolling on my shoulder as he slept.

I chose civility. A small roomette for one. A nice meal in the dining car. Steak with a half-bottle of Pinot Noir. I had a rather dapper and somewhat snobbish tablemate for dinner. Yet, his conversations were engaging. His name was Arthur.

He said he'd written books and essays on the American Mafia. I had not heard of him, yet he seemed to know his subject and its history. He talked about how the mob was no longer just in New York, Chicago, Boston, and Las Vegas. How it had taken over the secondary markets and rural areas. Drugs, prostitution, gambling, the building trades, and oil and gas products. The list went on. When he mentioned towns like Worcester and Springfield, Massachusetts, I perked up.

I asked about Springfield. "Ahh, the Raymond Patriarca family," said Arthur. "They ran numbers in Central and Western Massachusetts from their headquarters in Providence, Rhode Island." He explained how they barred any others from interfering with their businesses. With one exception. An agreement with the Gambino crime family. One of New York's big five. The sharing of the numbers in the area had something to do with satisfying an old family debt.

"They feuded," said Arthur. Especially over bookmarking opportunities, betting lines, and action on certain sporting events. My interest peaked when he said, "Including a big riff over a simple high school football game in the 1950s. Seems the Patriarca family wanted the action. The Gambino family wanted no part of it." I rolled it over in my mind. A simple high school football game. From the 1950s.

It had to be. Simsbury and Enfield.

The day after the game, Simsbury's football playing seniors and some juniors skipped school. Some stayed home and lounged. Others went to Hartford. To the movies. Returning to school on Wednesday, all were given detention. "Hated to give it to them," lamented Eliot Dodge.

In Enfield, the football players were treated as conquering heroes. Even as they practiced for their final game scheduled for that Saturday against The High School of Commerce in Springfield. They would win their game 22–0 and finish the season with a record of 5–1. The lone loss to a strong Longmeadow team, 8–6. A game where Enfield had six shots at the endzone in the final two minutes.

Their smallish quarterback, Mike Bromage, would go on to a successful four years for Fairfield University. All-purpose back Len Lavalette would know Simsbury's Bobby Holloway, as they would be teammates on the freshman football team at Central Connecticut State College. Lavalette would finish his education at AIC in Springfield.

Enfield players would go on to a myriad of schools and professions. Butch Fiore, small for a defensive tackle or middle guard, would win the coveted Charles Scalia Award as the team's MVP for his gritty play. Al Nosal would serve in Vietnam. He died as a result of his exposure to Agent Orange, which, for years, ravaged his body.

Like football, life can be a mean game.

In October 1975, I watched a good Windsor Locks girls' field hockey team shutout Avon, 3–0. I had planned to meet up with a friend from Windsor for a beer and a burger. We set a time to meet at a drab and nothing bar in the south end of Windsor Locks known as Charley 10. In fact, it was one of those places known as a ghost bar because it didn't have a valid liquor license. Still, local officials and police just left it alone.

The phone never stopped ringing. The guy seated next to me said it was probably bets on games being called in. The barmaid was also a local numbers taker and bag lady for the folks in town who made book on sporting events.

She came over to me with a phone in her hand. "You Rob?" she asked. I nodded. She handed me the phone, and I took the call. It was my friend Walt Hastings from Windsor. His family had been the longtime owners of "Barts" in Windsor. He also ran "Townline Marine" near the Windsor–Windsor Locks town line.

"Can't make it today," said Walt. "We'll do it another time." I thanked him for calling. Ordered another beer and continued munching on my greasy fries and overcooked cheeseburger. Sitting across the bar from me was an old-timer. Gray, balding, and in his twilight years. Cradling his glass with both hands. Crying in his beer. Moaning about lost lovers. A life where he had shamed himself and needed absolution.

He called out to me, asking if I was a priest.

"Do I look like a priest?" was my response.

He shook his head as if to say no. "A lawyer. You a lawyer?" I shook my head no. He droned on for about 15 minutes. Until his slurring voice mumbled something that sounded like, "And that football game I helped them win. It was wrong."

Suddenly, I became both priest and lawyer.

The wheels of justice will turn until someone with a wise eye for perception says that the squeaky wheel should no longer get any grease.

In the days following the 1959 Simsbury–Enfield game, that decision not to grease the wheel took just about a week. Simsbury High School Principal Eliot P. Dodge had called Charlie Rice for some legal advice. Rice called him back. His message was short and to the point.

Rice's message: "I did some probing. Nasty roads here, Elliot. They lead to and include both the Patriarca and Gambino crime families. Eliot, I'm telling you, as a friend and a lawyer, put this to bed and leave it alone."

Rice didn't even wait for a reply. He hung up the phone.

Not wanting to embarrass himself, Eliot Dodge canceled his next call, which would have been made to Judge Hall.

I learned that his name was Al. The old-timer moaned on about doing bad things. Stealing from a friend. Messing with another's wife. Stealing a car. Dressing up, making believe he was somebody he really wasn't. Like the times he was a football referee.

I prodded slowly, letting him dig his own holes. Bought him a beer. Paid his $4 tab and added a tip. I felt like Jimmy Stewart searching for information as part of a Chicago murder mystery in the 1947 classic film noir *Call Northside 777*.

Eventually, he began owning up to his aliases. His shame was too much to hold back. "Yeah, fake football ref," he admitted. "Lots of times, cuz dey wanted me to." I could only imagine the folks he was referring to.

I wanted to know what game. "I dunno. Some farm town," he slurred. I asked if it was Granby. He said no. Could it be Canton? He shook his head. Simsbury? "Yup, that's dem. Game ended in a big fight." He said that at the end of the game, "I wuz told to get lost before people started asking questions." Oh boy, had I accidentally stumbled upon a smoking gun before I ever knew what the term smoking gun actually meant.

He said he was paid $75 for his part in the game. His friend, the other fake game official, got $150 for his part because he knew someone named Ernie. A name I learned was the contact person responsible for finding the fake refs and engineering them into the game. How and by whose authority they were assigned to do the game was never learned. And how much money the Patriarca bookmakers made on the game was also never known.

In the summer of 1976, Walt and I stopped by Charley 10 for a beer. Curious, I asked the same barmaid about the old geezer from across the bar.

"He died," she snapped. "And good fucking riddens, too. That asshole son of a bitch owed me twenty bucks."

I lost my taste for beer. Paid my tab and left. Never went back.

Earlier in the story, I mentioned an 1815 poem, "The Destruction of Sennacherib," by Lord Byron. Tell you how it got associated with this story. It's said Byron's words in his verses were penned to the beat of galloping horses' hooves. Written as a biblical account of the Assyrians' unsuccessful siege of Jerusalem in 701 BC.

In the poem, Hezekiah, in the temple, prayed to Jehovah for strength and support. His prayers were answered. By dawn, most of the Assyrian army, over 185,000 battled hardened warriors, were, by Byron's words, smote (killed by force) in their encampment outside the walled city of Judah.

I came to see the story as a loose comparison of sorts. What I found was a bastardized version of Lord Byron's verses on the football team's pages in the 1960 Enfield High School yearbook.

It was included on the team pages to glorify the season's accomplishments in a somewhat skewered version of their win over Simsbury. Instead of the Assyrians, the word "Simsburians" was inserted. The Trojans, which defeated a corps of attackers, now lay "smote" and strewn about the football field. It was a fun adaptation to read. It was creative and slick. A nice addition to the yearbook.

Yet, like most stories of history and lore, not completely true.

The poem reads, "Where the might of the Gentile, unsmote by the sword, hath melted the snow in the glace of the Lord."

Now, due to Enfield's victory, it had become, "Now it just couldn't be that they were quite so frail, no, dear Simsburians, it was not that at all. You see, there was (school) spirit along with the ball."

Good stuff about the fighting spirit of the Enfield football players. And like most prose about the bible, there was nothing written about the phony gods wearing clown-like referee uniforms, who, like its participants, controlled the outcome of the battle.

I doubt Lord Byron would have been so understanding about the prose.

So, here we are, talking about a high school football game that was played 65 years ago. Still no closer to the truth of what happened than we were on that November day in 1959. Here's what I do know. When I was 13 years old, I went to a high school football game. Simsbury played at Enfield.

Enfield won the game, 20–12.

What I saw that day has stayed with me as a memory for all these many years. I understood the game and its penalties very well. What I observed that day was absolutely the worst officiated football game I have ever seen.

I saw a high school football team assessed 190 yards in penalties and believe that not even half that amount of penalty yardage was legitimate. And I have no way to prove it.

Simsbury had four touchdowns called back, one for a legitimate violation of a penalty from that era known as "backfield-in-motion." The three other penalties were for rules violations that did not exist in 1959. Don't exist today. Calls so egregiously bad they defied explanations.

Simsbury's All-State quarterback was injured when Enfield linemen fell onto his legs. An action that appeared to be intentional for the purpose of inflicting pain.

I saw two officials being hurried off the field by men in dark suits, in what appeared to be an obvious getaway, before the game ended.

I witnessed an on-field riot and fight that officially ended play before the official game time expired. A game with time remaining on the clock, never completed or officially declared over.

Over the ensuing years, I have met and spoken with numerous folks who have provided credible information that something very wrong occurred on that day so long ago. Including one individual whose hand was directly involved in the wrongdoing.

The information I've uncovered clearly tells me that something out of the ordinary did happen on that November day in 1959. An illegal effort of sorts to ensure that Enfield would be the winner of the game. Engineered by planted officials and their subsequent actions.

What we all witnessed … you just can't hide that many bad calls in front of that many witnesses.

It was obvious to me. Obvious to the man from Enfield standing next to me whose son was on the team. To the state policeman standing on the other side of me. To fans who were cheering for both teams. To the three honest officials who had lost control of the game and were not involved in making those phony calls.

To a motorcycle policeman whose dad was one of those three honest officials. The man on an Amtrak train, Arthur, who knew about the game and its betting lines. A medic in Vietnam who hailed from Springfield, Massachusetts. To an old sot I met in a nowhere bar, who admitted it to be true. And to those many others who witnessed it firsthand and knew something was not quite right.

In my heart, I believe these facts to be true.

Whether any Enfield folks, players, coaches, or fans were involved in what truly is a conspiracy, we'll never know.

Though, I firmly believe they were not involved.

I am quite sure the Patriarca family bookmakers, and those in charge of generating bookmaking action, are the ones culpable. Of that fact, if I may be remorsefully jocular, I am so sure of that fact that I would bet the farm.

The Enfield High School folks should have done a better job in their filtering and understanding of who the game replacement officials were. One had been kicked out of the officiating ranks years before for suspicious conduct. The other was never a registered official. He just had the uniform parts, whistle, and hat, like a clown in a circus.

Simsbury should have asked why five officials were on the field, not the standard four. And why some of those officials were making calls along the line of scrimmage. Calls they did not have the authority and responsibility to make. Calls that should have been made by other officials.

And why the other three officials didn't override those questionable calls.

And to those Simsbury players who took the field with honest intent, only to be, as Lord Byron penned, "smote and slaughtered" on a field of battle. Their efforts waylaid by unscrupulous and uncontrolled forces far beyond the realm of truism and honesty and by those who took the power of God into their own hands.

Coach Morisson talked to his team about letting down one's God. He was looking at the wrong apostles. He had only to look at those two phony gods in striped shirts with whistles. Amen!

In the end, innocence was lost. I never really looked at football in the same way after that game. I questioned every play and every call that seemed a tad hokey or not worthy of a penalty flag. Because on that day, I, too, as a young fan, along with so many others, were treated with little or no courtesy, concern, consideration, and respect.

I am sure of one thing. On that November day, the winners of that football game, Enfield High School, were the better of the two teams on the field.

I am also sure of one other thing. I watched many adults act woefully bad, making me ashamed that I had to be a part of that day. I made a promise to myself that I wouldn't engage in such behavior on a field or court of play. Either as a player or fan.

Throughout my playing days and ensuing years as a fan, I have kept that promise to myself. Remembering that day in 1959. At a high school football game. Because in retrospect, those who participated in or, like me, witnessed this travesty became metaphorically "smote" and soiled.

And by sundown, innocence had been lost and I had been burdened for a lifetime as a witness to my first "fix."

9

TOMMY THE
SLIPPERY BROWN TROUT

THE VALUE OF PATIENCE,
EVEN WHEN IN A HURRY

My dad made sure I knew how to fish by the time I was five years old. How to approach a small pond or lake. From the shore or from a boat. How to work and use special skills to fish a brook and its tantalizing holes. Know and understand the complexities of fishing a river.

He didn't just show me how. He taught me what to do. Because he always emphasized one day, I just might need these skills. Perhaps to survive. And no skill was more important than the virtue of patience. Because fishing is a solemn one-on-one responsibility where the test of patience is measured in the discipline of compliance.

My dad knew what he was talking about.

And wouldn't you know? All that learning from my dad. I learned how important that patience was going to be on a rainy and chilly Connecticut day in the spring of 1956.

I liked fishing in small streams and brooks. My dad preferred lakes and ponds. We often fished the manmade pond at Stratton Brook in the woods off Farms Village Road. What locals sometimes referred to as the "State Forest."

The original main pool was used by everyone in town for everything recreational. It wasn't a big pond. But functional. Nice sandy beaches on each side. Good water for swimming. Clean, clear, and cooled by the spring-fed brooks and underground springs. There was a dam and waterfall with a crossing bridge. A nice pavilion and hibachis for family cookouts. Oak, maple, and pine trees made up a small forest offering shade from the summer sun.

If you wanted to fish the main pond, you had to arrive early before the picnic and swimming crowds arrived. You could catch small trout. Sunfish, perch, and an occasional catfish. By 10 AM, it was usually getting crowded. You had to move to a different location.

There was a second body of water at Stratton Brook in 1956. Most referred to it as the "Swamp." Located to the northeast of the main pool, it was a larger body of water. Maybe four feet at its deepest. But almost unreachable. It was protected by a very thick berm-like line of bushes and briars. If you wanted to reach the water, you had to chop your way through the interwoven chaparral with a machete. It was that thick.

Once through, the water's edge was teeming with quick mud. You could sink up to your knees and need help to get yourself out. The rocks were ice-like slippery. It was a place for snakes. There were stories that the place had fish, big fish. Just not enough folks with the energy to cut through the debris to see if they could catch them.

To our surprise, the town of Simsbury, working with the state highway department, began removing some of the thick bushes in the summer of 1956. During a final stocking of trout in the main pond, a few fish were held out to be put into the Swamp.

My dad and I were fishing Stratton Brook on a Sunday. The local fish-stocking folks appeared near the far corner of the swamp. I recognized Ed Gostyla, who owned his own sports shop on Hopmeadow Street, directly across from the bottom of the hill that was Seminary Road.

He showed me the 10 fish he was going to put in the water. One was huge. A 12-inch brown trout with a damaged dorsal fin. He let me hold it in my hands. I swear that trout looked me right in the eyes and laughed at me. He squirted out of my hands into the water. He swam slowly past me, left to right. Looked at me and quickly swam away towards the center of the pond.

Gostyla laughed. Asked me why the fish had jumped out of my hands. I said something stupid about the fish telling me that I wasn't big enough to hold him. Gostyla asked, "Whad-ja say to him?" I turned at looked at Ed Gostyla.

Slowly, I spoke and said, "Told him his name was Tommy. And one day, I was going to catch him and cook him on the grill. Just takes patience."

Gostyla took a drag off his cigarette. Flipped the butt into the water.

More work was done on the swamp area in 1957. Small shrubs and trees were removed. A fill of mixed stones and large mulch was dropped along the shorelines. By late summer, the banks surrounding the entire waterline had been worked on and no longer was quick mud. You could now walk up to the water-line around the entire circumference of the pond.

I'd say something to my dad about how I wish they'd work faster to clear away the underbrush. He'd cast his line into the water. Look over at me and say, "Patience. It'll be done before you know it."

The plan was to eventually turn that former swampy area

into the new, larger swimming area for the growing family populations crowding into Stratton Brook. The same activities in the town of Simsbury began at the old Town Pool on Town Forest Road in 1960. The target date for completion of the Stratton Brook ponds was 1964, the same year as the Town Pool expansion.

The goal of the town's action was not only to increase recreational areas; it would also increase the size of the brooks. The spillway at the Town Pool would meet with the runoff at Stratton Brook. The larger brook would eventually meet up with Hop Brook, flowing behind the high school, which would combine in a flow-in from Grimes Brook, or what had for many years called Holly Brook. All waters would eventually flow into the Old Mill Pond on West Street. As kids, we fished every foot of those streams. Many a trout got away from the ponds into those brooks, and they became harder to catch.

On a cloudy Sunday afternoon in July, I fished the east end of the Swamp. I got a big hit using a nightcrawler. It bent my pole into a capital C. My five-pound test line pulled taunt. The line screaming as it was pulled from the reel's bail. Then, the fish on the line was gone.

I reeled in my empty line. The hook, once adorned with a big and plump nightcrawler, was naked. It's a term that fishermen have come to know all too well, that big hit that takes it all, hook, line, and sinker. Oh yeah. I knew who it was.

Tommy the Trout was always on my mind.

By 1958, the town had begun to develop the land around the old Swamp. A large area was bulldozed and leveled. A beach was built. New parking areas were created. Picnic tables and fireplaces were installed. The west end was now ready for recreational use.

The east end was ready for refining. But was still an undeveloped patch of rough terrain. Good for hiking. And with the connection to the larger brook, good for fishing. And I knew. Tommy was out there, probably laughing at me.

Patience. Yeah, patience. I was now learning about it with so many activities in my life.

I saw Ed Gostyla in front of Doyle's Drugstore. He puffed heartily on his cigarette and asked, "Catch that big trout, yet?" laughing as he blew out a big cloud of smoke.

I was 12 years old. Gave him my best stare. And walked away.

A few minutes later, I sat down on a bench outside Hall Brothers and Leader department stores. I felt badly for how I acted to Ed Gostyla. He was a nice man. I can't help but recall all the recent stories that had surfaced. Even my dad talked about them. How his business was suffering because he was being robbed blind by his employees. They'd steal inventory and sell it out of their trunk to people for bargain prices. Ed was a guy who liked customers. He'd sit and talk fishing and hunting, but he wasn't a good businessman.

It was Elmo Comotti who decided to make it right. He heard Gostyla was spending an afternoon in the bar at the Old Well Restaurant. His business was being run by one of the internal thieves. Comotti went to the Old Well and read Gostyla the riot act. Told him what was happening to his business. Gostyla was heartbroken.

Comotti later pulled aside one of the thieving employees. Told him to get lost or he'd beat the shit out of him. He had the thief empty his pockets of all his money and put it back into the cash register. He then threw him out of the store. Unfortunately for Ed Gostyla, it was too little, too late.

Ed's Sporting Goods closed forever at the end of the month.

On another day, I again ran into Ed Gostyla. "Mr. Gostyla, I'm sorry that I was ..." were my words until he held up his hand, meaning "stop." He gave that familiar smile. Said to me, "Yeah, kid, I know. It's OK. Just be patient and catch that big trout." Then, he moved on.

I watched him walk away. He was that man at the sporting goods store who had greeted you with a smile. His baseball cap visor pushed high up on his head. A cigarette between his fingers, the smoke slowly wafting upwards while he shared a story about ice-fishing in Vermont. The type of person every town needs. I had always known him as a fisherman. A hunter. A man who sold baseball gloves and bats. An outdoorsman. A man of patience.

It was said that when Ed Gostyla died, it was from a broken heart.

My dad and I went fishing at Stratton Brook on a miserable day in May of 1959. It was colder than normal. Gray, overcast, a steady rain fell. We were the only ones at the pond that day. I tried using fat nightcrawlers. The rain hitting the water made it too hard to see the line. Couldn't tell if something was nibbling on the other end.

I changed baits. Used a lure. A little golden-colored, S-shaped piece of metal with a double hook at the end. It was called a goldfish. With this type of lure, if something hits the line, you'd know it.

Amid a steady cold rain, I cast my line into the water repeatedly. The goal of a lure is to let it hit the water. Give it one to three seconds to slowly drop. Then, begin to reel it back to shore. You reel it in at a certain rate. Not too fast so it won't be too high in the water, just below the water line. Not too slow so it won't drop too deep and catch on the debris that is the bottom of every pond or lake. The goldfish, slithering and dancing through the murky water, seeming like a small live bait fish to a large trout.

Using my lure, I cast the line into the water for about 15 minutes. I could see my dad working his way around the far side of the pond. We would leave for home when he arrived on my side. I made a few more casts.

BANG ... a wicked hit. I knew it was Tommy.

My fishing pole bent into a capital C. Line stretched and taut. Almost yanked the pole right out of my hands. Only a nice largemouth bass, a stealthy-thin pickerel, or a big trout hits a line like that. I let the line unravel from my reel, giving the fish a loose line to run. Then, I closed the bail.

When the line went taut, there was a huge and sudden tug at the fish end of the line. So much so that the fish came up and out of the water. What fisherman call a "big one rising." It came out of the water and shot up two feet into the air. A silverly dark color. Wiggling and screaming. I could hear my dad cry out, "Whoa, big one."

It rose out of the water for a second time. Spit the lure out of its mouth towards me and was separated from the line. The line went limp. Tommy was gone.

I went down on one knee. Slapped the ground with my right hand. My dad was standing next to me. I looked up at him. He was smiling. It was that fatherly smile we all come to know. Supportive. Loving.

I said something like, "Yeah, he won today." My dad looked out over the pond. Water from the rain spilling off the bill of his cap. He nodded. Put his hand out to help me up. In a soft yet confident tone, he said, "Yes, he won today. But your day will come. Patience." We laughed and started walking down the path toward the car.

As we walked the path to the car, the rain slapped me in the face. I remembered a wooden plaque that hung on the wall in Eddie Knose's Top Hat Restaurant on Hopmeadow Street near the Simsbury–Granby town lines. A fish was looking at a baited hook with fear. The words said, "Even a fish won't get into trouble if he keeps his mouth shut." Oh yeah, patience.

The steady rain began to fall harder.

It was summer 1960. I hadn't planned on fishing, but my dad said let's take advantage of a nice day. He had played golf early that morning. Was home by 11 AM. He played just nine holes. Then, I remembered he had promised we'd go fishing on Saturday. Cut his golf game short and came home to keep that promise.

It was going to be a busy day. We were going to a cookout later that afternoon at the home of Fred Mildren. They had three kids. Bev was the oldest. Ray was three years older than me, yet I had played Little League baseball with him for two years. Their youngest daughter, Karen, was a year younger than me. I had known her throughout my grammar school and junior high years.

It was a perfect New England day in mid-July. Sunny with puffy white clouds that occasionally broke up the blaring sun. Temps were in the low 80s. A nice breeze added serendipity to the day. It was the type of day when the water is easy to read. The type of day when you use a nice fat nightcrawler for bait.

I found the first crawler under a log I turned over while looking for bait. It was a beauty. Thick and long with a nicely raised worm collar that is used to pin the bait to the hook. I made my cast out onto the pond of about 40 feet. Gently tugged on the line as the bait slowly fell from the waterline. Gave the line a slight jerk every eight to ten seconds to keep the bait moving.

At first, I wasn't sure if I had a nibble. Then, the line began rising. Dropped limp again. Once again began to slowly rise. I wasted no time. I lifted my pole from the Y-stick it was propped on. Yanked the line back to sink the hook.

WHAMO!

The tug on the other end was vicious. I knew it was Tommy.

It turned out to be an easy catch. After the initial hit, I just let my senses and all that I had been taught by my dad about fishing kick in. Patience! Keep the bail open until the right time. Re-sink the hook. Patience! Keep your line taut so the fish can't slingshot on you. If he rose out of the water, lift the pole and stretch the line. Patience. Bend the pole to the left or right in whatever direction the fish wants to go. Be patient.

I brought Tommy to the shore without using a net.

I was surprised to see my non-barbed hook barely in the large trout's lower lip. Another five or ten seconds, and I most likely would have lost him. My dad arrived and appropriately said, "Today, you and patience won."

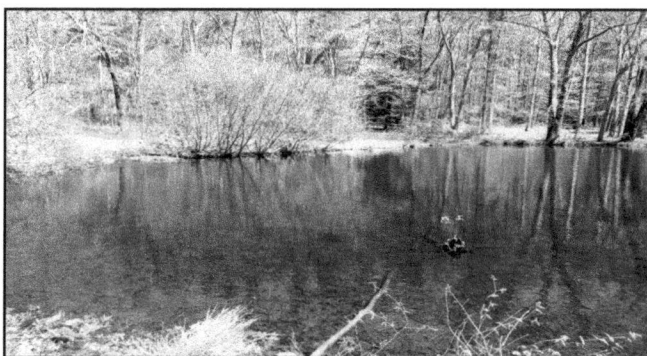

Rob Penfield Photo
Stratton Brook's North Swamp Pool Where Tommy Was Caught

A lady was standing a few feet away. Two kids in tow. A boy, perhaps six. The girl was four or five. She wanted to know if I was going to put the fish back into the water so her kids could watch it swim. I looked at my dad. He turned away with that look on his face that screamed, "This one is all yours."

I told the woman no. I was not putting the fish back. I would take it home. Cook it on the grill and eat it along with a salad and an ear of corn. She stood open-mouthed and said, "Oh my god."

I got up to leave. She was standing in the middle of the path. I said in a soft manner, "Lady, get out of my way." I could have sworn I heard the little boy say he wanted to eat fish. Honestly, it was funny.

As we walked back to the car, my dad said, "She's one of those people who thinks fish comes from a market."

Tommy measured 15 ½ inches long. A little under three pounds. The dorsal fin was damaged. Perhaps from being attacked by a larger fish as a young trout. Or a result of his pissing off one too many turtles. I was thrilled and sad. My dad sensed it. He mentioned something about there being lots more Tommys out there. "And you will have lots more days when the fish will be the winner."

Lots more times to test patience that would be a part of my life.

Sunday afternoon, we cooked my catch on the grill with hot dogs. Cooked it with the head on. Filled the cleaned-out area with bread stuffing. Cooked it first wrapped in aluminum foil with lemon. Then, put the fish directly on the grill. Gently singed each side for a minute or two. Spine and bones pulled away perfectly. It tasted good.

As my dad had said, "Your day will come. Patience! What you're after will most likely still be there. You'll eventually get to where you're going. The key is in knowing when to pull the trigger and make your move." He was right.

It truly was a meal that was years in the making.

For me, fishing has always been an investment of sorts. Like real estate, stocks, and bonds. Or, playing the odds at a game of chance in Las Vegas or Reno. Where the house always wins. It takes time to fully understand the games and strategies. The impact and payback. So much to learn. Every time I'd head out to fish, I couldn't help but hear in my head an instrumental song by the Vince Guaraldi Trio titled "Cast Your Fate to the Wind."

A little corny, but an investment in patience is an investment in life.

I came to learn that, just like catching fish, it takes time for an investment to develop and become a positive return on one's resources. And real investments come in so many diverse resources. Because it takes time to learn. Often, a lifetime. And sometimes, losing, or not winning, becomes a life-changing learning experience. Times of learning encapsulates humanity's seven capital virtues.

Each virtue is a by-product of another. One part tied together with others in no special configuration. A gestalt of sorts. A shape or format. Where the value of those virtues becomes stronger as the sum-total of its parts. Because each part feeds off the others. Making the whole of the virtues so much stronger than each individual part. Making the human thought process stronger. And, for me, it took a lifetime of learning to fit those pieces together. To find those rewards.

It took patience.

My dad said that it would make no difference what the situation would be. Fishing or the omnipresent lifetime responsibilities. Whether you're 13 years old or 75. But he always stressed patience. Just be sure you've thought it out and have a good plan before you make your moves.

Yes, I have made many general observations. Over the years, I've watched so many folks always in a hurry to seemingly go nowhere. Eventually, we all arrive at the same place.

One day, I put a large fish in the water, Tommy the slippery brown trout. Four years later, I caught that fish, as I had said I would. Using the learned skills of simplicity, pathos, and repetition. And patience, because virtues don't age. They just move with time.

No, I am not the most patient of people. Though, I do try and take my time and plan out my activities. As my dad taught me how to do. Not rush to action or judgment. Or travel too quickly to nowhere. Be ready when it comes time to pull the trigger. It seems to have worked out pretty well for me.

It's the complex simplicity that continues to amaze me. Amid all the struggles and the everyday learning situations. From my dad, I came to see and understand the capital virtues of life, humility, diligence, and kindness.

And especially patience.

Ya know, fishing teaches you a lot of lessons. If I did learn just one thing during those years, it's this: Even a bad day fishing is much better and more fun than a good day at work. Of course, perception will always be in how you manage it.

Patiently!

A very special lesson I learned from my dad, my friend. And from Tommy, the slippery brown trout.

10

WHEN ARE YA COMING BACK TO ENO'S POND, PATTI PAGE

LESSONS LEARNED FROM A GREAT OUTDOOR CLASSROOM IN LIFE

The music lazily wafted across the still waters of Eno's Pond. Sounds from a Zenith transistor radio. It was a hot July afternoon in the 1950s. Temperatures in the low 90s. The humidity was so heavy there was a thick haze. When you looked at the treetops across the pond, they seemed to be out of focus. Patti Page sang "Allegheny Moon." Her sultry voice seemingly floating over the pond's still waters that resembled a large pane of dirty glass in need of cleaning. Yet, the pond's waters still glistened with the sun's reflection.

My fishing pole was propped on a Y-stick. Standing on the pond's east side atop a sandy bank, my line out about 25 feet. A small nightcrawler as bait. I adjusted my baseball cap shading the sun's blinding rays from my eyes. My line hadn't moved. Probably now resting on the pond's muddy bottom. Mid-afternoons were not the best time to fish. It was the worst time. No matter what time you fished, Eno's Pond did not like to give up its watery inhabitants too easily.

Patience. The bane of youth. That was the discipline and the challenge.

But fishing is not what this story is all about. It's about Eno's Pond. About being a kid during summer, away from school. Freedom. Our time. Hanging with friends. Playing ball in the morning with the neighborhood kids. Afternoons, we fished Eno's Brook with a friend or two. Working your way downstream under the shade of big trees. From McGrath's Springs near the wild apple trees that dotted the meadows to the tall pines, wetlands, and elephant grass that quietly existed within a small basin that encircled Eno's Pond.

We'd stop along the way to cool off and skinny dip at what we called "Sliding Rock" near another notorious spot, the "Graveyard of Old Cars." After a dip in the cool, spring-fed waters of the brook, we'd find a nice spot on the high bank overlooking the old cars' graveyard and eat our lunch. Typically, a sandwich and cookies, washing it down with Kool Aid, Zarex, or fresh-made lemonade from our canteens. It was a part of our 18-hour classroom. That time of learning away from the military-like discipline that was those six hours of captivity in school.

Along the brook was a veritable wild garden of edibles like tomatoes, radishes, and cucumbers. We found ears of small-kernelled white corn, buried sassafras, and ginger roots. Sweet leaves for tea. There were wild tobacco leaves. Small leaf garden herbs and spices. Even wild marijuana leaves. We'd stuff our pockets and take the wild produce home to our moms. And always, cold, clear water bubbling up from the ground springs along most of the brook.

I don't know how many days my friends and I repeated this adventure. Too many to recall. It was like wearing a friendly old pair of worn-out Keds canvas sneakers. The dirtier and smellier they got, the more comfortable they were. Harder to throw away.

At the brook's end, Eno's Pond was waiting for us when we came out of the woods. And typically, from a lone transistor radio, music cutting through the afternoon din. It could have been Elvis or Little Richard. The Everly Brothers, Jerry Lee Lewis, Frankie Ford, or the Platters. It really didn't matter.

Maybe it was Patti Page singing, "Let Me Go, Lover!" No, we weren't old enough to know what those words meant. But just hearing them after our journey down the brook, that throaty, gentle warble. It made us feel comfortable. Like when you heard your mom call you home for supper.

Eno's Pond, a spring-fed pond, had origins dating back to the 17th century. Issac Owens, a multi-business entrepreneur from Tariffville, bought farmland during the Farmington Valley Indian wars (1660–70s), including the parcel that would become Eno's Farm.

The brook appeared from ground springs located near what, today, is the corner of Owners Brook Boulevard and Musket Trail Road in Simsbury. A small brook cut a swath and meandered through the fields in an easterly direction. It was woods then, eventually becoming cornfields in the mid-19th century.

From this stream, other brooks formed that emptied into the Farmington River in what are the Meadowlands today. That brook had many names, such as Hall's Run, Quarry Run, and Eno's Farm Brook.

All had small tributaries that also emptied into the infamous Northampton Canal. An ill-fated waterway for commercial water traffic through Simsbury, used from 1835 to 1847, from Northampton, Massachusetts, to Long Island Sound in New Haven.

Eno's Pond was a place for kids.

Adults and our parents made appearances. Usually in winter, during family ice-skating outings. From early spring till winter, you'd be hard-pressed to find anyone at the pond older than 15 or 16 years old.

For me and my friends, it was a total package. You rarely just grabbed your fish pole and cut a beeline for the pond. It was a journey through the neighborhood and the woods on the north side of what would become Barry Lane. Down what was known as McGrath's Hill to intersect with Eno's Brook.

Once there, you searched for fish bait. We'd dig for worms with our hands. Go through wet leaves and turn over logs. Bait could be a nightcrawler, blood worms, or small bugs, like a beetle or a caterpillar. It was the bait most used when fishing the winding spring-fed waters that ran about a quarter of a mile in distance.

The brook had small to middle-sized brown trout and lots of good holes. There was "Sandy Bottom," where you might find snakes sunning themselves on warm rocks. "The Pool" was a good-sized hole with slower water about two feet deep that ran for about fifteen feet. The hole had nice fish, along with a family of muskrats.

Rob Penfield Photo
**Eno's Brook Gently Meandered
Its Way a Quarter-Mile into Enos Pond**

Downstream was "Oak Bend," where the brook ran under a huge oak tree. Good fast water that was a trout motel. Our fish lines would always get hung up on underwater roots, and we'd lose lots of hooks. At "Skunk Cabbage Bend," the brook slowed and was shallow. There were fish, but you had to sneak up on 'em, real quiet-like, or they'd sense your steps as you walked towards the hole.

Also along this stretch was a myriad of antique car parts from the 1920s and 1930s. A trunk lid and fenders from Model A Fords. A front cowl from an old Pontiac. A rusted hood from an early '30s Chevy. We didn't know how all these cars and their parts got to this part of the woods. A considerable distance from any roads.

"Rockslide Falls" was a favorite spot for everyone. We skinny-dipped there. Boys and girls. The years of running water over the rocks had smoothed the surface to a glass-like finish. You could slide down the smooth rock into two feet of cold, spring-fed water. Atop the hill overlooking the falls was a great place to each lunch. We even camped out overnight at this location to earn our Cub Scout badges.

It was next to an omega-shaped canyon, the "Graveyard of Old Cars," filled with the remnants of antique cars from the late 1920s and early 1930s. As the story goes, people would drive their cars into the pond to discard them. The Eno family would pull the car from the water and toss it into the canyon. Folks would come from all over town to buy and then remove needed parts from the cars. The canyon was also infested with every type of snake imaginable. Often, it had some very mean cur dogs and stray barn cats.

You ventured into the canyon at your own risk.

The last fishing hole before reaching the pond was known as the "Jungle." You'd emerge from the woods into a thick underbrush that, by June, was impassable. If you decided to fish in the Jungle, you had to do so walking in the brook, usually stirring up mud and debris. The water was deep, up to your ass checks. When you decided you'd had enough, you had to walk backward to your original entry point, trying to follow in the same footsteps you used to walk in.

If you didn't get tied up in the thick briars, the bugs or the swarms of bees would converge on you. It was hot, humid, and marshy, so there were water snakes who did not like to be disturbed. And if trying to stay upright walking forward on the slippery rocks wasn't tough enough, then try walking blindly backwards on your way out. It usually ended in disaster. It's why we called it the Jungle.

Once out of the woods, you were now in the basin. Eno's Pond.

The first buildings at the Eno Farm site along what today is the 900 block of Hopmeadow Street were built (circa) 1800 to 1810. The farmhouse and barns would be expanded over the years. A second barn was built, as well as an icehouse to support the farm's needs and for commercial use. The farm's most productive years were from the late 1880s into the 1930s.

There were two entrances into the property. A rutted trail off the Post Road known as the College Highway and a small dirt road near the bottom of what would become Seminary Road. The farm had pastures for cows, horses, and goats. Bordered on the south by McGrath's Hill and the brook. On the west were thick woods and pasture lands leading to what today is Firetown Road. To the north, there was Williams Hill, a steep incline that ran up to the plateau that is Westminster School.

There was good bottomland for growing crops. Today, it's the first quarter mile of what is Owens Brook Boulevard. Water runoff from Williams Hill and the natural brooks and pond provided an ample water supply for living and ice-making.

Charlotte (Bidwell) Bacon remembered Eno's Pond. Living at the farm in the 1930s, playing in the barns and out in the fields. She fondly recalled when she fished the pond as a young girl, catching bullheads and sunfish. She would prepare her fish after soaking them in beaten eggs, dusted with cornstarch. She remembered that nobody else besides her cocker spaniel wanted to fish with her. Her dog would often jump into the water to retrieve her bobbin that had come loose from her line.

Rob Penfield Photo
Spillway Built (circa) 1890
Guided Water to the Eno's Farm and the Ice-House

In her nineties, Charlotte made a trip back to the homestead. In her words: "I braved the mosquitos, poison ivy, and snakes and found what was left of Eno's Pond. Marshy area now. The brook's old spillway is still there. You can't see any of what remains from Owens Brook Boulevard. You venture into the woods if you want to see any remnants of what remains of the old pond."

As she spoke, you could hear the emotions in her voice as she reminisced and recalled memories from her days as a young girl on the farm some 90 years earlier.

Following the death of Mary Phelps Eno in 1943, the Eno family moved away from the land. The farmhouse was rented out. More land parcels were sold. The largest, 40 acres, to Edgar M. Cullman, Chairman of the Board for Phillip Morris, Inc. His company, Cullman Brothers, would have a 40-year presence in Simsbury, Granby, and Tariffville, maintaining numerous tobacco resources.

In the 1960s, they would partner with American Shade Tobacco (AST). New fields were planted on the Eno property in the old upper pastures. The growing season in the fertile Simsbury and Farmington Valley lands would be 75 days from planting to harvest. The shortest growing season of quality tobacco in the world.

The land would produce the finest outer leaves for cigars known to man.

The golden years for the pond were the 1950s. The local kids were its lifeblood. We did just about everything at Eno's Pond. Except swimming. It was too dangerous to swim. If you needed to cool off, you went back into the woods to the brook at Rockslide Falls. Still, there were those knuckleheads who tried their luck swimming in the pond. Most ended up paying a price for their stupidity in one form or another.

I recall a classmate of mine, John Ahrens, who decided to test his fate. We warned him not to go into the pond, especially not at the place where he chose to enter the water. His reply to us: "Hey, I'm a Cub Scout, and I know what I'm doing."

He didn't listen. Within seconds, his ankle got tangled up with a submerged tree branch. He started flopping around in the water, yelling for help. Fortunately, he was only about ten feet from shore. David Iskra and Roger Thompson freed his leg and pulled him onto the shore. I remember a friend, Ray Nagy, saying, "Yeah, John, we're all Cub Scouts here, but you don't see our asses in the water." I never again saw John Ahrens go near the water on that side of the pond.

Fist fights were common events at the pond. One day, Stevie Pileski got into a fight with Bruce Elia. They went at each other for about a minute. Stopped and sat down under a shade tree to cool off and rest. Washed off at the water's edge on the pond's east side. Went back to their poles and fished for about an hour. Then, resumed fighting. The fight ended in a draw. The afternoon ended with both fighters sharing a ham-and-cheese sandwich and chocolate chip cookies.

The only time others would intervene in a fight is if one kid took advantage and began to fight dirty. Use a tree branch to hit their opponent or when kids would throw rocks. Then, no matter who's side you were on, we stepped in and stopped the fight. If a kid was known to carry a weapon, like a knife, he knew not to use it, or we'd report him to the police. It was simpler times, simpler solutions to resolve issues.

Occasionally, we caught fish. Mostly, bullheads and sunfish. Sometimes, we hooked a perch or eel. The smaller kids caught tiny pollywogs or little sunfish called pumpkinseeds. On those rare times when we hooked a nice eight-to-ten-inch brown trout, we'd take it home. Our moms would cook and serve it to us for that night's supper. For me, there was one exception. On those nights when I knew my mom was cooking liver and onions, I stayed away. Hated liver. Ate at a friend's house. Eventually going home to take my punishment that typically would forbid me from baseball or fishing for two days.

I did my punishment time. Occasionally, I would sneak away for a little baseball before dark on those evenings when Mom and Dad were away. I believe they expected me to. Then, go back home to watch the Red Sox game on WWLP, Channel 22, in Springfield, MA. Watch "Tall" Tom Brewer or "Yankee Killer" Willard Nixon pitch for Boston. Get to see my hero, Ted Williams, bat. Hoping for a patented majestic home run into the right-field bleachers. And others: Jackie Jensen, Sammy White, Frank Malzone, and my favorite Sox players, Mickey Vernon and Ted Lepcio. Always having to adjust the rooftop antenna to eliminate the fuzzy snow on the screen for a better picture.

I'd sit on the floor in front of the RCA TV we'd bought

at Holloways Appliance Store. Close to it. Usually, looking up at the tiny screen. Watching the game. Little League cap on my head. And always wearing my Spaulding baseball glove. It made you feel like you were a part of the game on TV.

The town of Simsbury reluctantly did some maintenance around the pond. The police did make daily visits via access on a rutted dirt road off Hopmeadow Street. The entrance was through a row of wild bushes growing at the location that currently is Owens Brook Boulevard. As Officer Lester Tuller used to say, "We like to drop by. For a quick look-see. Just to be sure all is OK."

The town's highway department would keep the access road open and do low-level maintenance to the surrounding grounds. Clear away rubbish. Take out dead trees and thick underbrush. They'd plow an opening in the winter for families who came to skate the pond and cook hot dogs over a small fire. One worker, Red Rust, would yell at us kids, "You little bastards. This is your fault that I have to come here and clean up your shit." Then he'd pull out his fishing pole, and for the next hour, he'd sit beside us, nipping on a half-pint of cheap whiskey, fishing for his dinner while on the town's payroll.

Twice yearly, the pond was stocked with trout. They purchased the fish from local fish-and-game hatcheries. The initial stocking was in early April, just before fishing season officially began. Most were quickly caught. Some trout got away by swimming upstream near the Jungle. A second stocking occurred in June. Some grew into nice-sized fish. You'd hear a story of a kid pulling in a 12 or 13-incher in the last half hour before darkness. The next day, 25 kids would show up with their fishing poles.

You could also pull in some good-sized bullheads. A blue-nosed or yellow perch was a common catch. There were lots of eels. Usually about three to four feet in length. If you caught a sucker, you never kept them and usually tossed your catch into the tall elephant grass on the pond's north side. By the next day, they'd be gone. Eaten by those woodsy creatures of the night. Raccoons, wild cats, or cur dogs.

There was also the belief the Mudders, those strange human-like folks that few in town knew about, would retrieve the fish for themselves.

The pond was a snake haven. Lots of medium-sized water snakes. Not poisonous, but their bite could get infected and make you sick. The blacksnakes were usually big and fat. Their bite was hard and deep and always became infected. Copperheads were everywhere. We were told they were poisonous. Doctor James Stretch lived near the pond. He said a copperhead bite could make you very ill. But it wouldn't kill you. You had to be careful when looking for bait. When you turned over a log or moved leaves. That's why you always used a stick to turn a log or a rock. Or when walking through tall grass.

There were bullfrogs and lots of snapping turtles. Really big ones. One of the reasons we didn't swim in Eno's Pond. Contrary to belief, snappers did not run and hide when folks got close. Like an angry turkey or a honking goose, they would attack. Some with their mouths big enough to snap off a kid's finger.

Cullman Brothers Tobacco also placed workhorses and a few wild bulls used for breeding in the upper meadows. Occasionally, they would show up around the pond. That sent everyone scurrying for the hills. Literally, the hills on the pond's south side. They wouldn't chase you because bulls won't climb hills.

Like with any place, Eno's Pond had its own stories. Passed down to those few who, over the many years, would listen.

Faded memories of our lost history. Stories of lore. Because, sadly, when the people who know and want to share the stories are gone, so, too, those stories are lost forever.

In 1951, a collie dog fell through the thin black ice on the pond's northwest corner. It was said that she swam under the ice to the brook's incoming flow. Surfaced in the stream near the Jungle. Climbed ashore. Shook off the water and took off through the woods. We later learned the dog's name: Survivor. She lived for many more years.

A 1959 story has remained a mystery. The police received a tip that there was a dead body on the pond's south side near the tall pines. Both police and fire department folks searched the area. The body was located. Dr. Owen Murphy performed an examination. He estimated the body had been dead for about six to eight hours. Murphy also found bite marks on the neck. Puncture wounds. Most of the blood had been drained. It's said the body was picked up at Murphy's office by "men in black" from New Haven. Today, the Simsbury police will tell you they have no record of this ever occurring.

No documentation of this event exists. Just stories.

It was 1958 when two men from Hartford came to salvage parts from the "Graveyard of Old Cars." In one car, they found human bones. Local doctors Owen Murphy and James Stretch were called in for professional evaluations. A coroner from Hartford was summoned. The bones were removed. Seems nobody in our town was privy to the final report. A call was made by Dr. Stretch to the state's Medical Examiner, a man he knew. Stretch was told by officials to "Drop it, Jimmy. Let it go!"

A man named Tom Collins, whereabouts unknown, is believed to have shot an alligator he saw in the water while fishing the pond in 1961. He did report it to the local police saying he thought the gator, about six feet in length, was probably a pet that got too big to keep and was released into the pond. No carcass was ever found. The police department has no documentation for this event.

On the side of the ledger marked "Very Weird" was the curious case of Pepe. He was Puerto Rican. A seasonal tobacco supervisor for Cullman Brothers in 1962. One evening after darkness, he came stumbling out of the heavy bushes near the pond and onto Hopmeadow Street at a point where today there is a traffic signal at the intersection of Owens Brook and Iron Horse Boulevard.

A local man, Harold Bradshaw, driving south, had to make a hard right onto the road's shoulder to avoid hitting him. Bradshaw stopped to help. Pepe, seemingly dazed and struggling for words, wanted to be driven to Tariffville. Bradshaw obliged, dropping his strange rider off in front of the Avion bar. En route, Bradshaw tried to question the somewhat confused Pepe to find out what happened.

Pepe, a tobacco field supervisor, had gone to lock up tool sheds along the pond's access road. He mumbled that he had no idea how he got from the tool shed area to Eno's Pond. Or how long he had been there. Only, he did recall bright blue lights from "that thing that flew over him." And a strange sense that he had been surrounded by "very little people." Bradshaw, his heart pounding in his chest, squeezed the steering wheel a little bit tighter. Nervously, he kept checking the rearview mirror on his ride home.

Harold Bradshaw was rather perplexed. A little scared. About a week later, he shared the story with my dad, George Penfield. The only person he ever told. My dad's reply: "Too many things out there we know nothing about."

It was, for a short time, called the "Pond of Frozen Money." On Christmas Day, 1960, kids playing hockey found money. Real green bills sticking up from the ice. There were five- and ten-dollar bills, even a few twenty-dollar bills. The kids and their parents harvested the booty from the ice. It was believed the total amount of cold cash found exceeded $300. Where it came from, well, now, that's one of those wonderful mysteries.

Those wonderful, endless stories of lore that were Eno's Pond.

I was bitten twice by snakes at the pond. The first time was in 1957. I was walking in the tall elephant grass on the north bank. I never saw the big black snake. I stepped on it. He reared up and sunk his fangs deep into my ankle. When my heartbeat slowed, I began to feel woozy. I headed for Doctor Stretch's house just over the rise on Hopmeadow Street.

His wife, Grace, met me at the back door. She called for the doctor. By the time he arrived, I was beginning to throw up. He made a quick diagnosis and loaded me into his big sedan. Drove me into St. Francis Hospital in Hartford. A friend he knew was working on a project for snake bite cures using venom mixed with other chemicals. He gave me two injections, and I drank a potion. Within 30 minutes, I fell asleep. Had to be carried out to the car for the return trip home.

Doctor Stretch told my mom and dad to keep me indoors for a few days. Said I'd probably be a bit queasy and a little out of it. He assured them I'd be OK. Told them about the injections and potion I'd been given. Experimental, yes, but it had already proved to be effective in others with bites. He said black snake bites were always nasty. Usually made a person sick from infection. Mom thanked him for what he did.

My parents never got a bill from Docter James Stretch.

A strange thing happened to me in June of 1964. It was one of the last times I remember going to Eno's Pond. I was 18 and had just graduated from high school. Had lots on my mind and wanted to get away and be alone. Being in the woods had always been a good place for me when I needed to think about things. I found my way to the pond. Sat under the big oak tree near the sandy beach.

I first saw her walking along Williams Hill near the elephant grass. Right where I had been bitten by a big black snake seven years before. She seemed lost and a little out of place. She saw me and waved. I waved back.

She made her way to where I was sitting. Sat down next to me. Her hair was blonde, more so than mine. She was pretty and had a nice figure. Smallish in size. She looked out over the pond and its quietness. She looked at me. "I'm Suzy," she said. I responded, "Hi, I'm Rob."

She again looked out over the pond as if she was searching for something. Like you do, looking for a path when you're lost in the woods.

We sat quietly for a while. She asked, "You come here a lot?"

My answer: "I used to, when I was a kid." She asked why I was here today. I told her that I had lots on my mind. Needed to get away. This was a place where I could think about stuff. Work things out in my head.

"Me too," she offered. "I do that. I have a place where I like to go and think. It's a nice community park."

She said she was from Northampton, Massachusetts, and I laughed. Told her that I had been accepted to Northampton Commercial College for the fall semester. My dorm room would be in the old YMCA on King Street. She smiled and laughed. Said she knew the school. Knew the old YMCA where, as a kid, she swam in the pool. She offered words of encouragement. She said it sounded like I was doing a good job at thinking. And, at living.

I thought that was an odd thing to say. I asked about her life. She sighed deeply and said she was a high school student. A senior-to-be. She seemed sad and spoke hesitantly. It was her next words that shot through me like I'd been struck by a bolt of lightning.

"Me, my life, well, I think that I'm already dead."

Well, I gotta admit. That's not what I was expecting to hear from a pretty girl on a nice summer's day. All I could offer was I really didn't understand and hoped it wasn't true.

That she'd find her way and there would be better days. She looked at me and smiled. Gently, she touched my arm.

She rose to leave. "You're nice," she said. "You'll have a good life."

I looked at her and said, "And you, what about your life?"

She just looked out over the pond. She smiled a sad smile and began walking towards the rutted trail. A pickup truck appeared on the crest of the hill. A young man emerged and waved to her. She walked to the vehicle. Turned, waved to me, and got into the truck. I could hear the truck's engine going through the gears as it made its way north on Hopmeadow Street. Again, I was alone and now, with lots more thoughts.

I entered Northampton Commercial College in September 1964. Struggled with academics. Played basketball. Rejected by just about every girl I asked out or tried to kiss. Christmas break turned out to be the peak of a mediocre semester.

It was February 1965. I happened to be in the college's dining commons, "The Cap and Quill." I found a copy of that day's local newspaper, *The Hampshire Gazette*. Thumbed through the pages looking for any info on our college basketball team, which had just lost a close game to Stockbridge College. What I found on the next page took my breath away.

It was a picture of Suzy. Suzanne Stieler. The girl from Eno's Pond.

She was dead.

Along with her male partner, Mark Warner, they were found together in a car at Look Park in the town of Florence, Massachusetts. Carbon monoxide poisoning. It took a few seconds, but I could feel the puke rising in my throat. I ran to the bathroom. I read the story presented in simple words that reported facts about the two people without empathy. Whether they innocently fell asleep while parking on a lover's lane or decided to die in a lover's pact, I wondered. What could be so bad that two people would want to die?

Then, I remembered her words from Eno's Pond. "I'm already dead."

A few days later, I went to the Forbes Library in Northampton. I wanted to look up suicides. I saw a local girl at the table next to me who was in one of my college classes. I asked if she knew the two people who had died. She knew of them but did not personally know either one. She did add that she believed they committed suicide. I asked why she thought that. Her reply: "Just a feeling. Guess we'll never know."

I knew shit like this happened. I wanted to know what would make somebody so sad that they didn't have the strength to take the next steps. That life itself was no longer worth enduring, and they didn't want to see tomorrow's dawn. Oh, God, did that make me sad. I dared not talk with anyone about it. Sometimes, it's best to forget some of the things we've been programmed to learn. Because we're then expected to act in a disciplined way by our elders, peers, and society. Perhaps as a form of payback for our continuing coexistence. To learn that sometimes our rewards for our actions are punishments. Boy, that's a lesson learned I will never forget.

It would be 54 years before I would return to Eno's Pond.

Winter at Eno's Pond was a whole new animal. Not better, but different. It was a place for families. Winters seemed to come earlier and were colder. The pond was typically frozen over with white ice by Christmas, ice that was at least a foot thick. And Westminster School, a private school for boys, would put up their low boards for their ice hockey teams. Let the games begin.

Ice skating took place every day. Big crowds on weekends. Folks built fires along the shore. Cooked hot dogs and warmed tea and cocoa. Music played, and people skated to the melodic sounds. The Ray Conniff Singers. Vince Guaraldi Trio. "Mr. Blue" by the Fleetwoods. Santo and Johnny played "Sleepwalk." Patti Page sang "Old Cape Cod."

David Kennedy was a history teacher at Westminster School and the ice hockey coach for the Sixth Form. He would put up hockey boards that were just 14 inches high and that we referred to as low-riders. He also installed hockey nets. Westminster School did not yet have an on-campus rink. Kennedy would prep the pond in readiness for those four or five home games against Choate, The Gunnery, Loomis School, Williston, and the Canterbury School.

Kennedy built a Rube-Golberg-like Zamboni to smooth the ice. Like

WS Yearbook Photo
David Kennedy
Hockey Coach

an old plow behind a horse, he'd mounted a 50-gallon barrel on wooden forks. It had holes punched into the container. Water would drip onto a blanket. He would then skate the ice, the wet blanket being pulled over the surface, making new ice for the next day's game. Kids from the neighborhood would help. His wife would make hot chocolate on a fire next to the pond. Nobody needed a permit for a fire. It was a time when such things were accepted practices. He would then place a sign on the ice. *"PLEASE DO NOT USE—GAME TOMORROW!"*

And we stayed off his new ice. It was simpler times!

I remember those times when nature called. Summer was easier, of course. Winter posed other problems. But there was a spot where if you had to go, boys or girls, well, you went. There was said to be a tradition at Westminster School. Everyone had to piss in Eno's Pond. I recall the many times when small crowds could be seen lined up along the shore, emptying their bladders. Players, coaches, and visitors. From the hockey team captain to Westminster's lead choral club singer and member of the drama club, whom I would come to learn was future actor Peter Fonda.

Families would have skating outings, birthday parties, anniversaries, and bar mitzvahs. Cub Scouts would earn badges and arrows with projects at the pond. All while skating around folks who had punched a hole in the ice for fishing. One Saturday, I watched a man who had driven out from Hartford drop to his knee and propose, offering a ring to his girlfriend. She accepted. Then, she flopped on her skates and fell on her ass.

The ice was usually good into mid-February. The Westminster coach would post a sign saying the ice was thinning and it was too dangerous to skate. A few idiots would still brave the thinning ice. Some fell through. Nobody drowned. Just a brief sadness that another year of skating had passed. But then, there was new anticipation for the coming fishing season.

Another year of learning the ways and means of Eno's Pond.

Eno's Pond began its slow and painful decline in 1961. Primarily due to changing times, human influence, and progress. Some good, some bad. There were politics, arbitrage, and competition for land. Power and greed in so many ways that it seemed to produce change for the sake of change.

The early changes to the pond and brook were subtle, almost unnoticeable. It began to shrink in size. At first, water was no longer exiting via the 1890s-built spillway in the southeast corner. Yet, the pond was getting smaller. Water will find its own way out and was doing so via underground channels that traveled out of the pond and east under Hopmeadow Street. An environmental impact. Most likely due to other building activities going on in the area. Even the small swamp next to the pond that had teemed with turtles and snakes was drying up.

Along Eno's Brook, "Sliding Rock" became overgrown

with moss. Then, one day, the "Graveyard of Old Cars" was gone. Cleaned out. Just a few rusted remnants of its existence remained. A broken seat spring, a rusted fender, a rotted-out wooden wheel.

Westminster School had built an on-campus ice rink. Players, coaches, students, and all that equipment no longer made those winter treks up and down Williams Hill to play their ice hockey games on the pond's always-shifting ice patterns.

After years of planning, the town began building a connector road west from Hopmeadow Street through the old pastures and meadows, connecting with Firetown Road. The new byway would be called Owens Brook Boulevard. Due to the positioning of the new road, it hastened the demise of the pond. It affected the flow and size of the brook we knew as Eno's Brook. It would be renamed Owens Brook. It would wipe away from the face of the earth the last remnants of the omega canyon we had always called the "Graveyard of Old Cars."

Land purchases and building permits would initiate the clearing of trees and the augmenting of land mass around the area that is today's Musket Trail and Winterset Lane. It would affect the natural underground springs that are the providers of the brook's water that had been flowing into the pond for over 250 years. The brook that had been the waterway of our youth would become but a mere trickle.

We, too, were changing. Growing up, growing older, and moving away from the lure of the pond. Those before us had moved on. Bob Pileski and Frankie Tetro. Tommy Hunt, Freddie Platt, Tommy Roach, Buddy Campbell, Bob Ferraresso, Bruce and Billy Beckwith, Ed Hanley, Eddie Trout, Orvie Winchell, my brother Pete Penfield, and all his friends.

Now, that 10-year window was coming to an end for us. Stevie Pileski, Jim and Bruce Hammond, Jim Lombard, Roger Thompson, Bobby Forsyth, Bobby Moran, Bruce Messenger, Joe Garrity, Ray Nagy, Donnie Kibbee, Butchie Clapper. And for me. We began to leave our childhood toys and mystical places behind us. Leave it for what we had hoped would be the next group to be the new keepers of the pond. Its secrets and its future.

During its final years, Eno's Pond just disappeared into time. Maynard Lydiard Jr. was a senior executive for Udolf Enterprises, and he, along with other builders, did construction during the mid-1960s on the lands that are today the Iron Horse Inn and the apartments on Hopmeadow Street overlooking the pond. Locally, land investor and builder Tommy Garrity, along with Stoddard, Moran, and Penfield, were involved in the change and support process.

The pond's final days were cruel. When building was completed, inspectors deemed it necessary for more backfill behind the buildings that sat on the hill above what remained of Eno's Pond. Over a three-month period, everything from rocks, unfiltered dirt, concrete clumps, stumps, and even industrial garbage was dropped down the hill behind the buildings. Then bulldozed into place to appease inspectors. Destroying what remained of the site's gentle ecology, all but sealing the pond's fate.

By spring 1969, Eno's Pond was gone.

Today, Eno's Pond is a small marshland. Fed by a few ground springs and a small trickling rill officially referred to as Owens Brook. You can't see it from the road. You'd have to venture into the woods to find this small, lasting memory.

For so many years and for so many reasons, both the pond and the brook were our classrooms away from school. An everyday living petri dish. It was there we learned math, English, history, and the sciences. Our group had its own hierarchy and pecking order. That subtle awareness of the skills of problem-solving, team building, and leaders and followers. We knew about the rich. And those who were not.

The kids came from nowhere; they came from every-where. From the central area between Hopmeadow Street and Firetown Road. From Seminary Road. Northfield Road and Barry Lane. From the south end in Weatogue and points north of the pond on Westwood Drive and Barnard Road.

They came from the meadowlands along Terry's Plains Road. From West Simsbury and Tariffville. Multiple personal-ities and memories I still have of those twelve-year-old kids, their young faces frozen in time. All experiencing the learning that was Eno's Pond.

We learned about war and peace. Life and death. That being of a certain age had its privileges and its responsibili-ties. We learned who the leaders were. We knew the good kids and the ones who were angry. I learned how and when to talk with people. When to stand and fight. When to cut your losses and retreat.

We all learned about the pond, as the pond learned about each one of us. Learned about fish, turtles, snakes, and the animals that were a part of our daily lives. Watched polly-wogs develop into frogs. Pumpkinseeds grow into sunfish. Flat shells grow into snapping turtles. We watched each other grow. We watched the pond grow all around us.

And then we watched it as it slowly died.

I grew to understand what the words meant when Patti Page sang, "Let Me Go, Lover!" The pain of losing a love. So much so that I sensed her words were meant only for me. I often remember those woods, the brook, and the pond. Where it was quiet and serene. How good and confident it made me feel. It helped me understand why I was angry. Another new tile piece for our mosaic of life and death. We soaked it in like a sponge. Because it was our place, our brook, our pond. Long before the local carpetbaggers came along and took it all away.

In 1984, I was assigned to a business consulting project in New York City. One evening, I was alone, having dinner in a small Italian restaurant. I somehow recognized I was sitting next to the internationally known orchestral conductor Seiji Ozawa. He, too, was alone and having a late dinner. I dared to interrupt his meal, and he was, to my surprise, receptive. I wanted to know how he was able to conduct a full symphony orchestra. Able to hear every instrument and know if one or two musicians were playing a wrong note or were off-key.

Ozawa smiled. Nodded at me. He was impressed with my question. A complex question, indeed. With a wry smile, he said my question had a surprisingly simple answer. He said when readying himself for rehearsal or a live performance, he'd find a comfortable spot in his mind. Nurture a gentle, reassuring thought that appealed and comforted him.

He added, "Your mind takes over. Transforms you. Takes you to a different level and to a place perhaps you never knew you had or could go to. It awakens all your skills, and while the orchestra plays, it allows you to hear the combined ensemble as if you're listening to each individual instrument. You'll hear each note played from each instrument."

It took me a few weeks to understand the complexity and discipline of his logic. But his answer was just like spending a day at Eno's Pond. Sitting there along the water's edge. Watching and listening to the ensemble all around you. Seeing the movements and hearing the sounds in the pond's basin. Tree branches swaying in the afternoon breeze. Birds flying. Watch a squirrel move through the trees. Raccoons foraging for food. Kids playing and talking. A fish rising in the middle of the pond, grabbing a fly. Making a splash in the water. Leaving a series of outwardly growing circular ripples en route to each of the pond's shores. The murmur of a light breeze blowing. A bullfrog's croak. A horse sounding off in the faraway meadows. A truck passing by on the nearby road. Patti Page singing.

The sounds of the Eno's Pond.

As Ozawa had said. Your senses, those skills you didn't know you had, transformed you. Took you to a different level. And when you combined all the living pieces together, yeah, you really could hear each individual component as a separate instrument playing each individual note.

You became a maestro of Eno's Pond.

During a trip north to Simsbury in December 2018, I made an early morning visit to the place where Eno's Pond had been. I walked west on Owens Brook Boulevard for about 800 feet. Entered the woods on the left side. Found the small brook and the area that had been "Sliding Rock." The remnants that had been the omega-shaped canyon known to us as the "Graveyard of Old Cars." Powerful memories and emotions stirred and were awakened within me. I trembled and softly said, "Oh God!"

I worked my way downstream, coming out into the open-air basin that had been the pond. The ground was frozen, so I was able to walk atop the marshy area that had been the pond. All the while thinking an arrogant, self-anointing thought:

"Yes, sacred ground. I am walking on the water of my childhood."

The ground was soft in some areas. Now, walking on what had been the bottom of Enos Pond. I found a few of the old memorable landmarks. The big tree trunk that had fallen in the pond during the 1955 hurricane. Rusted body of a late 1920s Ford Model A roadster. Remnants of the old low-boy hockey boards from Westminster School. Trinkets and toys. Hockey pucks. Pieces of fishing rods from long ago. I spied the 1890s-built spillway. Cracked, battered, but still in place. A walking area we called the "Left Bank." The swamp area where we caught turtles and sold them for $2 each to Arnold Daden, owner of the Old Well Restaurant.

As I walked about, I took in as much as my senses could command. I listened to the sounds of the pond. It hadn't changed. Just as Ozawa had said over 30 years before. You perceived it all combined. Or as one instrument playing one note. A learned discipline. Something we had been able to do before we were teenagers.

Rob Penfield Photo
Marshy Bottom of Old Eno's Pond
Looking North Towards Owens Brook Boulevard

Ya know, just for a few seconds there, I could swear within the cold, early morning breezes, I heard Patti Page singing the "Tennessee Walz."

Why, why was I able to do this?

I recalled a time my mom asked me how I was able to identify people and hear words of a specific conversation in a large room amid a group of a hundred people. Or the time my dad wanted to know how I was able to hear a machine in need of oiling in a noisy tool shop. People asked, "Why are you able to do that?" I never had an answer for them.

I learned lessons every day because my mom and dad understood the value and freedom of living and learning. Some of my ways were odd. No argument there. But they allowed me to be a little weird, creative, and somehow, I found my way down those undisciplined paths. Usually with more success than on those disciplined paths so many others wanted me to travel.

They allowed me to grow up by taking chances every kid from those times was allowed to take. Unlike today's forbidden paths of crash helmet overprotection on just about everything; albeit, we now live in rather different, scary, and strange times. We were learning as much from each other as we were from our teachers and parents. The good and all the bad. Learning how to sort it out because that was all part of the learning.

Maybe that's the answer to why I was able to hear those special things.

No, I didn't learn sociology and history from a book. Not from a science class, a lab, or a heavy textbook. Didn't learn decision-making from teachers in school. But I did learn lots of subjects and the critical importance of their ways because I spent every day living it. With all those other kids like me. Living in those outdoor classrooms of life.

And, no, I didn't find all that stuff under a log or rock in the woods. Then again, maybe I did find a little of what I learned there. After all, as maestros of Eno's Pond, we all turned over and looked under a lot of logs and rocks. And always, every day, there was something there to learn. Science, history ... life.

The paths of good, the paths of bad. A question of balance.

We were the kids of the world. The Maestros of Eno's Pond. It was the way of the times, and we all ended up teaching each other how to live. Because we had been taught by so many others. So, when we were out there on our own, kids being kids, we taught each other. Then, when it was our turn, we did our best and taught the world.

And on some of those long ago and forgotten days, the lessons we learned came to us for that one time in our lives, from across Eno's Pond along with and amid the sultry sounds from the lady inside the Zenith transistor radio.

She was, as memories will be, glorious and powerful. Leaving us with that haunting voice that echoed across the waters. Our daily bread. Our lessons learned.

And, what would be our forever unanswered question: "When are ya coming back to Eno's Pond, Patti Page?"

THE EPILOGUE
FROM ROB PENFIELD

WHY IT'S OK TO USE COMMAS IN A STORY ABOUT LIFE

Despite everything, I still remember.

I remember all the good and all the bad. To help me better understand what I remember, I've written stories about lessons learned while growing up. I hope readers enjoy reading my stories as much as I've enjoyed living and sharing them with you. The benefits and concerns I learned. The empathy I have for those lessons I should have learned.

All while "Sliding Down the Razor Blades of Life."

I wrote the stories because they and the lessons learned became the paths I traveled in my life. All had bumpy challenges, lots of old bones that I dug up, and many sharp razor blades I rode. Perhaps the same paths traveled by some of the readers.

I hope the goals in my stories are clear and concise to the readers and easily understood why I wanted to ... no, needed to share them with folks.

I still remember the lessons learned. Like when to talk, when to listen. How to survive and make decisions. When to smile or cry, when to stand your ground and defend your beliefs. When to fold and minimize your losses. When to move on, live to fight, and live to exist. Live another day of trying hard to remember how to forget.

Vietnam is there every day, no matter how hard I try to forget.

But most of all ... I remember.

I remember a wonderful column of thoughts written by a newspaperman in Maine. He wrote a story about using commas. He liked commas. Unlike The New York Times' stance of limiting the comma in its stories. He said commas were needed today because it seemed, as never before, we needed a comma to take a breath, complete a thought or a sentence. A comma to stop when needed and clearly explain our goals, objectives, our desires. He urged us to use commas, whenever, wherever, and in fact, suggested we should always carry a bunch of commas with us, perhaps in our shirt pocket, just in case we needed one.

I admired his passion for commas. Probably because, just like me, he, too, used lessons from his virtuous classrooms of life. And just like me, he, too, had life stories like the ones I have chosen to share with folks in this book.

I remember because my life felt like a series of periodic thoughts and experiences, often requiring restful breaks and separated by a pocketful of commas.

Joe Ehrmann is a thoughtful man. A gentle giant. A former All-American football player at Syracuse University. All-Pro player in the National Football League for Baltimore and Detroit. He's also a minister of faith. It was 1984, and in a tough section of East Baltimore, he began an urban ministry known as "The Door."

A place for boys and girls who have gone off course, looking for help and guidance. "The Door's" strength is simple. It's community based. "The Door" is located right in the middle of those troubled neighborhoods where its help is needed most. Family needs, equity in education and learning opportunities, social justice, racial reconciliations, and economic development. It's really all in one. Joe Ehrmann, East Baltimore, lessons in life. Lots of commas.

Ehrmann's book, *InSideOut Coaching*, is a roadmap of sorts. Like so many others before him, he had an epiphany about the troubles in his life and the direction he wanted to go. The styles of coaching. His attitude of life towards life.

He lamented about those one-dimensional coaches. People who are transitional. They use people "as tools to meet their own personal needs of validation and status. They, who always have an answer to suit themselves. They, the users of people with no positive solutions for others. They, who traveled on a roadmap to nowhere."

He admired and extolled the virtues of transformational coaches. "Their platforms of opportunities to impart life-changing messages to those in need. They, with answers, supporting directions, and solutions. They, caring, with thoughts, words, and deeds. They, traveling a roadmap with opportunities."

One day, Joe Ehrmann offered me wisdom. It took me a while to grasp the entirety of his message, but when I did, it was like answering a bell that tolls for you. His words were, "Rob, be a student and learn. Then, be a teacher. Build a better world and transfer that good, transformational knowledge you've learned to those in need, and do it with a clear conscience."

I felt wonder; I felt pain. Wishing I had lived my earlier years with that wisdom riding beside me. Perhaps I would have made better, if not more, decisions. But I didn't feel shame. Because when that bell had rung, I had always answered it without hesitation. And for what I believed were the right reasons. I had a good road map.

The disciplined yet free-flowing transformational lessons I learned from those many years in my classrooms of life.

For over 40 years, I've had a friend from Marlborough, Massachusetts. His name is Paul Pacific. I met him at American

International College in the winter of 1969–70. He was a hockey player. Not spectacular, but steady and dependable. Knew how to play the game. Used his lessons learned and did his job. Ended up playing years of professional hockey in numerous East Coast minor leagues. Won championships and friends. Was featured in a national ad with Oprah Winfrey. Always using a positive living thought process for life.

Paul Pacific is, in the words of Joe Ehrmann, transformational. He cares deeply for others, always offering life-changing messages. He is the author of a mind-opening book, *The Spirit Within.* He is not an overly religious person, though he believes in the strength of his God and in the journey of self-discovery. His roadmap is true and strong.

We hadn't seen each other in years and met at a golf tournament a few years back. He asked, "So, where are you these days?"

My answer was a tad snarky but sincere. "Somewhere in a space between space."

He smiled. Told me I was in a good place. Because I knew where I was and seemed happy with it. An answer that is truly inspiring and came from his heart. His beliefs, though complex, are simply interpreted as a message saying, "Heed the advice of your inner spirit. You'll never get lost, and you won't lose."

I once heard Paul say words I believe are embedded into his soul. "There is a great difference between a human being ... and being human." Boy, that one will make you stand up and listen to the music. When that bell rings, you'd better answer it.

Echoing Joe Ehrmann, Paul told me to be a student, learn, and then teach others. Transfer my knowledge, my learned experiences. My valuable thoughts about living and surviving. Use my words and my stories to tell people.

I remember all my lessons learned from my classrooms of life. Eno's Pond, Memorial Field, the Boneyard behind Central Grammar School, Riverside Park Speedway, South School, Enfield, Simsbury, James Memorial High School, Holly and Pharos

Farms, Stratton Brook. So many places, so many commas.

I'm not a person looked at by others as anything special.

I could fish by the age of five. Struggled academically in school. Knew the batting averages of all the major leaguers. Could talk to animals in the woods. Was cooking meals by age eight. I could type, sew, and iron clothes at a young age. Handled money well. Struggled in social environments. Improved academically as I aged.

I played sports and held my own against competition who were bigger, faster, and more skilled than me. Wounded twice and decorated for service in Vietnam. Graduated from two colleges. I was a sportswriter and covered the World Series, Super Bowls, and the NCAA Final Fours.

I worked worldwide as a business training consultant. I rebuilt and now maintain two antique Model A Fords I drive throughout the US. Maintain a house and a yard and have cats. And the best part, a wonderful lady named Bonnie brought me into her life. We've been married and together for almost 40 years.

Yeah, nothing special. Except to me. You see, I wouldn't have made it this far without the support from many and the lessons learned from those classrooms of life.

Sure, I would like to have done things better or differently. Perhaps with more empathy. Offering more transformational life-changing messages, as Joe Ehrmann speaks of in his urban-based ministry. Or heed that advice I hear from my inner spirit, as spoken by my friend, Paul Pacific.

I used all the tools in the box. All those wonderful tools that I had the good fortune to come into that resulted from all those lessons learned. Whether it was a good or bad situation, and when needed, all those wonderful tools I now had really worked!

And every time that bell rang, I always answered it and with a clear conscience.

Perception is judged by how you manage it. So, I keep on

paying all the bills of fare for all those forever debts. Those everyday tolls that continue to come due in my life. Probably in the lives of all of us.

Why? Because ... I remember.

And always while *"Sliding Down the Razor Blades of Life."*

ACKNOWLEDGEMENTS

I'd like to give special thanks to Tom Lehrer. He is a Harvard prodigy, an American musician, songwriter, satirist, mathematician, and professor. Through his benevolence, he's provided all his published works to the public domain. I'm allowed to use a sacred line from one of his songs as the title for this book.

The title words came to me during a very scary situation in Vietnam in 1968. I heard the song and the line, "Sliding Down the Razor Blades of Life." It was a perfect fit. I was living in the world of that song and knew its words would continue to be paths used by me during my lifetime travels. And they have.

Lehrer Archives Photo
Tom Lehrer, circa 1960

For me, Tom Lehrer's words are closer to real life than the infantile bantering of so many talking heads. Whether he sings the "Elements" song or mockingly harks out the line, "Poisoning the Pigeons in the Park," I have stuck to the script. And when I say thanks to people, I mean it because, as with Tom Lehrer, those folks have earned my sincere respect because they, too, understand the complexity of the learning they have experienced and endured.

There are so many wonderful people to thank for allowing me to barge into their lives and bang loudly on the pipes, asking questions about them from so long ago. First, thanks go to my loving wife, Bonnie. Without her support, I would not have made a three-year commitment needed to write this book.

I thank Jo-An Healy-Boehm, who provided me with stock car information about her husband, Ralph, from the 1960s. Former stock car drivers Ray Miller from East Granby, the late Don Moon from Southington, and my brother, Pete Penfield. To Fred Ciavola, his endless racing resources, and to the Eddie Flemke racing website.

In my story about bands from the 1960s, I sincerely thank Bruce Unger and Rich Linell from the Granby band The Shadows. They shared wonderful stories from their early days of learning the words to songs to the band's final gigs. To Bobby Bagshaw, drummer for The Misfits, and Jim Cooke, the band's bass player. Graciously, they both shared emotional memories from their times together.

A special appreciation and thanks to Jim Oberg and his brother, Dave, from the band I was a member of, The Chapparells. During our talks, so many memories were rekindled and brought back to life. To Robbie Brainard and the wonderful story about the area's best band, The Defiants. How they were born, how they lived, and how they died.

I owe humble thanks to many for a story about a high school football game from 1959. A story of innocence and cheating. To those who played in that game, thanks to Mike Bromage and Lenny Lavalette from Enfield High School. From Simsbury, I thank Dick Eckhart, Mel Ollestad, Ray Mildren, Hank Plona, Jim Bidwell, and Bobby Holloway for their memories.

Thanks for information goes to Ronnie Krogh, Gary Kuckel, Fred Young, Tim Connor, Vinny Cayne, Joe Bonczek, and Dave Seaman. They helped bring back the memory of a wonderful high school state baseball championship from 60 years ago. A story about winning that did not end without pain and suffering.

A personal thanks to a close friend and former Baltimorean, Al Fick, now living in Bath, Maine. For one story, I went looking for a man I had met when I was six years old. Al found him living in South Portland, ME. Through Al's persistence and 62 years after my first meeting this man, Al and I had lunch with a gentleman named Dick Carmichael. And we talked that day about memories for what seemed like 62 years.

To high school classmates from the class of 1964, Tony Connor and John Huckel, I offer sincere thanks to both for their opinions and thoughts from our high school days and graduation. They spoke the truth. That was the crux of the story.

There are another 100 people who provided bits and pieces to my stories. I would need a chapter to name them all. Please accept a group-type thank you. I appreciate your time, wonderful information, and your kindness to me. I hope to use your information during the ensuing times.

And to all those places I talked about in my stories, those very special places that were so much a part of my life. Some now gone. I am thankful those places were there when I was growing up. Those critical times of living and learning when I needed them to be there. And when I needed to be a part of those places.

You saved my life.

ABOUT THE AUTHOR

Rob and Bonnie Penfield

ROB PENFIELD is a Simsbury, CT, native with a passion for writing stories about his hometown. As he's done again with his newest book, *Sliding Down the Razor Blades of Life*. He's a graduate of Henry James Memorial High School; Northampton Commercial College, where he captained the basketball team; and American International College in Springfield, MA.

He's a twice-wounded Vietnam vet and a recipient of the Army Commendation Medal, Purple Heart, and the Bronze Star for Valor while serving with the US Army's 9th Infantry Division during the 1968 TET Offensive.

Rob was the *Farmington Valley Herald's* Sports Editor from 1973 to 1977, covering both girls' and boys' sports on an equal basis. The lone sportswriter in the state of Connecticut who was doing so at that time. He also worked for major daily newspapers and publications, including *The Sporting News* and *Sports Illustrated*. He has covered numerous World Series, Super Bowls, and NCAA tournaments and traveled with a WHA team while covering professional hockey, as well as reporting on golf, tennis, NASCAR, Little League and Babe Ruth Leagues, local stock car racing, and the 1976 Olympics in Montreal.

As a published writer, Rob has previously authored the riveting books *The Monsters That Never Die, The Last Echoes from Down 'N the Hole,* and the highly successful *A Life of Obstructions.* A story about Connecticut's first-ever girls' high school field hockey tournament in 1973.

His newest book, *Sliding Down the Razor Blades of Life,* is a continuation of his telling local stories of fact and lore. Sharing lessons learned that he's taken into his adult life. Capturing those long-ago memories before they are lost forever and presenting them to you, the reader, for your pleasure and opinions.

Rob and his wife, Bonnie Feudale, originally from Shamokin, PA, live a comfortable retired lifestyle in Phoenix, MD, with their cats and Rob's rebuilt Model A Fords he continues to maintain. A 1929 Roadster and a 1930 Rumble Seat Coupe. He enjoys fishing, collecting signed sports cards, working around the yard, and putting lots of miles on his cars while driving to car shows and cruise-ins throughout the mid-Atlantic region.

You can learn more about Rob at his website,
www.robpenfield.com.

MORE BOOKS
FROM ROB PENFIELD

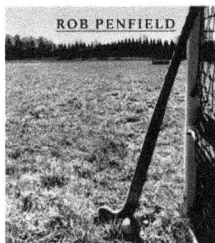

A Life of Obstructions

On November 17, 1973, the world changed, legends were born. A band of girls from tiny Granby Memorial High School won Connecticut's first-ever state field hockey tournament. It was a memorable season to a 50-year journey for field hockey in CT. Overcoming systemic opposition and institutional practices of gender bias and homophobia. A story of common people during uncommon times and their accomplishments. A small band of girls ... who became legends.

The Monsters That Never Die

A true story about a nine-year-old boy who heard an eerie voice beckon to him from the hurricane-ravaged waters of the local river. It was the voice of death calling out to him. A story about a young boy who went fishing one day and caught more than any kid can fit into his fish creel or his head. A 300-year-old river monster. A story about that boy who grew into a man. One who lives a life where he spends every day thinking about dealing with those Monsters That Never Die.

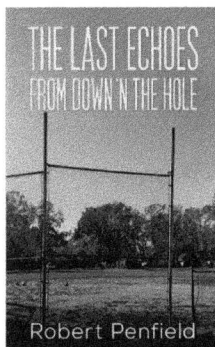

The Last Echoes from Down 'N The Hole

It was 1955. Little league season. The Giants were a team of no-names who weren't picked to make the playoffs. They won the championship. On a field that no longer exists ... down in a sleepy hollow that is no more. The reason they won, magic. Or maybe it was just one of those baseball things. It's why the author had to take a ride down some old roads, dig up some old bones and why he needed to remember just one more time before he forgot. And tell you a wonderful story from a long time ago.

ABOUT ATMOSPHERE PRESS

Founded in 2015, Atmosphere Press was built on the principles of Honesty, Transparency, Professionalism, Kindness, and Making Your Book Awesome. As an ethical and author-friendly hybrid press, we stay true to that founding mission today.

If you're a reader, enter our giveaway for a free book here:

SCAN TO ENTER
BOOK GIVEAWAY

If you're a writer, submit your manuscript for consideration here:

SCAN TO SUBMIT
MANUSCRIPT

And always feel free to visit Atmosphere Press and our authors online at atmospherepress.com. See you there soon!

www.ingramcontent.com/pod-product-compliance
Ingram Content Group UK Ltd.
Pitfield, Milton Keynes, MK11 3LW, UK
UKHW041910140125
453592UK00012B/125/J